Phoenix Rising

Robin T. Popp

Larkspur Lane Publishing, LLC

Contents

Chapter 1

PHOENIX LOOKED AROUND THE room stretching out before her and fought the urge to run. It had taken two chartered ships, three hyper—leaps and four wormholes to get to The Abyss. To say the bar wasn't what she'd expected was an understatement. Of course, she'd never been to a bar—never actually been off planet—before, so she really didn't know what to expect.

Tired and nervous, she stood inside the entrance, clutching the handle of her small duffle bag and bracing herself against the assault on her senses. In the back of the room, a band played a blaring tune, competing with the boisterous noise of the patrons. The odors of stale ale, sweaty bodies and the smoke of Euphorian—pipes made her nauseous.

She tried to think of this as part of a grand adventure, but she was out of her league. She wanted to turn and leave, but she had come to find someone and he was somewhere in this crowd. Too bad she didn't know what he looked like.

The bartender would likely know his patrons, so Phoenix started across the crowded bar to speak to him. People seeing her, and recognizing her flowing purple robes, cleared a path. Even in the Outer Fringe, it seemed, beings had a healthy respect for Xenobian High Priestesses. Or maybe it was fear that motivated them. Fear of a woman who'd honed her empathic abilities to the point where she could detect the truth behind even the most masterful of deceptions.

Not that Phoenix had any such ability. On Xenobia, Phoenix was a registered "null"; an empath without the ability to detect the emotions of others. A misfit in the land of harmony.

Phoenix had learned to compensate for her lack of empathic abilities with old-fashioned education and one thing she'd learned was that the universe could be a dangerous place without proper protection. So she'd "borrowed" a set of priestess robes from the temple and set out to find the man who would help her discover what happened to her father.

"I'm looking for Adrian Sun," she shouted to the bartender when she reached the bar.

His eyes widened in surprise but he quickly recovered, jerking his thumb in the direction of two men standing at the far right end of the bar. They had on the long black coats customarily worn by bounty hunters and Phoenix felt a thrill of excitement at seeing them.

As she made her way to them, she pondered how to get their attention. She needn't have worried. As soon as she reached them, they both turned to study her with matching sets of golden brown eyes.

They were handsome men, she thought randomly. She'd expected them to look rough, maybe with facial scars marring their appearance. The man on her right had short, unruly black hair and wore a bemused expression. The man on her left, with the dark blond hair, was scowling. Both were tall and exuded an aura of danger that made her question—again—her reason for being there.

"What do you want?" The rich, masculine timbre of the blond man's voice washed over her and it took several seconds before she could gather her wits to respond.

She returned his scowl with what she hoped looked like a firm and steady gaze. "I'm looking for Adrian Sun." She searched each face, hoping for a clue that would tell her which man was the one she sought.

"Why?"

"It's private." They were drawing attention and she looked around for an empty table. "Perhaps there's someplace quiet where we could talk, Mr. Sun?" She glanced at each man, still not sure to whom she spoke.

"You're wasting your time," the scowling one said.

"I beg your pardon?"

"Whatever you want, I'm not interested." He turned his back, dismissing her. She saw him raise his hand to hail the bartender, who quickly replaced his empty glass with a full one.

"Excuse me." Phoenix raised her voice to be heard over the loud drone of voices, but he showed no sign of having heard her. She looked to the other man and received a slightly mocking smile before he also turned his back to rejoin his friend.

Irritated to be so easily dismissed, Phoenix stepped closer to grab the blond man's arm. No sooner had her fingers brushed the cloth of his duster than he whirled around and seized her wrist in an iron tight grip.

Panic swept through her but she met the man's steely gaze head-on. Testing his hold on her arm, she felt his fingers tighten ever so slightly.

"You're hurting me." She spoke the words slowly, without inflection. This man reeked of danger and yet she sensed he meant her no real harm.

He continued to stare at her but then, as if her words finally penetrated, he looked at the hand gripping her wrist and his fingers slowly relaxed until she was able to pull free.

She glared at him, rubbing her wrist which was still tingling from his touch. "Adrian Sun, I presume?"

"You shouldn't be here." His tone was dark and foreboding.

"I have as much right to be here as anyone else." Phoenix refused to be intimidated. "And I'm not leaving until I talk to you."

He didn't capitulate but neither did he turn his back on her again. Feeling emboldened, Phoenix hurried to explain her reason for being there.

"My father told me that if he was ever in trouble, I should find you, here at The Abyss. Well, he's in trouble and I need your help."

"Yeah? And who's your father?"

"Skylar O'Mallen."

When had Skylar had a daughter? About twenty years ago, from the looks of it, but why hadn't Skylar ever mentioned her?

"Adrian—maybe we should sit down." Jack's voice penetrated Adrian's shock as he stared at the young woman claiming to be Skylar's daughter.

"There's a table over there." Jack motioned for the young woman to follow him as he cut through the crowd. Adrian followed, quickly finding himself mesmerized by the way her body moved beneath her billowy lavender robes. Xenobian Priestess robes, if he wasn't mistaken, and that just added to the mystery. Skylar had a *Xenobian* daughter?

For several long moments after sitting, no one spoke. Emerald green eyes studied him from across the table. He wished he could see more of her hair hidden beneath the drape of the headdress. What little was visible was auburn, like Skylar's. "Skylar never mentioned having a daughter," he said, more to himself than to her.

"Really? He talked about you all the time."

Adrian wasn't sure how to react to that, so he changed the subject. "How long have you been a Xenobian Priestess?"

"High Priestess," she corrected him. "Six Xenobian solar hours."

"Interesting. I would think being in a place like this would bother you. So many primitive emotions." He'd noticed a scene unfolding far behind her on the other side of the bar. Two drunken patrons had lunged at each other, fists flying while nearby onlookers scrambled out of the way. The sound of their fighting was drowned out by the rest of the noise in the bar, but a Xenobian High Priestess would have sensed the strong emotions.

"My training allows me to shield myself from the emotions around me, though of course my vow prevents me from blocking them completely."

One of the men pulled a trader's blade and lunged at his opponent, nearly slicing off the man's arm in a sweeping arc. The man screamed in obvious pain, but once again, the sound got lost in the ambient noise.

He gave the woman a slow studied look. "You're lying."

"I beg your pardon," she sputtered in what Adrian considered a moderately good performance.

"You're no more a Xenobian Priestess than I am."

She opened her mouth to protest, but Adrian cut her off. "Save your breath. We get all sorts out here in the Outer Fringe and they all lie better than you do."

She stared at him for a moment and he could almost hear the thoughts and lies tumbling around in her head as she tried to figure out what story to tell him next. To save her the trouble, he gestured to the scene across the bar. She turned and he knew the moment she realized she'd been caught in a lie when her shoulders slumped ever so slightly.

"Okay," she admitted, turning back to face him. "You're right. I'm not a priestess. I'm not even an empath. I'm a null, but I thought I'd be safer dressed this way." She gave him a defiant look. "But I wasn't lying about being Skylar O'Mallen's daughter."

She pulled off the headdress and long auburn hair cascaded down in thick waves. Something in Adrian's gut tightened.

"Can we start over?" she asked.

Adrian considered for a second, then nodded. "My name, you know. This is my partner, Jack Marsden. And you are…?"

"Phoenix Eemin."

"Not Phoenix O'Mallen?"

"I took my mother's name."

"Okay, so what makes you think Skylar is in trouble?" Adrian asked.

"Because he missed our game."

"Excuse me?" He didn't try to hide his astonishment. "Seriously?"

"You don't understand," she said. "Skylar and I play a game of virtual Strategem every other week. We've been playing ever since we met in a virtual game room ten years ago."

"Wait a minute. Have you ever met Skylar in person?"

"No."

"Then how do you know he's your father? For that matter, how do you even know it's Skylar you've been playing?"

"I know he's my father because he told me—along with the fact that he works for the government. As for whether he's really Skylar O'Mallen—how many men would send their daughters to find you if they were in trouble?"

"Okay, fine. I'll concede your point there, but one missed game doesn't mean he's missing. Maybe he got busy."

Despite his reassuring words, Adrian glanced at Jack, knowing his friend shared his concern. At Adrian's slight nod, Jack pushed away from the table and stood.

"If you'll excuse me, I have business to attend to." He offered Phoenix a pleasant smile. "It was nice meeting you." He didn't wait for her reply, but turned and walked out of the bar.

Adrian steeled his expression as he faced the woman. "I need to leave as well. What's the best way to reach you?"

"I'll give you my personal comm-code." She rattled off a series of numbers which Adrian didn't bother to enter into his comm-device.

"I've got great recall," he explained when she frowned. Pushing away from the table, he stood. "Shall we go?"

"So you'll help me?"

He inwardly winced at her hopeful tone. He wasn't sure what the exact relationship was between Skylar and this woman, but he'd be willing to bet Skylar wouldn't want her traveling around the universe looking for him and exposing herself to danger. "I'll see what I can find out."

She smiled and the force of it caught him off guard. It had been a long time since he'd been affected by a woman's smile and the fact that he'd been affected by hers did little to improve his temper.

They stood and Adrian immediately noticed the stares from the nearby patrons. "Better put that head-dress back on; you're attracting too much attention."

He was glad she didn't question him. Once the piece was again covering her long hair, Adrian felt better, though he missed the sight of it himself.

"Come on." Taking her by the elbow, he steered her through the bar, releasing her only once they reached the outside corridor.

They walked in silence while Adrian kept a constant watch out for the petty criminals who haunted the passages of the space station looking for their next victim. More than once, Adrian caught Phoenix sneaking looks at him, but she remained quiet—until they reached the docking station and she recognized where they were.

"Are we flying somewhere?"

"*We're* not. *You* are." The station master approached and handed Adrian the boarding pass Jack had purchased moments before. "I'm sending you home."

"What? But you said you'd help me."

Adrian ignored the hurt in her tone. "I am. I'm making sure you stay alive. The Outer Fringe is no place for a woman like you."

She thrust out her chin in a defiant gesture. "I can take care of myself and if you won't help me, I'll find someone who will." She scanned the area. Spotting a couple of traders, she walked over to them, Adrian close behind her.

"Gentleman, I require your assistance," she said in her best High Priestess imitation.

The traders glanced at her, clearly tempted to help her until Adrian moved closer, his hand on his laser and the threat of something dark and painful in his gaze. Without waiting to hear what she needed, the men walked off.

Realizing what happened, but not easily daunted, Phoenix scowled at him before approaching a group of dockworkers. Again, Adrian discouraged them with a look.

After the third failed attempt, she gave up. "Fine. You win."

"Clearly."

Escorting her onboard the ship, he saw her settled in her seat. An unfamiliar emotion flitted through him at the thought of never seeing her again, but he quickly suppressed it. There were more pressing matters to tend to.

"When I find Skylar, I'll tell him you're looking for him."

He left her scowling after him and waited on the docking bay until the ship's doors closed. Only then did he head back to the bar where Jack waited for him.

"What'd you find out?"

"I couldn't reach Skylar's ship," Jack said. "I contacted the Solaris Dominus Intelligence Agency headquarters. His ship never arrived."

"Damn it." They both knew what that meant. When they'd seen Skylar two weeks ago, the three of them had just captured Kinto Juarez, one of the SDIA's most wanted criminals. When they'd departed, Adrian and Jack had returned to The Abyss while Skylar transported Juarez to Veridian Prime. "Something happened to him en route." Adrian rubbed his forehead, a futile effort to wipe away the beginnings of a raging headache.

Skylar worked so deeply undercover for the SDIA that not even his own government would help him if he was in trouble. There was the added problem of the government's safeguard against an agent being captured or going rogue: a tiny time-release capsule surgically implanted in the agent's heart. It contained neo-cyanide, the fastest-acting, deadliest poison in the known galaxy.

At designated intervals, an agent was required to undergo physical and psychological evaluations on Veridian Prime to prove they were still of sound mind and body and still loyal to the government. Upon being cleared, the capsule's timer was reset. If they failed to either pass the evaluations or to show up at all, the capsule was allowed to release its poison, eliminating the agent before the agent could become a threat to the agency.

Skylar had once said he lived his life one Veridian Prime solar year at a time. Adrian knew the agent's last visit to Veridian Prime had been eleven months ago. That's why he'd volunteered to transport the prisoner rather than request transport; it was time to reset the capsule.

"How long to ready the ship?" Adrian asked, staring into a glass of black Smuggler's Swill, plagued by his troubled thoughts. He and Jack had a very narrow window of time in which to find their friend.

"An hour. Two at max," Jack replied. "What's our first stop?"

Adrian tossed back the contents of his glass and braced for the burn. When he set the glass back on the table, he met Jack's determined gaze with his own.

"Cloud City."

Chapter 2

THIRTEEN HOURS LATER, PHOENIX stared out the ship's front view screen, her thoughts replaying her meeting with Adrian Sun and his friend, Jack. The concerned looks on their faces when she'd told them her father was in trouble suggested they knew more than they'd shared with her.

If only they'd helped her. She hadn't traveled all the way to the Outer Fringe to turn back now.

As soon as Adrian had left the docking bay, she'd demanded to be let off the ship and felt no guilt asking the ticket master to refund her ticket or in accepting the credits he handed her.

Without the bounty hunter there to scare off every person she talked to, Phoenix soon found a new source of help in Mr. Zimmers, a transport pilot and self-professed independent businessman. Recognizing her outfit and thinking her a genuine Xenobian High Priestess, he had hurriedly offered his services after hearing her predicament. In exchange for a modest fee, he'd offered to fly her to see a man whose connections and influence were far-spread across the three galaxies. If anyone could find her father, this man could.

Grateful, Phoenix had accepted his offer, handing over Adrian's money without hesitation. Once settled on board Mr. Zimmer's ship, fatigue from her trip had caught up to her and she'd slept, albeit fitfully, for hours.

Now they were on final approach to the floating city known simply as "Cloud City" and Phoenix could barely contain her excitement. She remembered reading about it in General Galactic Studies but never dreamed she would one day visit it.

Gamma IV-II was the planet above which Cloud City floated. Decades ago, it was a significant source of the energy-producing Luminite crystal, but mining efforts had been ruthless, without thought to conservation. Now, the planet was virtually uninhabitable. The only city on Gamma IV-II was located several thousand kilometers above the surface, in the clouds. Hence the name. Phoenix had read about the technology that kept Cloud City from falling to the surface, but didn't understand it.

Docking took little time and once the ship came to a full halt and the stasis field was activated to hold the ship in place, Mr. Zimmers shut off the engines. Phoenix looked out the front view port, feeling a little uneasy at the sight of the flat, open platform that served as a landing base. There were no safety walls in place and she wondered what kept people from falling off. The surface of the planet was a long way down.

"Are you ready, Priestess?" The portly Mr. Zimmers gave her a comforting smile.

"Yes, thank you." Phoenix tried to adopt the worldly tone used by the real priestesses on her home planet. "I appreciate your assistance."

Mr. Zimmers bowed before her. "It is my pleasure."

Phoenix followed him off the ship and immediately noticed how thin the air was. She supposed the air generators used inside the floating city to make the atmosphere more comfortable didn't extend out this far.

Three men waited for them. They stood with the rigid posture of soldiers which seemed out of place in such a heavenly setting.

"Greetings, High Priestess," the older of the three men said, stepping forward. "My name is Marcus. Mr. Dante, the administrator of Cloud City, extends his warmest welcome and asks for the pleasure of your company. If you will follow me?"

Noticing that Mr. Zimmers was no longer beside her, Phoenix looked around and spotted him sandwiched between the other two men. Her excitement dimmed as a tendril of alarm snaked through her.

A touch at her elbow, gentle but firm, had her looking up into Marcus' serious expression. "Mr. Zimmers has other business. If you'll come with me?"

Sensing Mr. Zimmers might be in trouble, but unsure what to do, Phoenix allowed Marcus to escort her across the platform, leading her through wisps of clouds that dispersed as they passed through them. There was only the slightest breeze and the surrounding silence gave the place a calm, peaceful feeling. Looking over the side of the platform, Phoenix saw the fuzzy shapes of mountains and abandoned mining camps far below. A shiver traveled up her spine and she moved a little more toward the center of the platform.

"Has anyone ever fallen over the edge?" she asked nervously.

"No one has ever...*fallen*...over the edge," Marcus responded.

Phoenix appreciated a dry sense of humor but her smile faded when she glanced at his face and realized he wasn't joking.

She felt immediately better as soon as they entered the building.

Marcus led her through a complex pattern of corridors filled with people going about their business. He finally stopped before a set of large double-doors with guards stationed on either side. Marcus ignored them and knocked on the door.

From inside, a voice beckoned them to enter.

Marcus ushered her through the door and into a plush room with crimson carpet and black furniture. At the center of the room was a large sunken pit with cushioned, perimeter seating and low-level lighting. A retractable viewing screen hung from the ceiling near the left wall and a long conference table with chairs stood to the right side of the room.

"Is this the Priestess?"

"Yes, Mr. Dante," Marcus answered, gently urging her forward.

At the sound of the gravelly voice, apprehension stole over Phoenix. Looking around for the voice's owner, she saw him when he stepped out of the shadows.

Dressed in a black trader's outfit with dark hair streaked with gray, he may have been in his fifties or sixties. His once handsome face was battle worn with a particularly bad scar running down the right side of his forehead, disappearing beneath a patched right eye, then reappearing below the patch as it traveled across his right cheek. It stopped shortly below the right cheekbone. He looked like she'd expected the bounty hunters to look; dark and frightening – or maybe that was the panther at his side making her feel that way.

The large cat seemed content, though, to sit quietly while its head was stroked.

"How...how do you do?" Phoenix instinctively lowered her voice, not wanting to startle either the man or the animal. The thought that she should have taken Adrian's advice flickered through her mind.

"I do fine." Dante's words sounded calculated, as if polite conversation did not come naturally to him. "It is very nice to meet you, Priestess...?"

"Eemin," she supplied.

"You are looking for your father, are you not?"

His tone made her uneasy. "Yes. I was told you might be able to help me?"

"Perhaps. I have many resources, but I'm afraid nothing is free."

"I understand." She tried to sound as if she conducted business of this nature all the time. "What is your fee?"

"To search all three galaxies plus the Outer Fringe?" He paused as if to tally the numbers in his head. "A million credits."

Phoenix gasped. A million credits? She didn't have that kind of money. She fought to hide her frustration and disappointment. "I'm sorry I wasted your time, Mr. Dante. I'm afraid I can't afford such a large sum."

He smiled. "Few can, my dear. Few can. But perhaps we can work out a trade; an exchange of services."

"A trade?" Exactly what did this man have in mind? Stories as old as time flashed through her mind of young women sold as sex slaves. Before she could voice her concern or protest, Mr. Dante continued.

"In my line of business, I deal with hundreds of traders from all over the galaxy. I am fairly adept at discerning the liars from those who speak the truth. However, I am not infallible—but you are."

A slight nervous ringing began in her ears. Exactly what was he suggesting? "I'm not sure I understand."

"You are a Xenobian High Priestess, are you not?" He waved his free hand to indicate her outfit.

No, her mind screamed. "Yes."

He smiled. "It is impossible for anyone to lie to a Xenobian Priestess. So, in exchange for finding your father, an undertaking which, I assure you, is quite costly, you will put your abilities at my disposal." He smiled, his fingers stroking the top of the cat's head. "Do we have a deal?"

Her mind whirled. Could she do it? She was adept at reading body language, but was she good enough to pull off such a deception?

"No one is forcing you," Dante continued in her silence, "If you prefer, I will have Marcus arrange for your return to the Outer Fringe—or Xenobia. It is your choice."

She knew the only way she would find her father would be with his help and silently cursed Adrian Sun for forcing her into this situation.

"All right. I'll do it." *Please don't let this be a mistake.*

"Very good. I'm pleased you've accepted my offer. Let's start immediately, shall we? Marcus, show in Mr. Zimmers." Dante's voice filled the room as Phoenix tried to gather her scattered thoughts. Exactly what *had* she gotten herself into?

As Marcus crossed the room, Dante gestured with a wave of his hand to indicate that he and Phoenix should sit in the pit area. No sooner had she taken a seat than the double doors opened and Mr. Zimmers entered, escorted by the same two men who'd been on the landing platform. The portly little man's gaze darted around, meeting hers briefly before turning on Dante.

"Mr. Zimmers," Dante began pleasantly, still stroking the big cat. "Please join us." He gestured with his free hand to indicate that Mr. Zimmers should stand before him.

"I thank you for bringing Priestess Eemin to me. She and I have agreed to work together for the next little while, to our mutual benefit."

"You're welcome, Mr. Dante. I knew," Mr. Zimmers shot her another glance, "I mean, I'd hoped, um, well... glad I could help." His words trailed off and he fell silent.

The smile on Dante's face grew cooler. "Yes, well... there is one other matter I wish to discuss with you. It's about the shipment you delivered to Kathgar for me. Did you encounter any problems?"

"No, Mr. Dante." Mr. Zimmers spoke in a carefully controlled tone of voice. "No troubles."

"Wonderful." He drew out the word, then looked to Phoenix. She realized with a start that he suspected Mr. Zimmers of lying and expected her to tell him whether he was right or not.

She fixed her gaze on the little man, making note of his behavior: the way he played with his hands, how his gaze never fully met Dante's, the rapid blinking of his eyes and the way he leaned back, trying to put as much distance has he could between Dante and himself without actually stepping back. Everything about him reeked of duplicity; it didn't take a full Xenobian Priestess to know the man was lying. Phoenix felt certain that Dante already knew the truth, but she shook her head anyway.

Dante gestured to Marcus, who led the two guards from the room. The door closed after them with an ominous click.

Dante seemed satisfied to let the silence go uninterrupted while Mr. Zimmers shifted his weight back and forth from one foot to the other.

After several long minutes, the door to the room reopened and Marcus walked in. Behind him followed the two guards carrying something between them. The men stopped beside Mr. Zimmers and set the item on the floor.

"What the hell?" Mr. Zimmers jumped back, almost tripping over his own feet.

"Oh m—," Phoenix gasped, clamping a hand over her mouth and nose as she pushed herself back into her chair. She turned her head so she wouldn't have to look at the dead man's torso, but the acrid stench of rotting flesh assaulted her senses, forcing her to breathe in shallow gasps.

She'd never been exposed to anything so horrific and bile rose in her throat. She closed her eyes, glad there was nothing in her stomach to throw up and resolved not to look at all, but morbid curiosity won out.

The deceased man—at least she thought it had been a man—had obviously suffered a gruesome death, judging from the raw stubs where arms and legs had once been attached.

The panther, its tail twitching, rose to all four legs and growled.

"Shhhh," Dante soothed the beast. "Mr. Zimmers, do you recognize this man?"

The little man looked confused. "No, I don't. I mean, it's hard to tell."

"Rogers," Dante said in a voice that sounded tight. "His name was Rogers. He was one of my men. Kathgar's people intercepted him on a recent flight. Apparently they were not happy with the shipment of gemstones they received; the shipment *you* delivered."

Even without empathic powers, Phoenix felt the level of tension in the room rise.

"I don't understand," Mr. Zimmers said, his tone wavering. "I delivered the stones."

"It seems that while they paid for one hundred stones, they received only ninety-nine. As I personally placed the stones in the bag, I know that *I* did not short the count. Someone is lying—is it you? Or Kathgar?"

Phoenix knew Mr. Zimmers had finally realized her purpose there when he shot her a desperate look. His face grew pale and his breathing became rapid.

Finally, he spoke, his voice almost a whisper. "It was a very small stone. The smallest one there." His gaze darted back and forth between Phoenix, Dante, and Marcus, as if searching for an ally. "Please, your Eminence. I didn't mean any harm. I didn't think anyone would notice."

"I'm sure Rogers will understand." Dante's tone dripped with sarcasm. "I, on the other hand, am less understanding."

Fear leeched the color from Mr. Zimmers' face. "Please, Mr. Dante. I'll give the stone back."

Dante seemed to consider. "You still have it?"

Mr. Zimmers cast a nervous glance at the door. "Yes. I'll go get it."

"Marcus will accompany you." Dante gestured for Marcus to step forward. "To ensure there are no further... *misunderstandings.*"

"Oh, thank you, Your Benevolence."

At Dante's dismissive nod, Marcus escorted Mr. Zimmers from the room. Unbidden, an image formed in Phoenix's mind of the landing pad's rail-free walkway and the long fall to the surface below. She shuddered, shaking off the image. She was being fanciful. Dante would not kill Mr. Zimmers over something as minor as a missing gemstone. Would he?

Dante pointed to the dead man's remains and the two guards came forward. They lifted the torso between them with no outward sign that the task, the odor, or the sight bothered them as they carried it from the room. Phoenix felt the aftermath of the emotionally charged session in the ebb of her own energy level and slumped back in her seat.

Dante gave her a studied look and she held her breath. Finally, he nodded and smiled. "You did well, Priestess. I apologize for the unpleasantness—and I can see that you are fatigued. I will have a room prepared for you. In the meantime, I would be honored to have you join me for the evening meal."

He pushed a button on the end table beside him and almost immediately, an elderly woman appeared through a hidden door at the back of the room.

"Please have a suite prepared for Priestess Eemin. She will be staying with us for awhile. And let the cook know there will be two for dinner this evening."

The elderly woman nodded and left.

"Tomorrow, I will give you a tour of my city and then I have several business meetings that I would like for you to attend. Will that be acceptable?"

His tone suggested that the question was merely a courtesy. Her attendance at the meetings was part of their agreement. She couldn't refuse, not if she wanted to find her father. So she smiled and nodded.

"Good." Dante rose gracefully to his feet, offering her a hand. Standing, she noticed that he stood not much taller than she. As the panther rose beside them, Dante gestured to the door. "Shall we?"

She preceded him out of his audience chamber and then allowed him to escort her down the corridor until they reached a private dining room. A table already laden with food stood at the center and Phoenix eyed it, amazed she could feel hungry after seeing the corpse. Beside Dante, the panther seemed to grow agitated and Phoenix wondered if the cat was to eat with them—and if so, did it prefer its meal cooked?

Or raw and still fighting for her life?

She casually moved to the far side of the room, making sure the table was between her and the animal. She needn't have worried, though. A man appeared almost immediately and led the panther from the room.

Minutes later, Phoenix was enjoying dinner. The food was delicious and Dante proved to be an interesting dinner companion, entertaining her with stories of his travels throughout the galaxies and telling her of places she had only read about.

Afterwards, he escorted her to her suite. It was an internal room and therefore had no windows, but it was by far the most luxurious suite she'd ever stayed in. Her feet sank into the plush carpet and the bed, piled high with pillows, beckoned to her weary body.

"I hope you will find these accommodations comfortable. As you can see, your bag has already been delivered from Mr. Zimmers' ship. If you need anything, you have simply to press the intercom and ask."

Phoenix looked around, suddenly very ready to spend a little time alone. "Thank you, Mr. Dante. I'm sure I'll be fine."

"In that case, I will leave you. For your own protection, I suggest you lock your door. Our cloud city can be a dangerous place. I will have Marcus come for you in the morning. Breakfast is served at oh-eight-hundred sharp."

With that, he turned and left her alone.

After locking the door as suggested, Phoenix showered and changed into her nightshirt. Though the session with Dante and Mr. Zimmers had been stressful and tiring, Phoenix found she was too restless to sleep. Climbing into bed, she activated the vid-screen and scrolled through the streaming shows until she found one to watch. After an hour or so, she turned everything off and closed her eyes.

Though she was bone tired and the bed felt wonderful, sleep eluded her. Dozens of images flooded her mind, from Dante and his panther, to Mr. Zimmers and the dead man's corpse.

Ironically, though these images were troubling, it was the memory of a tall, dangerous looking man with dark blond hair and penetrating golden brown eyes that kept her awake.

Where was he now?

And why did she care?

Chapter 3

Morning came to Cloud City.

Finally.

Phoenix, who'd awakened long before sunrise, did the best she could to erase the effects of fatigue, first with a cold, wet face cloth and then by putting herself through the revitalizing, dance-like steps of the *Illuma Vidra Kata*, a series of movements designed to bring new energy and balance into one's being.

By the time Marcus arrived to escort her to the dining room, Phoenix felt ready to face the day—no matter what it held in store for her.

Breakfast, like dinner, was delicious and when Dante joined her, he regaled her with tales of the various celebrities he knew. When they'd finished eating, in keeping with his earlier promise, Dante gave her a tour of his city. As they walked, he kept up a constant dialogue, often asking her questions about herself.

"Priestess Eemin, did you enjoy your visit to the Outer Fringe?" he asked, leading her down a corridor.

"I don't know if 'enjoy' is the word I would use, but it was interesting." As she spoke, Phoenix studied her surroundings, trying to find something about this corridor that differentiated it from the dozens of others she'd walked through that morning. Unfortunately, they all looked alike.

As if sensing her frustration, Dante smiled indulgently. "Cloud City can be quite confusing when you're new. I'm sure it won't be long before you've learned the layout. Until then, may I suggest you not wander around alone?"

Phoenix couldn't help but smile. "That won't be a problem. I have no desire to get lost."

The corners of his mouth turned up slightly as he took her arm and escorted her down another crowded corridor. She was amazed at how many people lived here.

"Your city is much more crowded than I expected," she said, turning to watch several bounty hunters walk past in their long, dark coats. She studied their faces, looking for one in particular; strangely disappointed when it wasn't there.

"Because Cloud City lies outside the Galactic Assembly's jurisdiction, we attract a certain—criminal element, shall we say?—to the city. It is another reason why you shouldn't wander about unescorted."

This information caused Phoenix to consider the people around her in a new light. Any one of them could be a criminal. Would she know if they were?

A shiver ran down her spin. *You shouldn't be out here.* Adrian's words echoed in her mind.

They reached the end of the corridor and when they turned the corner, Phoenix found herself standing at the entrance to a large grassy, outdoor area. Full of light and energy, it was artistically landscaped with colorful flowers and trees. Phoenix fell in love with it immediately.

"It's beautiful," she breathed.

"I'm glad you like it. This is our park. Many come here to relax."

Phoenix smiled. "I can see why."

Dante led her to the perimeter wall so she could look out over the planet.

"My apologies, Priestess. I must speak to someone over there, privately. Do you mind if I leave you to enjoy the view? I assure you, I will have you in my sights at all times so you will not be alone."

"Not at all."

In fact, she was glad to have a few minutes to herself. She watched him leave and felt herself relax. She enjoyed the feel of the cool breeze against her face and the heat of the sun on her skin. It would have been perfect if it weren't for the nagging sensation that someone was watching her.

She scanned the park but no one appeared to be paying attention to her. Shrugging off the uncomfortable feeling, she walked to the wall and looked out over the planet. Normally, she suffered a fear of heights, but the glass retaining wall was high enough, she felt safe. Soon, Dante returned and escorted Phoenix from the room. As they walked, Phoenix studied him out of the corner of her eye, trying to read his mood. It stayed safely hidden behind that cool hard expression of his.

"It's time for us to return to my audience chamber. I have several meetings that I would like for you to attend."

"Of course," she agreed, turning her thoughts to the sessions ahead.

Phoenix shuddered when they entered Dante's audience chamber. It looked much the same as it had the day before, absent the panther—and the corpse. Dante took his customary chair in the pit group and gestured for her to take the seat adjacent to him.

"Do you require anything?" he asked.

"No, thank you."

"You understand that anything you hear within these walls must remain private. Tell no one."

"Yes, of course. I won't really be listening to the words. My attention will be focused on reading energy and emotion."

"Very well, let's get started."

He reached over and pressed one of the buttons on the end table. Soon the door opened and a trader strode in, coming to stand before Dante.

They began discussing some issue they had with another group of traders, but Phoenix's attention was concentrated on the man's body language. He seemed at ease and faced Dante squarely. The session continued without incident and not once did the man's actions suggest deceit. When Dante glanced her way, she nodded. The conversation concluded and Phoenix felt a weight lift from her shoulders. She could do this.

Another man entered almost immediately after the first left and this one seemed harder, more dangerous. Phoenix tried not to let the man's appearance sway her as she focused on his stance and hand gestures. After several minutes of animated conversation, Dante looked to her. She hesitated.

"Priestess, I need to know." Dante spoke quietly.

"Need to know what?" The trader glanced sharply from Dante to her, his eyes narrowing.

"I need to know if you're telling me the truth," Dante replied, sounding very matter-of-fact.

"What the hell?" The trader shouted. "You brought in a Xenobian High Priestess?"

Dante ignored the trader's outburst. "Priestess, what is your verdict?"

"His aura is very dark," she began, not sure what to say. "An honest man would not have cause to be uneasy, therefore I must conclude he is lying."

Dante scowled at the trader. "Our deal is off. Leave my city immediately."

"What?" The trader shouted. "Because of some priestess mumbo-jumbo, you're canceling our deal? I've already paid for the shipment. Who else am I going to find to buy two thousand kilos of Clairvoyance? It's not like I can sell it on the open market."

"There's always Purgo-Max," Dante said, referring to the black market planet that once was a maximum security prison for the most dangerous prisoners. The trader swore, turning to jab a finger in the air at Phoenix. "You're responsible for this. Watch your back because—."

"Be careful who you threaten." Dante's words rang loud and clear, though he never raised his voice. "Priestess Eemin is under my protection. Any threat against her will be taken personally by me."

The trader glared at Dante, then turned and stormed out of the room.

Phoenix was shaken. She'd never been threatened before and needed time to recover. Dante gave her none. Already the door was opening for the next business associate to enter.

The rest of the sessions progressed more smoothly, but the image of the irate trader haunted her throughout the day, his threat replaying over and over in her mind.

Had she been wrong about him? Her charade could have serious consequences that she'd not considered before. She should never have agreed to work for Dante. At dinner, she would tell him their deal was off and figure out another way to find her father.

That evening, Dante's duties prevented him from dining with Phoenix, so she had her meal delivered to her room. With it arrived a bottle of sweet Ramian nectar and a note from Dante, congratulating her on a job well done.

After eating, Phoenix soaked in a deep bath, sipping the nectar and letting the warmth of the water seep into her bones to chase away the chill of fear. She might be under Dante's protection but who would protect her from him?

Finally, dressed in her nightshirt, she crawled into bed and allowed her mind to grow numb watching the vid-screen. Her thoughts turned to Adrian. She didn't know why she'd felt safer with the bounty hunter, when he was clearly dangerous, but she had. Unfortunately, he wasn't there.

Taking deep, steadying breaths, she focused her thoughts inward, seeking the inner balance and peace that was the crux of the Harmonious Accord's philosophy. A sense of calm eventually stole over her and she fell into a troubled sleep.

Hours later, she jerked awake, wondering what had awakened her. Then she heard it—the rattle of the door.

The trader's threat came back to her in sharp clarity and she struggled to sit up in bed. Leaning over to the nightstand, she flipped on the small light. This time, when the door rattled, she actually saw it move. If someone wanted to speak to her, they would knock, wouldn't they? So whoever was on the other side of the door clearly had ill intentions.

Fortunately, she'd locked the door before going to bed, but wondered if the lock would hold. She should call Dante.

Glancing around the room, she spied the intercom. Scrambling out of bed, she rushed to press the button. "Please, help me. I think someone's trying to break into my room."

Static greeted her words. She tried again, but with no better results. Had her intruder deactivated the intercom?

She looked around but there was nowhere to hide and no other doors through which to run.

Then the rattling stopped.

Phoenix waited, not daring to breath. Had the intruder given up? Gone away?

The silence was short-lived. A small muffled explosion caused the door to shudder in its frame just before it burst open. The brighter light from the outside corridor silhouetted a figure blocking the doorway. When he stepped into the room, the light fell on his face.

It was the trader she'd called a liar.

Chapter 4

"WHAT DO YOU WANT?" She demanded, afraid she already knew the answer and glad her voice, at least, sounded strong.

"Because of you, I lost millions of credits." He closed the distance between them, catching her easily because there was nowhere to run. "You owe me. I'm here to collect." When he spoke, his moist, fetid breath fanned across her face.

He shoved her up against the wall, his hands grabbing her breasts, his mouth coming down on hers in a brutal mockery of a kiss. Panicked, she beat at him with clinched fists, struggling to get away. Then, in a desperate move, she bit his mouth as hard as she could.

He howled in pain, instinctively stepping back, but there was little time to enjoy her victory. She saw his raised fist just before everything went black.

Phoenix came to almost immediately, her head exploding in pain from the blow she'd received. Something wet and coppery-tasting coated her lips. Blood. Maybe his, but more likely hers. It didn't matter.

She realized she was on the floor, lying across the threshold of the bathroom door. The trader was straddling her, with one hand beneath her nightshirt, groping for her panties.

In the next instant, he ripped them off, leaving her exposed.

A new horror filled her, but despite the hopelessness of her situation, she renewed her struggling.

She remembered the bottle of Ramian nectar that Dante had sent, now sitting on the floor beside the tub.

When the trader started to undo the fastening of his pants, she seized the opportunity to reach blindly across the floor.

Please, let it be within reach.

Just as she heard the sickening zip of his pants coming undone, her fingers touched the smooth cool hardness of the bottle.

Putting all her strength into a final shove against the trader, she gained enough maneuverability to grab the bottle—and slammed it against the side of his head as hard as she could.

For a moment, time seemed to stop. The bottle didn't break, but the trader froze; momentarily suspended in place. Then his eyes rolled up into his head and he toppled to the floor.

Instantly, Phoenix released the bottle and forced herself to stand. Unsure what to do next, she hesitated.

The sound of the trader's moan as he regained consciousness sent her racing from the room.

Desperate to put as much distance as she could between her and her attacker, she raced down one corridor and then another, with no clue—or care—where she was going. She ran until she was out of breath and only then did she slow to a walk.

When she rounded the next corner, she found herself at the park. Without the sunlight, it was dark and ominous – but there were places to hide.

She was half-way across the park when a muscled arm caught her about the waist from behind, ripping a scream from her throat as it lifted her off the ground. She kicked her legs and flailed her arms in a futile attempt to get free. Then a hand clamped over her mouth, silencing her.

"*Krauk*, woman, do you want to wake the whole city?"

The familiar deep tones penetrated her fear and she went limp with relief.

His hand fell from her mouth and the hold around her waist loosened enough for her to slide down until she was once again standing. Turning inside his embrace, she looked up into Adrian's familiar brown eyes and threw her arms about his neck in a desperate hug.

"I'm so glad to see you," she mumbled against his neck, inhaling his clean musky scent.

He stood rigidly at first, then slowly, as if it were something he rarely did, he wrapped his arms about her in an embrace.

"I thought I might have frightened you." His voice sounded rougher than usual.

She gave a small laugh. "You scared the hell out of me."

His hands fell away and she immediately missed their warmth. He pulled her arms from around his neck so he could look at her, but didn't let go. "Did something happen?" His gaze fell on her lips and his hand cupped her jaw in a surprisingly gentle hold. The softness of his gaze turned hard as he ran a thumb over her bleeding lip. When he spoke, his voice sounded colder and more deadly than a winter's night on Isinburg V. "Who hit you? Dante?"

"No. A trader did." She tried to shrug, but her shoulders and neck hurt too much. "Dante decided not to do business with him based on my reading and now he blames me. He broke into my room and tried to—" She had trouble saying it out loud, but as it turned out, she didn't need to. Adrian figured it out.

She sensed his entire body tense. "Where is he?"

"I'm not sure. I managed to knock him out with an empty bottle of nectar and then I ran." Afraid he might leave her to go after the trader, Phoenix changed the subject. "Not that I'm not grateful, but what are you doing here?"

"We stopped for supplies and information. I couldn't believe it when I saw you in the park. I knew Dante would never let you walk out of here, so I came to get you." He glanced at his watch. "We need to get to the rendezvous spot. Jack's picking us up."

"My things are back in my room. We need to get them."

"No time," he told her, then fell silent as his gaze raked over her, making her suddenly conscious of the way she looked. She tugged at the bottom of her night-shirt, trying to stretch it lower to cover more of her legs. "No, you can't go around dressed like that." He shrugged out of his long, black duster. "Put this on." He held it while she slipped her arms through the sleeves, then turned her around so he could button the front.

Phoenix was tall for a woman, but Adrian's coat was still big on her and she was very aware of his scrutiny as he took in her appearance. Then he gave a half-shrug.

"It'll do."

Then, taking her by the hand, they left the park.

Adrian couldn't believe he'd found her so easily and knew that as soon as Dante discovered she was gone, he'd have his guards out searching for her. He led her down several corridors, knowing that at this time of night, no one would be about—except possibly the trader who'd attacked Phoenix. Adrian welcomed the opportunity to run into him. Just the thought of the man touching Phoenix had Adrian seething.

"Where's the rendezvous place?" Phoenix asked, breaking into his thoughts.

"Opposite side of the city."

Reaching the door to the stairwell, he stopped.

"Why are we stopping?" she asked, casting a nervous look behind her.

"We need to get to the lower levels." Adrian palmed the door panel, but it didn't open. Locked.

Releasing her hand, he pulled a knife from his back pocket and pried off the panel cover. It popped off easily and within moments, Adrian had cut and stripped several wires.

"What are you doing?"

"Fortunately, not all the technology in Cloud City is modern. I've just rewired the system to run a continuous maintenance loop which will allow us to bypass security, but it won't last long, so let's hurry."

He replaced the cover and when he tried to activate the door, it opened.

"Let's go." He followed her into the stairwell and let the door close behind them.

"Where do these stairs lead?" Phoenix whispered.

"They run beneath the city. If we're lucky, we won't have to go top-side until we reach our destination. Just keep quiet and stay close." He pulled the glow-rod from the side pocket of his pants and used the small beam to light the darkened stairwell.

"Give me your hand."

Together, they descended the steps and Adrian couldn't help but notice how delicate her hand felt in his. At the bottom of the stairs, they opened the door and stepped into another maze of corridors.

Several times, they were forced to backtrack a wrong turn, but throughout their trek, Phoenix never complained, for which Adrian was grateful. The longer they stayed in the lower levels, the more he worried. There was no way to tell what was happening above them; no way to know if Phoenix's absence had been noticed. The last thing he wanted was to go upstairs and walk into the middle of a search party.

They backtracked another dead-end and took the only other available corridor that led to an unmarked door. He stopped to listen. After a full minute of hearing nothing, he opened the door and stepped inside.

Shadows against the wall made the room seem eerie. Using the beam of his glow-rod to look around, he saw large crates stacked on one side of the room. On the other side, lengths of chain hung from the ceiling and mounted on the wall was an assortment of metallic devices that Adrian recognized with a sickening feeling.

Taking Phoenix by the hand, he guided her across the room toward the opposite doorway, hoping she wouldn't notice anything—and if she did, that maybe she wouldn't understand what she saw.

They'd only taken a few steps when the sound of voices drifted to them from outside the room.

Quickly looking for a place to hide, Adrian's gaze fell on the nearby stack of crates. He pulled Phoenix behind them just as the voices grew louder.

Looking through the gaps in the crates, Adrian saw Marcus walk in and cross to the wall holding the collection of whips and chains. As he studied the display, two guards entered, dragging a struggling victim between them. Adrian recognized the little man as Zimmers, a weasel of a man who haunted The Abyss from time to time.

"...but I didn't mean to hurt anyone," Zimmers was whining. "I didn't think anyone would miss it."

Marcus remained silent as he selected a particularly nasty looking metal-spiked leather whip.

"Wh... what are you going to do?" Zimmers asked, clearly worried.

A small smile played at Marcus' lips when he turned to face the little man, testing the weight and length of the whip by cracking it in the air. Zimmers paled and would have run had the guards not restrained him.

Adrian and Phoenix exchanged glances and he saw that her eyes had gone wide. Afraid she might make a noise that would give them away, he lifted a finger to her lips, reminding her to keep quiet.

"No, please," Zimmers pleaded, his voice growing louder and more urgent, drawing Adrian's attention back to the group. "It won't happen again."

"I'm sure that it won't." Marcus walked up to him and ripped the shirt from his body. Then he stepped back while the guards turned their prisoner to face the wall and secured the metal cuffs around his wrists.

When the whip came down, Zimmers screamed. Beside him, Phoenix jerked, but Adrian barely noticed. He stared at the blood welling along the torn flesh. The whip cracked again, drawing more blood and screams of agony and fear.

Adrian braced, waiting for the monster within him to rise; fought not to feel the rush of sick pleasure that was the legacy of Zarek's years of conditioning. He refused to let Zarek win and clamped down on his emotions with iron determination. His gaze fell on Phoenix and her expression of stunned horror.

When Marcus brought down the whip again, she jerked and gripped Adrian with trembling hands. He didn't think she was even aware of touching him. When the whip snapped again, she flinched and cried out.

The sound of Zimmers' tortured cry at the same moment kept them from being discovered.

On the next downward strike of the whip, her knees buckled and only Adrian's quick actions prevented her from falling. She clutched his arms, holding on as a drowning woman would a lifeline, and managed to stay on her feet. She wasn't an empath, he reminded himself, so it must be the sight of such violence that was overwhelming her.

Adrian wished he could shield her from it. More important at the moment, he needed to distract her, otherwise, her next cry could be their undoing.

Still holding her close, he turned her head until she was gazing up at him. Her emerald eyes held a haunted, lost look and he found himself unable to turn away.

He lowered his mouth to hers. The kiss was hesitant, chaste. The next one was less so. It ignited a hunger within him and when her lips parted on a sigh, he pressed his advantage.

Phoenix had been kissed before, but never like this. The rest of the room and its occupants disappeared. Poor Mr. Zimmers was forgotten. She felt only a need so primitive it would have scared her had she the presence of mind to think about it. She didn't.

At the moment, Adrian was her entire world. She wrapped her arms around his neck and surrendered herself to him, trusting him completely to keep her safe. Embracing her with one arm, his free hand moved to her hip, pulling her tightly against him until she felt the hard ridge of his desire pressing into her. Instinctively, she rubbed against it and felt, rather than heard, Adrian's low growl.

His hand moved from her hip, up along her waist and then higher, until he cupped her breast through the heavy fabric of his coat.

Her desire continued to build and her hands clutched at him as each successive squeeze of her breast grew harder, more demanding, until the next one brought enough pain that she cried out.

Suddenly, Adrian set her away from him. A chill washed over her in the absence of his warmth and she thought she saw a wild, desperate look in his eyes just before he turned away.

Embarrassed and confused, Phoenix stared at his back, trying to calm her reeling senses. What had just happened?

She looked past him through the opening in the crates and noticed they were once again alone. She hadn't even heard the men leave.

"They're gone," she told Adrian, watching him closely.

He moved out into the room and looked around. "Come on," he said after a few seconds, not bothering to look at her. "Let's get out of here before they return." His voice sounded rougher than usual and Phoenix wished she knew what he was thinking.

At the doorway, Adrian stopped to listen. Apparently satisfied that no one was in the corridor beyond, he stepped out, gesturing for her to follow.

They continued in tense silence until they reached another stairwell. They took it up and found the door at the top unlocked.

They stepped out into a windowed corridor. The sun was just beginning to rise and light filtered in through the glass. The few people about at this hour ignored them.

"We're almost there," Adrian told her as they rounded the next corner and stood at the opening to a small landing bay full of ships. Adrian was looking around the area when Phoenix suddenly felt him tense. He put a hand out and moved her back behind him. Looking over his shoulder, she saw several armed guards.

"Change of plan." His words were tense. "Come on."

He retraced their steps until he found an empty stretch of corridor along the perimeter of the building. Stepping close to the window, he pressed the comm-device on his wrist.

"Where are you?"

Phoenix couldn't hear the voice coming through the device, but knew it was Jack.

"Yeah, I saw them," Adrian said. There were a few more seconds of silence followed by a terse, "I don't like it, but I don't see that we have any other choice. Okay." He looked up and down the corridor. "Give us five minutes to get there." He pressed another button on his comm-device to end the call and started walking. "This way."

"Where are we going?" She had to hurry to keep up with him.

"The Outcrop."

"What's that?"

"It's a restaurant that extends out perpendicular to the city over the planet. Good food and a great scenic view. Fortunately, it doesn't open for breakfast, so we shouldn't run into crowds."

Phoenix followed Adrian in silence, wondering if Jack was planning to land the ship on the roof of the restaurant. She hoped it wasn't far. Emotionally drained and physically exhausted, she was functioning on pure adrenaline.

As Adrian had predicted, they found the restaurant closed and locked.

"How are we going to get in?" Phoenix stared at the entrance, noting the absence of a panel like the one at the stairwell.

"We're not going inside." Adrian walked past the entrance and continued down the corridor until he reached the first window.

Phoenix joined him and looked out. From here, she could see the side of the restaurant jutting out at a right angle to the space city. Then she noticed the narrow ledge halfway up the wall, running the length of the structure.

"Please tell me Jack is picking us up on the roof."

"The roof is several floors above us. There's no time to reach it. We'll have to go out here."

She turned to Adrian in disbelief. "You're joking."

"I never joke."

Phoenix crossed her arms and shook her head. "Well, you can forget it. I'm not going out there."

"We don't have a choice. There's no safe place to land the ship and nowhere else that Jack can bring it close enough for us to board."

"No. You're crazy. That tiny scrap of metal is not wide enough to walk on."

"Sure it is," he assured her, working on the window latch. When it popped free, he looked at her. "Opening this has activated the alarms. We now have five minutes to get to the ship before Dante's men are all over us." He paused and Phoenix thought she saw a slight softening in his expression. "You can do this."

Without waiting for her to agree, he slid open the window, swung a leg over the sill and climbed out onto the ledge. "Come on." He leaned down and held out his hand to her.

"I... I can't." She took a step away from him.

"Phoenix, we don't have a lot of time." She could tell it was a struggle for him to keep his tone even.

"You don't understand. I can't go out there."

Adrian leaned further inside. "I'm not leaving you, Phoenix." He kept his hand extended, his gaze holding hers.

"I'm afraid of heights." She heard the panic in her voice.

"I'm right here with you," he promised. "I won't let anything happen to you."

Again she shook her head, too afraid to move.

"Trust me."

For what seemed minutes, they stared at one another, but Adrian's gaze never wavered. The fear of facing Dante again proved stronger than her fear of falling. Reluctantly, she took a step forward and placed her hand in Adrian's.

As she swung her leg over the sill, Adrian moved back to give her room. He seemed perfectly at ease, perched on a ledge that seemed much too narrow, no matter what he'd told her.

"Don't look down," he warned as she stepped out beside him. "Put one hand against the wall to steady yourself and hold mine with the other. We're going to take it nice and easy. It gets a little windy the further out we go, but as long as you stick close to the wall, you'll be fine. Ready?"

She took a deep breath, keeping her gaze trained on Adrian. "Okay."

He smiled. "That's my girl. Nice and slow now." He began to side step along the ledge, never releasing her hand as she followed after him.

Just as he predicted, the further out they moved, the stronger the wind blew. About halfway to the end of the building, Phoenix made the mistake of looking down. Instantly, vertigo hit as the world spun out of control.

She leaned into the wall and shut her eyes, afraid she might lose her balance. Her breathing grew ragged and her feet froze, refusing to move, even when Adrian tugged gently at her hand.

"You're doing fine." His calm voice carried over the sound of the buffeting wind.

"No, no." She kept her eyes shut. "I can't do this. Please, get me back inside."

"We can't go back." Adrian's tone was gentle but firm. "We're almost there. I won't let anything happen to you," he promised. "Do you hear me, Phoenix?"

She nodded, but couldn't speak.

"Listen to me, you're doing fine. Open your eyes, but look only at me. Open them, Phoenix. That's my girl. Now, concentrate on the sound of my voice. You can do this. Trust me."

His words became a litany that he repeated over and over as he led her along the ledge. Phoenix refused to think of anything except the sound of his voice which was calm and assured. It anchored her and gave her the strength to move.

The time it took to reach the furthest point of the ledge seemed interminably long. The wind whipped at them mercilessly and more than once, Phoenix feared it would knock her off. She felt childish clutching Adrian's hand so desperately, but she couldn't let go.

Then the ship appeared. She stared in fascination as it drew close and then hovered only a few meters away. The thrusters added a new level of difficulty, blasting them with hot gusts of wind and plastering the duster to her body. She pushed herself more tightly against the wall, afraid the weight of the coat might drag her over the edge.

A hatch opened in front of them and she waited for a platform to extend toward them, but none came. How were they supposed to board, she wondered? Jump?

She saw the answer in Adrian's gaze even before he said the words.

"No. It's too far," she protested, shaking her head. "Adrian, please." Her eyes pleaded for understanding even as fear paralyzed her.

"Phoenix. You have to jump—now."

Then everything seemed to happen at once. Adrian swore and, pulling out his laser, fired at her. No, not at her—past her. She looked back and saw Dante's men shooting at them.

The searing heat of a laser's beam on her arm told her she'd been hit—or at least grazed. If she didn't jump, the next shot might kill her and she'd die right there on the ledge.

"Jump!"

The urgency of Adrian's tone propelled her from the ledge just as a searing pain lanced through her side. For one brief moment, she was sailing toward the ship, the open hatch beckoning to her.

The next moment, she was falling through the air with the planet's surface rushing to meet her.

Chapter 5

ADRIAN CONTINUED FIRING AT the guards climbing out on the ledge after them. Just as the last one fell after being hit, Adrian caught sight of a familiar face through the window.

Kinto Juarez—the one man who knew what had happened to Skylar—smiled and raised a hand in mock salute.

Before Adrian could decide how to react, Phoenix's scream pierced the air.

When he turned toward the sound, he felt the cold hand of fear squeeze his heart. Phoenix, with arms flailing, was plummeting toward the planet's surface.

Slapping his weapon into its holster, Adrian dove head-first off the ledge.

There was a fair distance between them, but the coat she was wearing was acting like a parachute— albeit, a very poor one—resisting the wind and slowing her descent.

Snapping his arms tight against his sides to reduce his drag, he kept his gaze focused on his target. He sliced through the air with increasing speed and flexed his arms and hands as needed to adjust his position.

Drawing closer, he became aware of another problem. She was panicking, flailing her arms and legs about so it would be impossible to get close enough to grab her. He'd only have one shot at this. If he missed, there'd be no second chance.

He yelled at her to be still, but the wind slammed his words back into his face. Watching his slim opportunity for success dissolve in the tide of her panic, Adrian did the one thing he hadn't done in a long time—he prayed.

He prayed for her to be calm in the face of her worst fear; prayed for her to trust he would save her. Mostly, though, he prayed for a miracle.

He was less than three meters above her, with the ground approaching fast, when she suddenly grew still. Before he could do more than be grateful, Adrian hit the burble—that pocket of dead air directly above a falling body. With the wind resistance suddenly gone, he slammed against her, wrapped his arms around her and locked them in place. She didn't move and he couldn't see her face to know if she was conscious or not. He'd been falling head first while she'd been falling feet first. With his arms wrapped around her waist and his face pressed against the juncture of her legs, it was an enviable position—under different circumstances.

He started a slow mental count.

Ten.

Nine.

The timing had to be just right. If he acted too soon – or too late—they would both die.

Seven.

Six.

With extreme effort, he twisted around so now his feet were below him and hers were falling back over his head. The coat covered his head, nearly blinding him. Only if he looked straight down through the gap beneath his armpit could he make out the surface of the planet.

Four.

Three.

Two.

Adrian snapped the heels of his boots together.

The small thrusters embedded in the thick soles fired. Adrian braced his legs against the impact and felt their descent slow.

No one visited Cloud City without taking precautions against "accidents". Some wore anti-gravity belts. Others wore tunics that converted into parachutes. Adrian preferred thruster boots. They survived a fight with an opponent better than the other two choices.

When they were about a meter off the ground, Adrian snapped his heels again to deactivate the thruster and they fell the last short distance.

The landing was rough and Adrian stumbled a bit, but he kept upright, Phoenix still clutched in his arms. They were alive.

As some of the tension left his body, he changed his hold on Phoenix, swinging her up so he could cradle her in his arms. He felt her body trembling against his and looked down into her face, steeling himself against the effect of her haunted green gaze.

"Are you hurt?"

She didn't respond but pushed at his chest until he—reluctantly—set her on her feet. She moved slowly; awkwardly, as if the effort to do anything was too much.

"Let's go!"

The sound of Jack's voice drew Adrian's attention to the ship hovering a few meters away. Jack stood in the hatchway, motioning for them to hurry.

Adrian turned back to Phoenix in time to catch the flat of her palm smartly against his face.

"That's for almost getting me killed." She turned and stalked toward the ship, miraculously recovered from her earlier paralysis.

"I saved your damn life," he hollered after her, rubbing his jaw. The woman was stronger than she looked. "You should be thanking me," he muttered.

Phoenix stopped in her tracks, whirling around to face him, hands on hips. "Thank you?" She bit out the words. "I shouldn't have been out there on the ledge in the first place. Thank you? I should have hit you harder."

She turned on her heel and finished crossing the distance to the ship where Jack helped her climb aboard. Adrian followed more slowly.

Damn, she was sexy when she was mad.

Phoenix sought refuge in the first room she found after climbing aboard. Once inside with the doors safely closed, she collapsed onto the bed. She'd just survived a near-death experience. The fall from the ledge had traumatized her – and yet, the only thing she could think about was the slap to Adrian's cheek.

She touched her fingertips to her cheek where the echo of the slap still stung. An empathic sting; something a true null wouldn't have felt.

The pain wasn't imagined, though. Nor, she realized now, had the pain she'd felt each time Marcus had splayed the whip across poor Mr. Zimmers' back.

Was it possible that the empath tests she'd taken as a child were incorrect? That her empathic abilities had merely lain dormant until triggered by exposure to—what? Something stronger than the passive emotions of Xenobians? Or maybe the development of her abilities had been delayed due to her half-human genetics.

Whatever the reason, she was starting to feel the emotions of those around her—and it was more than distracting. It was dangerous.

She touched her side, finding it undamaged. The searing pain that had caused her foot to slip when she'd jumped for the ship had not been the result of her getting shot.

Adrian?

A part of her wanted to make sure he was okay.

She stayed where she was and forced herself to take a calming breath. If she checked on Adrian, she'd have to explain why and she wasn't ready to share this new development with anyone. Not until she understood it herself.

Why hadn't she paid more attention in school when they'd taught controlling one's emotions?

She thought back to that moment when she was falling, engulfed in mind-numbing terror and felt that first brush of calm assurance.

Had that come from Adrian? He'd been the only other person around, so it must have.

She closed her eyes and massaged her temples with her fingertips. This was all so confusing.

Adrian sat back in his seat, watching the stars fly by as Jack piloted the ship.

"What do you think?"

Jack's question broke into his thoughts.

"I think she's trouble." When he felt Jack staring at him, Adrian turned to find himself the recipient of a raised-eyebrow. "Sorry, what was the question?"

"What do you think about flying out to Dominion to see what leads we can pick up?"

"Oh." Disgusted with himself for letting that woman dominate his thoughts, Adrian considered Jack's proposal. He'd told Jack about spotting Kinto Juarez, but neither of them was inclined to go back to Cloud City to find him. The next best thing would be to go to one of Juarez's favorite haunts and wait for him to show up. "Let's set a course for The Black Hole," he said, referring to the only city on a planet Dominion. "Even if Juarez doesn't show up, someone there is bound to know something – and share it for a price." He paused. "Set our course by way of Sanctuary."

"Sanctuary? You think Skylar took refuge with a bunch of religious missionaries?"

"No, but we can't take Phoenix to Dominion."

"Sanctuary isn't exactly on the way," Jack pointed out. "It's six standard hours away. I don't think Skylar's got that kind of time, do you? Besides, what makes you think Phoenix will stay there?"

"He's right."

Adrian and Jack turned in their seats at the sound of Phoenix's voice and found her standing at the entrance to the bridge. She still wore his coat and her hair was mussed, but she appeared composed and calm.

"I will continue to look for my father; with your help – or without it."

Frustrated, Adrian ran his fingers through his hair. Taking Phoenix along would only complicate their efforts to find and rescue Skylar.

The sudden surge of the ship broke his train of thoughts and he turned to glare at Jack, more than ready to transfer his irritation to his partner.

"What the hell are you doing?"

"I'm taking us to Dominion. You know as well as I do, she's right. Skylar's time is running out. Now, don't you have a message to send?"

With a final glare at Jack, Adrian left the bridge.

Phoenix had returned to her cabin several hours ago, seeking the solace of her own company, but now it felt like the four walls of the room were closing in on her.

Standing up, she paced along the short space at the foot of the bed but it did little to relieve her pent up energy.

She longed to go to the bridge, but Jack had retired to the other cabin to rest and she knew Adrian would be there alone. It was easier, safer, not to be near him. Every time they were together, the air between them fairly crackled with emotions. With her new abilities raw and exposed, it was hard enough to deal with her own emotions, much less his.

She took a deep cleansing breath and let it out slowly, but it didn't help. Needing a change of scenery, she left the cabin.

Unsure where she was going, she walked along the short passageway, reaching the bridge sooner than expected. There, she paused.

Adrian sat with his back to her. Even without her new abilities, she'd have sensed his fatigue from the way he sat and moved. It gave her an idea. Maybe there was a way she could ease the tension between them. A peace offering of sorts.

She hurried past the bridge in search of the galley.

It was a small room, but efficiently laid out and stocked with all the basics, including what she needed. She set to work and soon had brewed two cups of K'feinno.

Carrying one in each hand, she made her way back to the bridge.

Adrian glanced up when she walked in, but when she offered him one of the cups, he simply stared at her skeptically.

She blew out an exasperated breath. "It's not poisoned. I was making a cup for myself and thought you might want one also."

"Why?"

"Because you look tired." She waved the cup in front of his face. "Do you want this or not?"

"Fine," she said when he continued to stare at her. "Forget I offered."

She stormed off the bridge, still holding both cups, and headed back to her cabin. She'd made an effort and he'd blown her off. She wouldn't make that mistake again.

Alone on the bridge, Adrian tried to figure out what had just happened. He'd been thinking about Phoenix, something he'd been doing too much of in the very short time he'd known her, when suddenly she was there, standing beside him, holding out a cup of K'fein-no.

The gesture had taken him by surprise. He couldn't remember the last time anyone—other than Jack, maybe – had done something nice for him without there being a catch. He'd taken too long trying to figure what she wanted and she'd misinterpreted his silence as rejection. Why couldn't he just accept a kind gesture when it was offered?

He knew the answer to that all too well. Damn Zarek to hell, he thought, for teaching him to be distrustful. Not only had he offended Phoenix, but now he'd have to fetch his own K'feinno.

Setting the ship's navigation on autopilot, he headed for the galley.

Six hours later, Jack walked onto the bridge.

"Any problems?"

Adrian thought back to the one and only time he'd seen Phoenix. "No."

"Good. I'll take over. Go get some rest."

Adrian rose from his seat, rubbing his tired eyes. "Mind if I use your cabin? Phoenix is using mine and I don't think she's of a mind to share."

"Yeah, sure." Jack shrugged. "Help yourself."

"Thanks."

Adrian headed down the short passageway, stopping in front of his own cabin door along the way. He mentally reviewed its contents and concluded there was nothing in there he needed, but instead of continuing on, he lingered, unable to explain why he felt a need to check on Phoenix. He only wanted to make sure she was all right—and maybe apologize for being rude earlier.

Before he could talk himself out of it, he raised his hand and knocked on the door. When there was no answer, he tried the handle. It turned easily and he pushed the door open.

He spotted her immediately, lying on his bed, asleep with her auburn hair spread out on the pillow like a halo about her head. She looked so peaceful and enticing that he was tempted to walk over to take a closer look, but knew he wouldn't. Closing the door so as not to waken her, he continued on to Jack's cabin.

Within minutes, Adrian had stripped off his shirt and shoes. Still wearing his pants and feeling a bone weary exhaustion that was as much emotional as physical, he stretched out on the cot and let sleep overtake him.

He was sixteen, asleep in the cell that had become his home. When he awoke, he wasn't alone.

A nude woman sat beside him on the bed. She was every young man's fantasy, with long blond hair, blue eyes, generous curves and flawless features. She held a tray of food on her lap and because Zarek's conditioning had left him dull-witted and starving, Adrian fell on it.

Too late, he discovered Zarek's duplicity. The food was laced with the powerful aphrodisiac Pheromone 14. As the drug took hold of him, his determination to resist the woman faded. At his first touch, she shivered, so he muttered words meant to be soothing as his hands explored her body.

When he tried to kiss her, she shrank from him. Aware only of an insatiable need to taste her, he gripped her jaw and crushed his mouth against hers. The action merely whetted his appetite and he forced her head back until her mouth fell open and immediately, he swept his tongue inside.

At her submission, a sense of satisfaction engulfed him. He had done well. He embraced the new feelings and listened to the voice in his head that urged him to continue; to be masterful.

When his fondling turned rough and she cried out from the pain, he felt superior; invincible. Spurred on by his growing need, he quickly had her below him, his member plowing awkwardly into her soft folds. He took her roughly, aware only of his own pleasure. Only once, when she cried out, did he try to withdraw, sensing something might be wrong. The effort was exhausting and in the end, a misunderstanding. Her cries were cries of passion; he must see to her needs.

He soon found his climax and cried out, but with Pheromone 14 pumping through his system, this was just the beginning of a long night. Each successive coupling grew rougher as he seemed to need more vi-olence to maintain the same level of satisfaction. Af-

ter his fourth climax, his need ebbed and a kernel of awareness fought its way to his brain. He was being manipulated and an innocent woman was suffering because of him.

Disgust and horror combined to give him the strength to push himself off the woman. Even as he did, searing pain shot through his head; a clear sign of Zarek's displeasure, which meant the man was watching – as usual.

Adrian wanted to go to the woman, who lay on the bed soundless and still. He wanted to apologize; to explain, but he was physically too weak and it took the last of his energy to fight the effects of the drug and crawl to the far corner of the room though blinding pain seared his brain.

"Go back to her, boy." Zarek's voice boomed into the room across the intercom. "Finish what you started. That one likes it rough and I promise you'll enjoy it."

"Krauk you," Adrian whispered, his body curling into a fetal position. The worst was yet to come. He knew that.

Zarek didn't disappoint him and the pain proved to be too much. He passed out, finding peace at last.

When he came to, he waited for the pain to return. When it didn't, Adrian risked opening his eyes to look around. Alarm hit him like a crushing blow at the sight of the woman still lying on the bed. He wasn't sure he *had it in him to resist Zarek again and needed to warn her to leave before it was too late. He opened his mouth to call to her, but his voice refused to work.*

Stumbling to his feet, he shuffled across the room. When he got near enough to really see the woman, he felt a momentary confusion. This was the same woman he'd attacked, but her once blond hair now lay auburn across the sheets and green eyes, not blue, stared sightlessly from a familiar face.

Phoenix!

Then he saw the dark red stain spreading out from between her legs and across the mattress.

Blood! It was everywhere and the color stood out in stark contrast to her unusually pale skin.

She had bled a long time before death claimed her and he knew he was responsible.

Zarek had finally succeeded. He had turned Adrian into a monster just like himself.

Remorse and self-loathing built until Adrian couldn't hold it in any longer. He threw back his head and roared in rage at the fates; and most of all at Zarek.

The high-pitched sound of a woman's scream ripped Adrian from the clutches of his nightmare. He bolted from the bed and automatically grabbed his laser as he raced from the cabin.

Phoenix was in danger.

Chapter 6

Adrian burst into Phoenix's cabin ready to face whatever threatened her. Light from the passageway spilled across the bed, providing him with enough light to see her huddled against the headboard, her gaze darting wildly about the room. Still shaken from his own nightmare, he momentarily let his hungry gaze devour her, assuring himself that she was, at least, alive.

He quickly turned his attention to the room, scanning it for anything unusual. Seeing nothing, he started toward her, but as he did, she shrank away from him in horror.

"No! Stay away from me!"

Her words caught him off guard, stopping him in his tracks. "Phoenix, what's wrong?"

At that moment, Jack raced through the door, his laser held before him, ready for use. "I heard screaming."

"Don't let him hurt me," she pleaded.

Jack looked about the room. "Who are we protecting her from?"

"I think me."

Jack narrowed his eyes, pinning Adrian under a gaze that was equal parts suspicion and curiosity. "What'd you do to her?"

Adrian shook his head. "Damned if I know."

It was some time later that Phoenix sat curled up in a chair on the bridge, staring out the view port, unaware of the stars passing in front of her. Only now, with her mind clear and fully awake, did she allow herself to consider what had happened.

She'd had a nightmare, but one that had seemed so real it terrified her. It was like she had been standing in the room, watching helplessly as another woman was raped. Not only had she "felt" the woman's pain and fear, she'd also "felt" the rapist's lust and heard his thoughts as he congratulated himself on his actions.

She'd tried to force herself awake, but the nightmare scenes continued, drawing her further into the violence and pain until her own identity slowly faded, melding with the woman's until she was the one being brutally raped. Worse, she'd looked up into the rapist's face and recognized Adrian.

Phoenix raised the cup of K'feinno Jack had brought her and took a sip, letting the drink's warmth chase away the bone-deep chill left in the wake of the nightmare. Considering the experience more objectively, she realized there was nothing prophetic about it. It had been a dream, nothing more. And it hadn't even been hers.

Growing up, she'd heard the tales of children, still adjusting to their empathic powers, psychically eavesdropping on other people's dreams and nightmares. That's what had happened to her; it was the only logical explanation. Unable to control her own powers, she had simply eavesdropped on someone else's nightmare. In this case, the obvious "someone" was Adrian.

Phoenix found the conclusion almost as unsettling as the nightmare itself. Why would Adrian dream about something so horrible? Was it the manifestation of his subconscious demons needing to be exorcised? Or some private sexual fantasy? She found neither possibility reassuring. They all pointed to a deeply disturbed man; one into whose hands she had entrusted her life and that of her father's.

The image of her dead self on the mattress again flitted across her mind and she shivered. While her first reaction to the nightmare had been fear, her second was rapidly turning into anger and frustration.

A noise caught her attention and still lost in her thoughts, it took a moment to realize that Jack had spoken.

"I'm sorry?"

"I said—I don't know what's going on between you and Adrian, but I want you to know that if he hurt you in any way..." He let the suggestion hang, unfinished.

"I thought he was your friend."

"He is, but I don't condone violence against women and frankly, I didn't think Adrian did either."

Something about how he said that pricked her curiosity. "Don't you know? I thought you two had been together a long time?"

"Five years."

"I would think in that time, you would know whether a man was capable of rape."

Jack leveled his gaze on her, his face suddenly very serious. "Before I go beat the crap out of my best friend, let me make sure I understood you correctly. Are you saying that Adrian raped you?"

"No, no!" Phoenix regretted her slip immediately. She had no doubt that Jack would do just as he threatened. "Adrian didn't do anything."

Oh boy. How was she going to explain herself without confessing her newly discovered powers?

"He kissed me, earlier, and it was..." How did she describe what she'd felt? Maybe she shouldn't try. "I guess it affected me more than I realized." She felt her face turning red and waved her free hand dismissively in the air. "Anyway—the rape—it was only a dream."

She watched as some of the tension left Jack's body.

"Adrian Sun would never rape a woman." His conviction was strong and left no room for doubt. "If he was a little rough with you, it's probably because we don't get that many—gentle—women out here in the Outer Fringe." He cocked his eyebrow and gave her a wink.

Jack didn't seem to notice her stunned silence and went on. "He might be a little rough around the edges, but Adrian's a good man, I'd bet my life on it—and have, many times."

In his cabin, Adrian turned and paced back to the other side of the room. He was suffering this self-imposed confinement in order to give Phoenix time to recover. Recover from what, exactly, he wasn't sure. What had he done this time to upset her?

Several memories came to mind.

Exposed her to a man being tortured. Kissed her. Got her shot at. Nearly let her fall to her death.

It was enough to give anyone nightmares, but if she'd done as he'd told her in the first place and gone home, she wouldn't have suffered through any of them.

So he really didn't see how he was to blame—and he shouldn't have to hide away like a criminal.

He headed for the bridge.

"What are you doing here?" Jack's tone sounded slightly confrontational, which only added to Adrian's irritability.

"I will not be ostracized from my own bridge." He looked over at Phoenix who watched him with a furrowed brow. "I would like to talk to you." He forced himself to add, "Please."

She rose from her chair and walked toward him. For a second, hope blossomed that she'd come to her senses, no longer blaming him for some imagined offense. Then reality set in as she pushed past him without saying a word.

His irritation rose a notch and he turned to follow, but Jack's hand on his arm stopped him.

"Let her go, Adrian." His tone was firm, protective and it grated on Adrian's nerves because he was acting like Adrian was an actual threat.

The thought made Adrian go cold. Never before had Jack, by action or word, made him feel like the monster he sometimes feared he might be. That Jack did so now, because of this woman, cut him deeply.

"Get your hand off my arm." He spoke slowly, with a deadly calm that had Jack widening his eyes. He recovered quickly.

"I can't let you go after her."

"Really? And just how do you plan to stop me?"

Jack's tone grew more serious. "I don't want to hurt you."

Adrian gave Jack a fierce look. "Be very careful what you say and do next, friend," he stressed that last word. A part of him was stunned at how quickly they both had resorted to near violence. It was unlike them. Taking a deep breath, he let it out slowly, looking for the icy calm that used to dominate his life—prior to Phoenix. "I didn't do anything to her and I only want to talk to her."

Jack studied him for a moment longer, then nodded and removed his hand.

Adrian left the bridge and headed for his cabin, the one Phoenix had slept in. When he didn't find her there, he checked Jack's cabin and prayed that he wouldn't find her there either.

Finding Jack's cabin empty, Adrian headed for the galley – the only other place on the ship where she could be.

He found her sitting at the table, sipping a drink.

"I want to talk about what happened earlier."

She stood and emptied her drink into the sink. After she placed the dirty cup in the washer, she turned to face him.

"There's nothing to talk about. Everything's fine."

Having expected a fight, she'd caught him off guard. "Excuse me?"

"You heard me," she bit out. "There's nothing to talk about."

Anger mixed with frustration. "Yes, there is. What was all that crap back there?" He took a step forward as he waved his arm toward her cabin. "Oh Jack, don't let him hurt me," he mimicked. "When have I done anything to hurt you?" Other than taking you out on a ledge a thousand meters above the ground and letting you fall? The question silently mocked him.

Her gaze went from controlled to heated as she moved away from the counter, squaring off to face him. "Don't you make fun of me when it's your fault in the first place."

One eyebrow cocked, he took a step closer. "There! That's exactly what I'm talking about. How do you figure this is my fault?"

"Forget it. I'm not going to stand here and do this. I'm going back to my cabin." She made to move past him and his temper exploded.

"You're not going anywhere until we've had this out," he shouted, storming forward until she was backed against the wall. "You treat me like I'm some kind of felon, practically turn my best friend against me and then you say there's nothing to talk about, yet somehow it's my fault?" He slammed his fist against the wall beside her head, using the pain to focus his anger and frustration away from her. Leaning against the wall, he gripped her upper arm with his other hand and held her as he brought his face close to hers.

Seeming more furious than frightened, she shoved at his chest, but he refused to move. "You want to know why I was afraid?" She yelled. "Because I dreamed that you raped a woman. Only somehow that woman became me and I died from your brutality." Her anger spent, she punched him, but there was no strength in her effort. She gave a little sob. "You killed me."

He stared at her in disbelief. How could she know about his dream? Yet if it was true, it explained a lot. Of course it had frightened her. Hell, it had frightened him.

He took a deep breath and released it slowly, feeling all the fight drain from his body.

"It wasn't your nightmare," he told her. "It was mine. I've been having it ever since..." He paused, afraid the truth would frighten her more. "It's a recurring nightmare. I was having it when your scream woke me. How is it possible for you to have had it, too? Unless you lied about being a null." He gazed at her, suspicious now of what she'd told him.

"I didn't lie to you," she said. "As a null, my abilities don't measure high enough to count. I don't know why now, all of a sudden, they decided to manifest. Maybe it's the stress." Her last statement dripped with sarcasm.

He ignored it. "When did you first notice them?"

She dropped her head and wouldn't look at him. "When we watched Marcus whip Mr. Zimmers."

Adrian thought back and realized now that her cries hadn't been of horror, but of pain.

"Have there been any other incidents?"

She nodded. "Standing on the ledge. I felt like I got shot. I didn't, but I felt the pain of whoever did right when I jumped for the ship. That's what caused me to slip. And now your dream."

"Nightmare," he automatically corrected her, unwilling to tell her the truth and really scare her. It hadn't been a nightmare at all, but a memory.

She didn't look soothed. "I haven't known you long enough to star in your recurring nightmare," she pointed out. "Especially one where you rape me. And I'm positive that I don't want to share the experience with you."

"Ah, Phoenix," he sighed, letting his forehead dip until it rested gently against hers. His hands came up to cradle her face as he inhaled her warm, fresh scent. "I may be a monster, but I would never hurt you," he said softly.

She grew still and his gaze focused on her lips, remembering their taste. A need more powerful than his anger and frustration slammed through him and, for a moment, he thought of nothing but the woman before him. He longed to take her into his arms, to share more than a kiss.

In that moment, he realized that she had every right to be afraid of him.

"You need to go now." He found it difficult to speak and the words came out sounding harsh. He dropped his hands from her face and stepped away, giving them both space, expecting her to bolt, feeling surprised when she didn't. She looked at him with something like concern.

"Adrian?" She sounded hesitant, like she wasn't sure how he might react to anything she said.

"You're right to want to stay away from me, Phoenix." He took another step back, putting more space between them, wondering if it would be enough.

"I don't think you're a monster." Her sweet words tore through his soul.

"Sweetheart," he growled. "You have no idea what kind of monster I really am. Now walk away while you still have the chance."

He didn't move from his spot until long after the sound of her footsteps faded.

Phoenix walked into Adrian's cabin and, shutting the door, leaned back against it. She remained that way for some time, listening. When she heard the sound of footsteps passing by, she knew instinctively they belonged to Adrian.

When he'd found her in the galley, she'd been prepared for his anger. What she hadn't expected was the wave of desire that flooded through her as he held her trapped between his arms. He'd wanted to kiss her. She hadn't needed to be an empath to sense it. Ironically, it hadn't been fear that had pulsed through her system at that moment, but excitement, anticipation, and something more. She'd wanted to feel his lips on hers.

That, more than anything, worried her, because remnants of the nightmare still lingered in the back of her mind. She had not set out on this adventure to get sexually involved with anyone, especially someone whose psyche was an emotional vortex. She was on a mission to find her father.

Phoenix walked over to the bed and sat down. She rested her elbows on her knees, letting her weary head drop onto her hands. Closing her eyes, she took a few deep, steadying breaths. She was much too inexperienced in the ways of men to know what to do.

She blew out a breath and forced her thoughts away from Adrian.

It was a big universe and her father was out there, somewhere. The odds of finding him were against them, yet she felt reassured now that she knew Adrian was looking for him.

"Hang on, Father," she whispered. "I'm coming for you."

Planet Dominion

"Agent O'Mallen," came a benevolent sounding voice. "The names of the SDIA agents working in the Elysian Rift please."

Skylar managed to laugh, despite the fresh wave of agony that accompanied Zarek's words. "You'll find out soon enough, when they shut down your operations."

He had no idea if what he said was true, but didn't see why he should be the only one to suffer the doubt, though to be sure, his suffering was the greater.

"Pity," Zarek said, without sounding in the least bit upset. "I had hoped to spare you further discomfort, but I see you require convincing."

The now familiar tingling started slowly, giving Skylar time to anticipate just how bad it would get. A part of him saluted the other man's technique—he'd never met anyone with such a knack for inflicting pain or so effectively waging a psychological assault.

The tingling turned to burning prickles running across his body. Soon, every nerve-ending felt raw and on fire. It grew unbearable, but of course, that was the point. Skylar suffered through it silently, biting the already raw and bleeding flesh of his inner cheek as much for distraction as to keep from crying out.

Under normal circumstance, he might have used his own special mental skills to fight back, but Zarek had taken precautions. In addition to abusing him physically, he'd rendered Skylar incapable of sustained coherent thought. The electrodes attached to Skylar's skull probed deep into his brain, manipulating his thoughts until he could no longer separate reality from the virtual world. He believed he was committing heinous acts against people who couldn't defend themselves and no matter how strongly he tried, he couldn't make himself stop.

The pain increased until Skylar writhed in agony, wondering for a split second if maybe this time, he'd reached his breaking point. Skylar suffered no illusion about his ability to resist Zarek's torment. Eventually, he would break. If he lived long enough.

Time was his one advantage for the simple reason that he had very little left.

He'd been captured before he could refresh the timer on the poison capsule in his heart. The clock was ticking on his last days and the bitch of it was, no one even knew he was missing—except maybe Phoenix and there wasn't anything she could do against a man like Zarek – nor would he want her to. His daughter was one of the two things he'd done right in his life. Saving Adrian had been the other.

That's one thing Zarek will never forgive me for should he find out.

So long as Adrian remained alive, even if Skylar died, he'd still beaten Zarek. Despite the pain he was in, the thought made him smile.

Chapter 7

PHOENIX FELT THE JOSTLING of the ship as it settled on the landing pad. She had read that the perpetually dark and cloudy atmosphere of the Black Hole gave the dismal-looking city its name. It was the start of the evening hour and with the setting sun came a drop in temperature, or so Jack had warned her earlier when she'd sat on the bridge to watch their final approach to the dark planet.

Now, as she waited in the cabin for Jack and Adrian to secure the ship, she was filled with uncertain anticipation. She knew they hoped to discover information about her father here. There'd been a discussion about leaving her on board while the two of them went into town, but Adrian insisted she go along—probably because he didn't trust her to stay out of trouble if left alone.

He'd not said so specifically to her face; in fact, he'd not talked to her at all since the episode in the galley, which was why she was so surprised when a knock sounded on her door and she opened it to find him standing outside.

There was a moment's awkward silence and then Adrian cleared his throat. "It's time to go."

"Okay, I'm ready." She started to step out into the passageway but he put out a hand to stop her.

"You can't wear that."

She looked down at the jumpsuit, which she'd found in his closet. "Why not?"

"It's too revealing."

As Adrian pushed past her to walk into the room, she looked down at her jumpsuit again. How could it be too revealing? She was covered from ankle to neck in thick, heavy fabric.

She turned to argue with him but found his back to her as he stood at the closet searching its contents. A second later, he pulled out a shirt and pants.

"Here, put these on."

She had no choice but to take the clothes because he forced them into her hand. She held them up as she looked in the mirror. "These won't fit. They're too big. Whose are they?"

"They're mine and don't argue with me. You can either put them on out here or go change in the bath-room."

He was crazy. Why should she take off something that fit to put on something that was clearly too large?

"Want help?"

Giving him a scowl, she went to the bathroom. After closing the door, it didn't take long to strip out of her jumpsuit and put on the clothes. Of course, they swallowed her.

She rolled up the shirt sleeves so her hands would be free to hold up the pants. Adrian's back was to her when she stepped out, so she cleared her throat to get his attention.

He turned and slowly let his gaze travel over her from head to toe. "Not bad." She thought she saw the hint of a smile cross his face but he hid it quickly. "We need to do something about keeping those pants up, though.." He went back to the closet and dug around until he found an adjustable belt. He also pulled out a pair of boots for her feet that actually fit once she stuffed the toes with extra socks.

Seemingly satisfied at last with her outfit, Adrian crossed to the closet one last time to pull out a duster similar to the one he wore.

"I want you to wear this. It'll keep you warm and the added bulk will help hide your appearance."

"Why do I have to wear all these clothes?" She struggled to get her arms through the sleeves.

"Because out here, we only get three kinds of females—hardened criminals, prostitutes, and droids—and you couldn't pass for any of them. If you go out there looking like you did in that form-fitting jumpsuit, you'd attract a lot of attention—all the wrong kind."

"But you'll protect me," she blurted without thinking.

He gave her a scowl as he gripped her duster at the shoulders and tugged on it to readjust the way it hung. "So now you trust me? Your faith in me is touching, but I'd rather not have to kill anyone tonight." She started to correct his misbelief on her faith, but he held up his hand to silence her. "We'll do it my way."

He buttoned the top button of the duster, which she'd left undone, and then popped the collar so it stood high around her neck, providing more cover. Then he stepped back and studied her for so long that she grew self-conscious.

"One last thing." He walked over to a drawer and found an elastic band which he handed it to her. "Braid your hair. You can use this to secure it."

While she did as he instructed, he dug in the pocket of his coat and took out a common stretch hat. When she finished with her hair, he helped her slip the thick braid down the back of her shirt and she tried not to think about how his fingers felt as they brushed against her neck.

"Here." He handed her the hat. "Put this on and let's see how you look."

She went to stand in front of the mirror and as she pulled the hat on over her head, Adrian came up behind her to study her appearance. Her face was almost completely hidden between the hat and the collar, the sleeves of the coat were longer than her arms so her hands weren't showing and the duster was so long, it almost touched the floor.

"I look like a boy playing dress-up in his dad's clothes. How is looking like this supposed to attract less attention?"

"Because you don't look like a woman." Adrian buttoned the duster he wore and stood beside her. Once he lifted his collar so it stood up like hers did, they bore a superficial resemblance to each other. She didn't think she looked nearly as dangerous in her coat as Adrian did in his, but with him along, she doubted anyone would stop to bother her.

They left the ship and joined Jack, who stood outside waiting for them, also wearing his duster with upturned collar. Both men looked serious and the power that emanated off them left Phoenix's senses buzzing.

The Black Hole was much as she expected from Jack's description. The city's population was primarily a transient one with only the business owners living there on a permanent basis.

The city boasted no cutting-edge technology and there was little in the way of obvious material wealth.

The "what you own is mine to take" mentality did not foster trust in its residents or visitors. Everyone, more or less, kept to themselves.

Adrian and Jack took one last look around the landing field. Apparently satisfied with what they saw, or with what they didn't see, they started toward town.

Stuck walking between the two men, Phoenix cast a quick glance at Adrian. He never took his eyes off the streets ahead of them, yet she had the impression that he was aware of everything going on around them.

Inadequate lighting dimly lit the walkways, leaving dark shadows in doorways and alleys. There was no shuttle traffic on the streets, but the pedestrian traffic picked up the closer they got to the center of town. Phoenix thought it interesting that no matter how dense the crowd, the two bounty hunters were always given wide passage.

After walking several blocks, they stopped outside a building with a sign hanging out front that identified the place as "Spacer's Den."

"This is a downgraded version of The Abyss," Jack warned her as he opened the door.

He was right. The minute she set foot inside, a cacophony of emotions bombarded her. Predominantly male patrons filled the room, some sitting at tables while others stood in small groups scattered throughout. Interspersed amid shouts for more drink and food were the explosive bellows of laughter and loudly broadcasted quarrels that, in at least one instance, ended in a fistfight.

The place was wall-to-wall people and, looking about, Phoenix saw no open tables. As she wondered where they'd sit, Adrian led them through the room to an occupied table near the back wall. The men sitting there, clearly irritated at the intrusion, turned and started to say something, but the sounds died in their throats when they looked into Adrian's and Jack's faces. Immediately they stood and, gathering their drinks, went in search of other seating arrangements.

Mesmerized by everything going on around her, Phoenix did not at first register that Adrian was talking to her. "I want you to stay here with Jack while I secure supplies," he told her. "We'll eat when I get back."

The thought of his leaving made her uneasy and she realized with some surprise that she felt safer with him around. *How was that for a twist,* she silently chided herself.

"How long will you be gone?"

He gave her a curious look. "An hour. Maybe two."

She realized she was clutching his arm and forced herself to let go. "Be careful."

Once outside, Adrian pulled the collar of his duster tight to block some of the icy wind creeping down his neck, Adrian headed down the street to the supply depot. He kept part of his mind alert to all movement around him while another part was puzzling over what had happened at the pub. Phoenix had actually sounded worried about his leaving. She confused him, but he guessed that wasn't hard to do. He hadn't spent much time around women.

Putting her from his thoughts, he quickened his pace. The depot he was going to stayed open around the clock and was operated by a Bevlean refugee. A slender bipedal humanoid with skin the color of pale-green pond scum and large amber-colored eyes, Morris stood a meter tall; taller when he was perched on top of the raised platform behind the counter of his store.

The merchant seemed surprised to see him. "Mr. Adrian?"

"Hello, Morris. I guess it's been a while. How have you been?" The little man cast a nervous glance around his store, which appeared empty. "Is there something wrong?"

"You shouldn't be here."

"You'd rather I took my business elsewhere?" Adrian asked, confused.

"I'd didn't mean the depot, Mr. Adrian. I meant you shouldn't be here in Black Hole. It's not safe."

"Morris, you're not making sense. Black Hole has never been a safe place."

Morris held up his hand, silently asking Adrian to be patient. Then he pulled out his handheld computer and spoke into it using his native language. He laid it on the counter and a second later, a floating computer screen appeared in the air above it.

It wasn't the best likeness of him, Adrian reflected, studying the image in the upper left corner, but it was good enough. Of more concern was the context in which his picture appeared. Morris had pulled up an underworld site where contract killings were posted. Someone had put a contract out on him.

It was small comfort that the pay-off for bringing him in alive was larger than bringing him in dead since the difference wasn't enough to worry about.

One million credits. Who the hell had that kind of money to pay?

Unsurprisingly, the icon at the bottom of the screen denoted that the contract had been picked up. He'd have to watch his back.

"Thanks for the heads up. I'll be careful." Adrian wasn't worried that Morris might try to collect on the contract. Such a move would be bad for business – not to mention extremely unhealthy.

"What can I do for you?" Morris asked.

"I need a few things." He tapped the screen of his comm-device to send a list of items to Morris' computer. A moment later, the list appeared on the computer screen. "Can you fill this order?"

Morris studied the list. "Yes, yes. Of course."

"How much?"

He waited for Morris to calculate the total and then paid him in credit chips. He would have rather rather transferred the amount from his account to Morris', but the Black Hole was a chip-only city.

"How soon can you fill the order?" he asked.

"Two, maybe three, hours."

Adrian counted out a sizeable tip and handed it to Morris. "Make it two hours."

"I'll do my best," Morris said, pocketing the money. "Be careful out there, Mr. Adrian. You've always been a good customer. I'd hate to lose your business."

"Thanks, Morris. See you soon."

Stepping outside into the icy wind once more, Adrian inhaled deeply. He pulled his duster closed and headed back to the Spacer's Den, making a point to look over his shoulder as he went.

Sitting in the bar, Phoenix felt great. She'd been nervous when Adrian first left them, but Jack proved to be good company, entertaining her with outrageous tales of some of his more daring deeds. He'd made light of them, but they'd still sounded dangerous.

Laughing at his latest recounting, Phoenix took another sip of her juice, savoring the taste. "I had no idea Edenberry Juice was so delicious."

Jack raised his glass and tapped it against hers in a toast, smiling. "Neither did I, but in my case, it's the company and not the berry that makes this juice particularly enjoyable."

She smiled at his compliment but couldn't keep her thoughts from straying to the memory of Adrian as he stood over her in the galley. She blushed, remembering her reaction to his nearness, and when Jack winked at her, she let him think he was the cause.

Nearby, a group of men engaged in a friendly battle of strength. Phoenix watched the first two rounds of arm wrestling as if it was the most fascinating thing she'd ever seen.

"This is wonderful. I've never experienced anything like it." She heard the excitement in her voice as she looked around the room. "Those men are drunk, aren't they?" She pointed to a nearby table. For some reason the sight of grown men rocking back and forth with raucous laughter struck her as funny and a small giggle escaped.

"You've never seen anyone drunk before?"

"No," she admitted. "Xenobians don't drink. Alcohol dampens one's ability to reason while heightening one's pleasure centers. It creates an imbalance and..." She struggled for the right words. "Xenobians believe in a balanced existence."

Jack offered her a smile. "Sounds boring."

Pleased to hear her own thoughts voiced, Phoenix smiled back. "It is."

"So, what do you do for fun?"

Phoenix thought about it and giggled. "I ran away from home. What do you do for fun?"

His smile grew broader. "Whatever the hell I want."

At that, they both laughed and took another drink of the Edenberry juice.

"Seriously," she continued. "Don't you have a hobby or something you do to relax?"

He considered it for a moment. "I guess you could say that my hobby is computers. I enjoy writing code."

Phoenix raised an eyebrow. "Are you any good?"

Jack smiled. "Good enough."

"What about Adrian?" She asked. "What does he do for fun?"

Jack's smile faded. "Adrian doesn't have fun. At least, not since I've known him."

"How did you two meet?" Momentarily distracted by loud shouting from the nearby table, Phoenix turned to see several drunken patrons shoving one another in obvious disagreement over something. Absorbed in watching them, she lifted her glass and took another swallow of juice, then shifted her slightly unfocused gaze back to Jack as he told his story.

"Six years ago, I took a job with a Tigrerian South-hemi to smuggle weapons. They were in the midst of a planetary civil war; southern versus northern hemispheres. I thought the shipment was artillery—the Tigrerians are an aggressive race—and there was most likely someone smuggling the same thing for the other side. When I found out that the merchandise was a new bio-toxin, I refused to transport it.

"The South-hemi found someone else to haul their shipment, but when it arrived, the other side had been tipped off and set a trap. Several of the canisters exploded and thousands of citizens on both sides died before the biotoxin could be contained. Ironically, the incident united the two warring sides because they had to work together to rid the planet of residual poisons.

"When the planetary officials wanted someone to blame, I suddenly found myself accused. They put a price on my head and Adrian was the bounty hunter who found me."

"What happened?"

"He tried to take me in and I resisted. We started fighting and neither of us saw the Tigrerian war hounds until it was almost too late. They'd been hired to follow Adrian with the intent of killing us both once I was found. Turned out the government wanted their revenge, but didn't have the funds to pay the reward.

"We teamed up to fight off the war hounds and by the time we finished killing them, we no longer felt like killing each other. So instead, we went for a drink. By the end of the night, he'd talked me into giving up smuggling to become a bounty hunter. We've been friends ever since."

Phoenix stared at Jack. "That's incredible."

He laughed. "What's incredible is that the man has any friends at all. He's uptight and has no sense of humor. As the saying goes, all work and no play, makes Adrian boring as shit—doesn't it, Adrian?"

With her back to the door, she hadn't noticed Adrian's arrival. Odd that her heart gave a slight flutter at the mere sight of him. If she hadn't been so relaxed, the reaction might have embarrassed her.

He stood frowning down at them – she supposed because of Jack's comment. It struck her as funny and she giggled. Jack's smile grew broader and Adrian's frown deepened.

"Are you both drunk?" He sounded incredulous.

"No." Jack couldn't seem to stop smiling. "No way. We've been drinking Edenberry juice all evening."

Clearly not believing them, Adrian lifted Phoenix's glass to his nose and took a tentative sip.

"Strange," she thought she heard him mutter as he set the glass back on the table.

"It's very good," she commented.

Across from her, Jack suddenly rose to his feet and stepped around the table to stand beside Adrian. Phoenix turned in her seat to find the men standing with their backs to her and their attention focused elsewhere. There was a sliver of space between them and she struggled to see through it.

What she saw was a man in a black duster, standing just inside the tavern's entrance. His short, spiky hair was pitch black, looking almost blue in the room's lighting. With his hands held loosely at his side, he reminded Phoenix of Dante's panther; dangerous and ready to pounce at the first provocation.

His gaze traveled over the room, missing no detail. He spotted Adrian and Jack and his lips curved in a predatory smile. When he raised three fingers and touched his forehead in a mock salute, Phoenix felt a chill run down her spine.

"Time to go," Adrian said. He glanced back down at her and scowled, seeming to finally notice that she wasn't standing beside them. Grabbing a fistful of material from between her shoulder blades, he hauled her unceremoniously to her feet and without releasing her, herded her deeper into the bar, away from the entrance.

"We're going the wrong way," she felt obligated to point out.

"Keep walking. We're going out the back," Adrian said from behind her.

They navigated through the tables until they reached a short hallway that eventually led them to the warehouse portion of the bar. Adrian pulled her to a stop before the outer door.

"Stay here. I'll check it out."

She nodded, watching him pull his laser from its holster. He pushed the door open a crack and peered outside. Phoenix wasn't sure what he expected to see. It was dark outside. Before she could share this bit of logic, Adrian had slipped outside. Jack now stepped forward to take his place. Their extreme caution was making her nervous.

"What's going on? Who was that man?" She asked in a whisper, glancing back toward the bar to see if they'd been followed.

She was only talking to herself. While her head was turned, Jack had slipped through the door as quickly and quietly as Adrian had.

Frustrated, she wanted to storm through the door but knew better than to do so. Instead, she waited in the dark warehouse, alone.

How long would they make her wait? What if something happened to them and she didn't know?

The seconds ticked by.

One.

Two.

Three.

Fo—

A hand grabbed her and pulled her through the doorway. The small yelp of surprise that escaped her lips was quickly stifled by another hand over mouth.

"It's me," Adrian whispered, his warm breath brushing her ear.

She looked around and saw Jack standing not far away, laser drawn as he studied the entrance to the alley in which they now stood.

Turning back to Adrian, she tried to ignore the hard feel of his body against hers as he held her close to his side and studied the opposite end of the alley.

"Would you please tell me what's going on?" she whispered loudly.

"It's no longer safe for us to stay here."

"Why?"

"There's a contract killer in the bar." He started walking toward the alley entrance, pulling her along with him.

"A contract killer?" Her thoughts immediately conjured the man in the black duster. "Who's he after?"

"Me."

She would have stumbled had Adrian not still been gripping her arm.

"Something you want to tell me, partner?" Jack asked, having overheard their conversation.

"It would seem someone has put an active contract on me," Adrian replied as calmly as if he was discussing the weather.

Phoenix had no time to absorb the shock of his announcement before they were moving down the street, avoiding the more brightly lit areas. Phoenix, imagining unseen dangers lurking just out of view at every doorway, moved closer to Adrian, seeking his protection.

There were still a few people out, but none paid them any attention. That didn't stop the prickly feeling that they were being followed. When she could stand it no longer, Phoenix turned to look behind them and caught a fleeting glimpse of a figure in a long coat disappearing around a corner.

The man at the bar.

Phoenix didn't need to see his face to know it was him.

They'd reached the end of the third block when Adrian's arm shot out, bringing the group to a sudden halt.

"Is that who I think it is?" He asked Jack in a low voice, gesturing with his head to the group of men gathered midway up the next block. From the sound of their voices and laughter, they were drunk.

Jack studied the men. After a second, he swore under his breath. "You think he's still mad?"

"Who?" Phoenix asked, confused by their exchange.

"Wouldn't you be?" Adrian asked in return. "I don't think he's noticed us. Let's take the alley."

"Who?" Phoenix asked again, this time more insistently.

"A bounty we picked up," Jack replied.

Her next question died on her lips, her curiosity suddenly replaced by a feeling of dread.

The alley was long and narrow, lined on both sides by buildings with no windows to allow light to filter through. The alley was lit by a single lamp mounted above a doorway halfway down. Its bright glow helped them to see but it also cast darker shadows in the places where it didn't reach. Phoenix's senses went on hyper-alert as she followed the men.

They were nearly a third of the way in when she realized there was no opening at the end of the alley. Their only way out lay through one of the doors or back the way they'd come.

Almost as if he shared her feeling of being trapped, Adrian's steps slowed to a stop as he looked around. Phoenix couldn't stop herself from mimicking him, although she wasn't sure what she was looking for. As far as she could tell, they were alone in the alley.

Then she heard it—the barest whisper of sound. It was gone before she could identify it.

Adrian gestured for her to remain where she was, then he and Jack walked further into alley, lasers drawn. The large trash dumpster several meters ahead seemed the most likely place for someone to be hiding.

Phoenix held her breath as the two men approached it cautiously. So intent was her attention on the men that it took a second before the movement at her side registered. Turning to look, she studied the building with confusion as the wall blurred and swelled outward before her eyes.

Alarm shot through her even as her mind argued she was only suffering the lingering effects of the Edenberry juice. The wall continued to bulge outward, taking on a new shape.

When she recognized what it was, she gasped.

At the sound, Adrian and Jack whirled in her direction.

The flash from twin laser beams lit the alley, temporarily blinding her. When she could see again, a body – humanoid, but not human—lay on the ground against the wall.

She fought not to look but her gaze was drawn to the fallen figure who was nude and whose skin bore a striking resemblance to the color and pattern of the stonework against which he'd been standing. It was the perfect camouflage and explained why none of them had spotted him.

Then she noticed his skin was changing; turning a darker color. Between one breath and the next, the figure's skin changed to match the color and texture of the street. Even knowing where he lay, it was difficult to see him.

What type of being was this?

Then it occurred to her. A chameleon, of course. She'd read about them.

These thoughts raced through her head before she'd had time to catch her breath. About to ask Adrian to confirm her guess, she realized that he and Jack were standing back-to-back with her between them, lasers held at the ready and their gazes searching the alley for...what?

More chameleon assassins, she realized with a shiver.

A flicker of movement, caught in her peripheral vision, caused her to look up. Had the sign on the building moved?

She heard the crunch of gravel. It sounded like it was coming from the far end of the alley, from deep within the shadows.

Both men fired their weapons. Jack shot at the wall sign while Adrian fired into the dark where his beam temporarily lit up the night revealing a solitary dark figure.

Adrian fired again. At the same time, he shoved Phoenix to the side so hard, she lost her footing and fell.

A laser beam burned a hole in the building behind where she'd just been standing. The shadowy figure at the end of the alley had fired—and nearly killed her.

The night grew unnaturally silent.

Adrian stood before her, shielding her when he was the intended target. She knew it would do no good to point it out. Instead, she looked over to where Jack was bent over the chameleon at his feet, his fingertips pressed against the figure's armpit. A moment later, he glanced over at them and made a slicing motion across his throat.

The assassin was dead.

Adrian pointed toward the alley. Jack nodded and disappeared into the darkness.

Phoenix, feeling exposed sitting on the ground, started to stand. Pain shot through her temples and she sat again abruptly.

Adrian glanced down at her, clearly concerned. "Are you hurt?"

"No, I didn't think so." Even to her own ears, she didn't sound convincing. "Just a little dizzy—I guess from all the excitement."

She tried again to stand, and this time managed to get to her feet without pain. She looked down the alley to the far end, even though she couldn't see anything. "Jack?"

"There," Adrian said, sounding relieved, as Jack stepped out of the shadows and started walking toward them. "We good?" Adrian asked when his partner had joined them. At Jack's nod, Adrian holstered his weapon. "Let's get out of here, then." He gestured to one of the doors and the group started toward it.

"Not so fast."

At the sound of the man's voice, the group turned. Coming toward them, his laser drawn, was the bounty hunter from the bar.

"Lazureth." Adrian spoke the name like a warning. "What are you doing here?"

"Just conducting a little business. Don't take it personal."

Phoenix stood beside Adrian, petrified. Her head was ringing and she could barely focus on what the men were saying.

"You disappoint me, Adrian. I thought you were smarter than this." Lazureth turned his attention to

Jack, who'd remained quiet. "You fucked with the wrong person."

He pulled the trigger of his laser and shot Jack in the head.

Chapter 8

PHOENIX SCREAMED AS JACKS' body crumpled in a heap and the odor of scorched flesh filled the air. Adrian's roar of outrage gave voice to her own as he launched himself at Lazureth, heedless of the weapon still clutched in the other man's hand.

They fell to the ground, fighting, while Phoenix waited in grim resignation for Lazureth to pull the trigger and kill Adrian as he had Jack.

For whatever reason, Lazureth didn't fire the weapon.

"It's not what you thi—"

Adrian grabbed Lazureth by the throat, choking off his words, and punched him hard enough to split his lip. With an agility and strength that suggested he wasn't entirely human, Lazureth tossed Adrian aside and scrambled to his feet before Adrian connected with a second punch.

"It wasn't Jack," he shouted at Adrian, angrily wiping his lip with the back of his hand. "Look for yourself." He had to say it twice before the words sank in.

Phoenix expected Adrian to renew his assault and watched in confusion as he instead went over to Jack's body—slouched against the building, lifeless eyes staring outward. He squatted down and stared for a long, hard second before abruptly standing.

"Phoenix, stay here," he said to her. Turning to Lazureth, he jabbed a finger at the man, centimeters from his chest. "Don't you dare touch her."

Phoenix opened her mouth to protest, but he'd already pulled his weapon and was walking toward the end of the ally. In seconds, he'd disappeared into the shadows as Jack had done earlier.

Left alone with the bounty hunter, Phoenix's mind raced with thoughts of committing murder, though she wasn't sure who was more deserving—Lazureth for killing Jack or Adrian for abandoning her with a killer.

"It's not what you think," Lazureth repeated, as if he'd read her thoughts. "Adrian, Jack and I are friends."

"You have a twisted way of showing friendship."

"It wasn't Jack."

He gestured once more to Jack's body and she couldn't stop from doing a double-take. This time, she saw what she'd missed earlier.

Jack's features were growing blurry, like they were melting off his face, leaving behind a blank canvas. No, not blank she realized looking more closely. Stone-like.

The same type of stone in the wall against which his head was resting.

"A chameleon," she breathed, aghast. She glanced at Lazureth, who confirmed her guess with a nod. Had he been telling the truth after all? "How did you know it wasn't Jack?"

"I was on the roof, watching. Waiting to see if Adrian and Jack needed my help. When Jack walked to the end of the alley, I saw the other chameleon attack him." He shrugged. "My mother is Felinian, so my eyesight in the dark is better than most – but not good enough to get off a clean shot without getting closer. By the time I got down here, the chameleon had already assumed Jack's likeness and joined you." He sighed. "I really thought Adrian would have caught on quicker than he did. He must have been distracted."

He gave her a look that said he suspected she was the source of Adrian's distraction. Trying to redirect the conversation to safer ground, she extended her hand in greeting.

"My name is Phoenix Eemin."

"Lazureth. No last name – and I'd rather not shake hands, if you don't mind. Adrian's already gotten in one lucky punch. I don't want to give him any excuses to try for another."

Phoenix thought he was joking but when he made no move to take her hand, she finally lowered it.

She heard the sound of footsteps and turned to see Adrian step out of the darkness supporting a wobbly, and largely unclothed, Jack. There was blood running down the side of Jack's head. Seeing it, Phoenix recalled the burst of pain she'd experienced right after Adrian had pushed her and knew now it must have been his pain she'd felt, not her own.

She hurried forward to meet them and hesitated only briefly before slipping beneath Jack's other arm to help support his weight.

"How badly is he hurt?" She asked Adrian, cautiously avoiding looking at Jack. Where were his clothes? Then she remembered that the chameleon had been wearing them.

"It looks worse than it is," Jack answered. "Bastard caught me off guard. I'm just a little dizzy."

"You're lucky you weren't killed," she said. Then to Adrian, "is there someplace we can go so I can clean his wound? Someplace safe?"

"Over here." Lazureth was standing before a sturdy brown metal door a short distance away holding Jack's coat, which he'd taken off the imposter.

"What is this place?" She asked as they joined him by the door.

"A safe house." Lazureth knocked and then stepped back. Phoenix looked around for a camera or some other form of surveillance scanner. What she saw instead almost made her laugh. A short distance up the wall, a small window opened and a head appeared.

At recognizing Lazureth, the man smiled and waved. Then he withdrew inside and the window closed. A few seconds later, Phoenix heard the grinding of door locks just before the door opened.

"Mr. Lazureth, welcome home," a very tall, thin man greeted them. Upon seeing Jack, his expression turned to one of concern. "Looks like you ran into trouble."

"Just a scratch, Reed. You should see the other guy," Jack quipped. "Although that might be hard to do since they won't become visible for another thirty-six hours."

Reed's eyes momentarily widened, then understanding dawned. "Damn chameleons. How many?"

"Three," Adrian answered. "All dead."

"Well, that's going to smell," Reed muttered mostly under his breath. "Never mind. I'll take care of it."

He led them up a set of stairs to the second floor and opened one of the doors.

"Food and drinks are on their way up. I'll have one of the staff bring medical supplies – and an extra set of clothes for Jack."

"Thank you, Reed," Lazureth said.

The man nodded and quietly closed the door behind him as he left.

"Over here," Adrian said, gesturing to one of the chairs at the table.

"I take it you three are already acquainted?" Phoenix asked as she helped Adrian get Jack settled.

"You didn't already tell her?" Adrian looked accusingly at Lazureth, who merely shrugged.

"I did, in fact, but I don't think she believes me. Did you forget to tell her you were meeting an old friend—at *your* invitation, I might add."

Lazureth smiled but Adrian's expression remained stoic, though Phoenix thought she detected a gleam in his eyes. How dare he find this situation humorous. Exasperated, she looked at Jack.

"Lazureth is an old friend of ours who happens to have a safe house here," Jack said, taking pity on her. "Adrian sent a message from the ship to see if he was around and letting him know we were coming. We were supposed to meet up at the bar, but as you know, our plans changed when Lazureth told us about the three assassins waiting out front for us."

Now she was totally confused. "When did he tell us that?"

Adrian held up three fingers and then touched them to his forehead in the same mock salute Lazureth had given Adrian at the bar.

Three fingers for three assassins.

"Oh. I thought he was—never mind." She stopped, feeling the stares of the men on her.

Adrian shrugged and turned to Lazureth. "What did you find out?"

The two men started talking, but Phoenix wasn't interested in listening. When the knock sounded at the door, she crossed the room to answer it.

As she stood aside, a man entered—at least, Phoenix thought the being was male—walking in an uneven gait and wearing a royal blue tunic and pants. His cloven hooved feet had no need for shoes. His skin was pale grey and where a nose would have been on a human, this man had two slits. His dark round eyes seemed disproportionately large for his head while his pale-pink lips framed a mouth that was very homosapien-like.

In his three-fingered hands, he carried medical supplies and clothing.

Phoenix watched in fascination as the man set about cleaning Jack's wound, working with far greater gentleness and dexterity than she could have done.

With the wound cleaned and a bio-patch applied, the man gathered his supplies and left without ever having uttered a word. Jack wasted no time getting dressed.

The trays of food arrived shortly after that, carried in by two human women. They laid out place settings and dishes of hot food. One carried a seal bag which she handed to Lazureth. He set it on the floor beside his chair as the women left.

"Shall we eat?" He asked as the door closed.

They needed no further prompting and were soon sitting around the table, enjoying a hot meal. While they ate, the men talked about people they knew and caught up on current events. Phoenix listened with avid interest. Near the end of the meal, the subject turned to assassins and contracts. For Phoenix, their conversation was surreal. Only a week ago, she'd been listening to conversations about transcendental meditation.

"What about the contract on Adrian," Jack probed. "Any idea who put it out?"

Lazureth finished his bite of food before answering. "According to my sources, it was Juarez."

Both Adrian and Jack nodded, so she assumed this wasn't news to them.

"What I want to know," Adrian said, "is where he got one million credits to fund it. Juarez doesn't have access to that kind of money."

"It's not his money," Lazureth said. "Juarez works for Zarek, now. It's his money."

"Zarek!" Adrian's tone was sharp and wary.

"Damn it," Jack swore.

Lazureth looked from one man to the other. "Yeah, I thought you knew—why? Is that a problem?"

"Massive understatement," Jack muttered under his breath.

"No," Adrian corrected him, sounding matter-of-fact. "It's a dust storm, not a black hole. We can handle it."

"Are you mental?" Jack retorted. "If Juarez is working for Zarek, then that means Zarek has Skylar—which makes this mission over—buddy."

"I said, we can handle it." Adrian's tone was firm and Phoenix didn't miss the way his gaze darted over to her.

A small chime sounded, ending the argument. Lazureth glanced at the underside of his arm where a subcutaneous comm-unit was emitting a pulsing green light.

Lazureth noticed her interest. "That's Zoe. She's signaling me it's time to go."

"Zoe?" Phoenix asked.

Lazureth looked thoughtful. "I guess you could say she's Jack to my Adrian. I would stay, but she'll be irritated if I don't bring her this food soon." He picked up the sealed bag and stood.

"I'll go with you," Jack abruptly offered, pushing away from the table. "Someone should be at the ship when the supplies are delivered."

Adrian gave Jack a quizzical look. "We're nearly done if you want to wait."

"Stay and finish your meal. I've got this."

"What about your head?" Adrian asked.

"It's fine." Jack waved his concern aside. "And I'll let Morris do all the heavy lifting."

"Okay," Adrian agreed, not sounding fully convinced.

Lazureth turned to Phoenix. "Ms. Eemin, it was a pleasure meeting you. If there's ever anything I can do for you, let me know."

She offered him a wary smile. Like Adrian and Jack, he was dangerous—and she couldn't erase the image of him shooting Jack.

If Lazureth noticed her hesitation, he didn't call attention to it.

"I'll buzz you when the supplies are stowed," Jack said. Then he and Lazureth left and the room seemed suddenly filled with Adrian's presence.

Phoenix waited to see if he would explain any of the earlier conversation, but he seemed content to sit and finish his meal.

"Who is Zarek?" she finally asked.

Adrian's expression remained passive, controlled. "He's a sick, sadistic bastard who also happens to be the crime lord controlling Previon, a city on the other side of the planet."

"He's worse than Dante?"

Adrian gave a soft snort of disgust. "Zarek makes Dante look like a Junior Space Scout."

"Worse than Marcus?" The image of Mr. Zimmers being whipped flashed through her head.

"No one does torture better than Zarek," he said with conviction. "Between the physical abuses, starvation, use of drugs and virtual immersion tactics, his talent is unsurpassed."

"And you think he's got my father." It was a statement, not a question and he didn't correct her. Something in his tone when he'd described Zarek caught her attention. "You described him like you were speaking from personal experience. Were you?" She saw from his expression that he was. "I'm so sorry. How long ago?"

"I was ten."

Phoenix was so appalled, not even a gasp escaped for several seconds. "So young."

Adrian nodded. "Zarek thought he could mold me into his image through a carefully applied program of torture and reward. I, of course, rebelled—for which I was repeatedly punished."

"Where were your parents? Couldn't they protect you?"

"My mother tried and was murdered for her effort. Zarek never understood how that strengthened my resolve to defy him. Anyway, when I proved too resistant, Zarek drugged my food and when I fell asleep, medics surgically implanted a neuro-chip in my brain. After that, he used a discipline wand to remotely activate the chip to produce intense pain or pleasure, depending on his mood. At the highest setting, the pain was so bad, I'd pass out. Those hours of being unconscious were the only respite I got. Sometimes I resisted just for a chance to pass out."

Phoenix felt her heart breaking for that young child who'd been so badly abused. What a terrible childhood, to know nothing but sadness and pain. "How did you escape?"

"When I was sixteen—"

"You were imprisoned for six years?!"

He shrugged like it was nothing, but Phoenix knew better.

"That's horrible. How did you finally escape?"

"I didn't. Not really. Eventually, Zarek's methods of persuasion worked. He succeeded in turning me into the monster he wanted me to be."

The statement caught her off guard and she didn't know how to respond.

"After that, there was no need to keep me locked away. One day, in a rare moment of clarity, I slipped out without Zarek's knowledge. Once I reached the village, I caught a shuttle going off planet. By the time Zarek discovered I was gone, I was beyond the range of the discipline wand. I took a job on a trading vessel but on my first voyage, Rogue Traders attacked the ship. We tried to fight them off but they outnumbered us.

"I was wounded in the fighting and knocked unconscious. When I came to, I learned I was the only survivor. I tried to repair the ship, but didn't know much about mechanics at the time. The communications system was working, though, so I took a chance and sent a distress signal. It was a gamble. For all I knew, the Rogue Traders would pick it up and come back to finish me off. Instead, I got lucky and Skylar found me. He took me under his wing and taught me how to take care of myself. I didn't know he was a government agent for the longest time; I thought he was a bounty hunter. He took me with him on several hunts and I discovered I had an aptitude for it—no doubt thanks to Zarek's careful conditioning."

She shook her head, feeling totally dismayed. "Do you still have the chip?"

"Yes. Several years ago, I tried to get it removed. The medics told me that over the years, my brain has grown around the chip. It's too deeply embedded to be safely removed without damaging my brain. I'm not willing to risk it."

"Is there any danger of leaving it in?"

"Not unless I come in range of a discipline wand."

Now she understood Jack's reaction. "Which is what will happen if you try to rescue my father."

She didn't need his answer to know it was true, just as she didn't need him to tell her he was going to try to rescue her father despite the danger. His sense of conviction was like a strong ocean wave crashing over her, drowning her in a sea of emotions that were hard to untangle: love for her father, loyalty for a friend, resolve, determination—but strangely, neither fear nor cowardice.

Overwhelmed, she pushed away from the table and crossed the room, turning her back to him so he wouldn't see her tears.

"Phoenix?" Concern filled his tone as he followed after her. His touch, when he placed his hand on her shoulder, was gentle. "I'll get your father back. I promise."

"You think I'm crying because I'm worried about my father?" She turned and looked up at him through tear-filled eyes.

"You're not?" Now he sounded confused.

"Adrian, I don't want anything bad to happen to you."

"You're crying because you're worried... about me?"

His surprise that she might care made her even sadder. "Zarek could kill you."

He rested both hands on her shoulders near the base of her neck, holding her in place as he gave her a solemn look. "Skylar saved my life. If I die trying to save his, I'm okay with that—but I couldn't live with myself if I didn't even try."

"But I don't want you to die." She sniffed as fresh tears welled in her eyes and threatened to spill over.

Adrian gently pulled her to him, enfolding her in his arms. She went to him as if it were the most natural thing in the world, her earlier fear of him gone.

Adrian was in a state of shock—and something more. No one other than his mother had ever shed a tear out of concern for him. That Phoenix seemed genuinely upset touched him more deeply than he wanted to admit.

The smart thing to do would be to set Phoenix away from him; put some distance between them, both literally and figuratively—only she felt so damn good.

With more effort than he thought it would take, he took a step back. His brain said to let go and walk away, but his hands moved of their own volition, cupping her face; the pads of his thumbs wiping away the tears trailing down her cheeks.

His gaze fell on her lips, pale like the delicate pink of a Previon orchid. They drew him in like a tractor beam. He offered up a cursory resistance and then eagerly gave in to temptation as he moved in so close he could feel her breath across his face.

At the first touch of Adrian's lips, Phoenix felt her entire body come alive. Her feelings for him might be confusing, but she knew she wanted this.

His kiss was like the man himself; strong and purposeful. It left her dazed and craving more. She leaned into him, her arms encircling his neck, and responded with an eagerness spurred by an unfamiliar primitive desire. She'd not kissed many men and none who'd been as robustly male as Adrian.

As they kissed, one of the hands that had been cupping her face grabbed the cap off her head and fumbled with the band securing her braid. Soon, he was running his fingers through her loosened hair, sending shivers down her spine.

"Tell me to stop," he whispered hoarsely when they finally came up for air.

His request confused her. "No."

With a growl, he bent his head and once more captured her lips with his.

Phoenix felt her world tilt and held onto Adrian, letting him be her anchor. She had a brief moment of clarity when she felt a hard surface press against her back and realized that Adrian had lowered them to the floor.

With his weight pressing down on her, Phoenix had never felt so aroused. She kissed him with the desperation of a Torian desert dweller seeking that last drop of moisture in a *Fellum* straw. Her entire world centered on the contact of their lips.

Then she felt Adrian's hand fumbling between her breasts. It was a surprisingly awkward gesture; endearing because she hadn't expected Adrian to be a novice when it came to sex. A cool draft of air chilled her newly exposed breasts, revealing Adrian's true mastery at seduction. What she'd mistaken for fumbling had been the deft unbuttoning of her shirt.

That was her last conscious thought before Adrian's rough palm cupped her bared breast. Her nipples drew to stiff buds beneath the assault as an inferno of need exploded inside her. He broke their kiss, but before she could protest, he'd wrapped warm lips around one nipple and began running his tongue over it in quick, powerful strokes.

Phoenix held him to her as she cried out in pleasure. Tension coiled low in her belly, sending quivers down both legs. Her pulse beat so loudly, the sound filled her head.

"*Krauk*," Adrian swore, jumping to his feet and racing for the door. He reached it just as it began to open and pushed it shut again.

"We came to collect the food and dishes," a voice shouted from the hallway.

"Come back in a few minutes," Adrian hollered back, leaning against the door. No longer caught up in the moment, his brain began to work again.

What was he doing?

Rutting on the floor like an animal? Hell, he hadn't even tried to seduce her but got straight to it like she was a sex droid and he was paying by the minute.

He turned his attention to Phoenix, wondering what to do next. She was sitting with her back to him, buttoning her shirt. Wiping a hand down his face, he knew he had to make the first move.

Pushing away from the door, he walked over to her and held out a hand to help her stand. She looked up with reddened face and reluctantly accepted his offer.

"Phoenix, I'm sorry," he began, but then stopped. "I mean, I'm not sorry that I kissed you or... " This wasn't going well. "I wanted to kiss you," he began again. "It's just... *krauk*, I didn't expect to lose control after one kiss. Something about you..."

He saw the hint of a smile touch her lips and forgot what he was going to say, every fiber of his being yearning to have one more taste.

"*I'm* not sorry." She spoke shyly as if she was embarrassed to admit she'd enjoyed it. "It's probably just as well that we were interrupted, though. We don't really have the time to... " She waved a hand in the air to encompass the various, unspoken activities in which they might have indulged themselves. "Jack will be calling soon."

Jack! Krauk—he'd forgotten about Jack. What time was it?

He pulled his comm-device from his pocket and saw that Jack had been gone almost an hour. More than ample time to load supplies, yet he showed no missed calls or messages. That was odd.

He punched a key and listened, but all he heard was the buzzing of an unanswered signal. Jack wasn't answering and it gave him an uneasy feeling. "We should go."

"Is there a problem?"

"I hope not, but we'll find out soon enough."

He ran his gaze over her, making sure she was dressed. She'd buttoned her shirt and pulled the duster closed. She hadn't braided her hair—probably because he'd destroyed the band when he'd pulled it off—but had piled it on top of her head before pulling the cap on. He missed the sight of it and wished the feel of those long strands flowing between his fingers wasn't still such a vivid memory.

Satisfied with her appearance, he led her from the room.

Outside, Adrian flagged down a shuttle and paid for a ride to the landing field. Without Lazureth or Jack along as back-up, it was safer than walking.

After the shuttle dropped them off, Adrian hurried past several docked transports to the spot where they'd left the ship.

Only it wasn't there. Jack had left without them.

Chapter 9

DAMN JACK AND HIS misguided sense of loyalty, Adrian thought, looking around the landing field.

Phoenix stopped beside him, breathing hard after hurrying to keep up with his long strides and fast pace. She stared at the empty spot. "Isn't this where we left the ship?"

"Yes."

"Where is it?"

"Gone," Adrian replied.

She looked around the landing field. "Maybe he moved it to a safer location?"

She sounded hopeful and he hated to disappoint her. "No, he left us."

Did Jack really think he could rescue Skylar by himself?

Knowing Jack, he'd try and probably be killed for his efforts.

"But why?" Phoenix asked.

"I saved his miserable life once and now he thinks he owes me. Leaving us stranded here while he flies off to rescue Skylar alone is his way of paying me back."

"So—we wait for him?"

They could go back to Lazureth's safe house. This time, he'd ask for a room with a bed so they could finish what they'd started.

It was a tempting, but unrealistic, idea.

If only they had the luxury of time. They didn't because Adrian knew damn well Jack wouldn't be able to rescue Skylar without him.

"We need to find a ship willing to take us to Previon," he told Phoenix as they started back across the landing field. "I don't suppose you have any money on you? I spent most of mine on supplies and the ride over."

"Not unless you left some in one of these pockets. These are your clothes, remember? Everything I own is still sitting in my room on Cloud City." She reached into pockets of the duster and pants, but he knew she wouldn't find anything. "What about Lazureth? Wouldn't he give us a ride?"

Adrian heard the hopeful note in her tone and hated to be the one to quell it. "I don't see his ship. We're on our own."

They were halfway across the field when he noticed a familiar ship. The Sansholox Zie. The ship's owner was a small-time smuggler, as unpleasant in personality as he was in appearance, but he was greedy and Adrian knew he could work that to his advantage.

"I may have found us a ride," he told Phoenix, picking up his pace. "Let's see if I can talk the ship's captain into taking on two passengers."

Reaching the airfield's main building, Adrian paid out a few more of his dwindling supply of credit chips hiring a shuttle to take them back to the Spacer's Den. It was with a strong sense of déjà vu that they walked through the door ten minutes later.

A handful of the patrons glanced up at their entrance. Adrian noticed the calculating looks they received and, unbuttoning his duster, made a show of pushing it open to reveal his lasers holstered at his sides. Many of the patrons immediately turned their attention back to what they had been doing. The remaining few followed suit more slowly.

During his visual sweep of the room, Adrian spotted the ship's owner sitting at a nearby gaming table. Crossing to the opposite side of the man's table, he waited until the smuggler glanced up. In a subtle move, Adrian signaled with his head that he wanted to talk and waited for the man's slight nod.

Then Adrian led Phoenix to an open table several meters away. After a few minutes, Abe Sansholox ambled his massive form over to them and wedged himself into an open chair. He spared a brief, interested glance at Phoenix before turning his dark gaze on Adrian.

"You wanted something, Sun?"

"Yeah. A ride to Previon, as soon as possible."

"That's not exactly a scheduled stop for me."

"I understand." Adrian wondered how much this would cost as he watched the other man make his mental calculations.

"Passage for one?" Abe looked at Phoenix. "Or two?"

"Two." The imaginary clicks of a credit counter sounded in Adrian's head.

"Two million credits to take you and your... friend... to Previon."

Adrian heard Phoenix gasp, but ignored her.

"One," he countered.

The big man smiled with confidence. "I'd get one million credits for delivering your dead body to Previon. Surely it's worth paying a few more credits to arrive at the planet alive."

"Are you threatening me?" Adrian offered the man his coldest smile. "You must have a death wish."

"I'm not the one who walked into a room full of criminals with a contract on my head."

"Do you really think I'd do that without some type of protection?"

Abe scoffed and gestured at Phoenix. "Her? She must be faster and stronger than she looks."

"Oh, she is—and she won't have to do more than think about hurting you."

A startled expression crossed Abe's face as he glanced at Phoenix in awe. "A Psychotran? I've never run into one before."

"Those who do usually don't live to tell about it, do they?" Adrian worked hard not to smile. Best known for their work in the niche market of professional assassinations, Psycotrans were a race of telekinetic beings whose quick and savage tempers often led to deadly consequences.

Abe turned back to Adrian. "I think you're bluffing."

Adrian smiled. "Perhaps you require a demonstration. Phoenix, love, do you see the man in the red shirt at the third table? I believe he called you a whore when we passed him earlier."

Adrian caught Phoenix's startled gaze and silently entreated her to play along. To her credit, she didn't question him but shifted her attention to the man he'd indicated.

For a second, it seemed that time stood still as nothing happened. Then the man in the red shirt toppled from his chair onto the floor and lay still.

Abe gasped and would have jumped from his seat had his girth not prevented it.

"One million to deliver me and my bodyguard to Previon—alive," Adrian said. "Do we have a deal or would you rather take your chances bringing me in dead?" He shrugged. "You're a gambling man, Abe, and you look like you've been staying in shape. Maybe you can move faster than the time it takes to form a single thought."

Adrian watched the emotions race across the big man's face.

"Deal," he grumbled, clearly not happy. "One million credits, but I want the money upfront—in chips."

"Agreed. We'll meet at your ship in two hours. I'll pay you then." Adrian waited for the big man to nod. "And Abe—if you try to double cross me, I *will* kill you."

All three pushed back from the table and stood. "Just be at the ship in two hours," Abe said and ambled off.

Adrian felt Phoenix watching him and turned to her.

"We don't have that kind of money," she said softly.

"Not yet," he admitted, leading her from the bar. Outside, he pulled out his comm-unit. "Call Morris," he addressed the unit. A second later, the call went through.

"Morris, it's Adrian."

"Mr. Adrian? Is there something wrong with the supplies I delivered?"

"No, they're fine. Listen, I need to raise a lot of money, fast. Do you know where I might find an Endgame match in town?"

Morris, who kept his thumb on the pulse of activity in town, told him there was a private high stakes match taking place across town.

"Is Bradden still operating out of the smoke house?"

"Yes, but Mr. Adrian, if you need money, I would be happy to extend you a line of credit."

"Thanks, Morris, but even you don't have the kind of money I need to get a spot at the table."

He disconnected the call and turned to Phoenix. "There's a match of Endgame going on across town. It's a form of gambling," he added, seeing her confused expression. "Unfortunately, a spot at the table isn't cheap, so we need to run across town to see a guy I know about a loan."

He hailed a ground shuttle and when it arrived, they climbed into the back.

Sitting beside Adrian, Phoenix felt herself relax. It was the middle of the night and she was exhausted. It didn't take long for the rumble of the engine to lull her asleep.

"Phoenix, wake up. We're here."

Much too soon, Adrian's voice wakened her. When she felt his hand gently caress her cheek, she realized that sometime after she'd fallen asleep, she'd slid sideways until her head rested on his shoulder. She might have been embarrassed if she felt more awake.

Reluctantly, she roused herself and let Adrian help her from the back of the shuttle.

She wasn't too asleep to notice that Adrian paid the pilot with the last of his money. She hoped this plan of his worked and made a mental note to ask him to explain it in more detail to her later.

"Your friend lives here?" She asked as the shuttle flew off, leaving them standing in front of a three story office building.

"I wouldn't exactly call Bradden a friend," he replied, placing a hand at her back as they walked to the front door.

"What would you call him?"

"A loan shark."

They didn't have loan sharks on Xenobia, but she was familiar with the term. The concept, as she understood it, was simple. Adrian would put something of value up as collateral and the loan shark would give him cash. Adrian would have to pay back the full amount plus interest. The consequences for not paying back a loan were a bit sketchy, but what she'd gleaned from the literature, physical injury was involved.

Adrian pressed the buzzer in the front door's security panel.

"Who is it?" a disembodied male voice asked a minute later, sounding bored and not at all upset to be bothered in the middle of the night.

"Adrian Sun. I'm here on business."

"Mine or yours?" the voice countered.

"Yours. I need a loan."

They heard the sound of the front door unlocking and went inside.

The lobby was dimly lit, making it difficult to see what the inside of the building looked like, not that Adrian gave her time to look around. He headed across the lobby to the lift and they stepped inside. When they reached the third floor level, the elevator doors opened and an attractive man with brown hair, loose fitting pants tied around his waist, no shirt and a long, open robe greeted them with a warm smile on his face and a laser held in each hand.

"Adrian, it's good to see you again," he said, gesturing with one laser for them to walk into the next room.

"Really?" Adrian sounded doubtful. "I expected a warmer reception from you, Bradden, considering the last time I saw you, I helped you out of a difficult situation."

"I haven't forgotten," Bradden assured him. "Which is why I haven't pulled the trigger—yet—but one million credits is a lot of money. You must've really pissed off someone important."

"Kinto Juarez put that contract out on me."

"Juarez doesn't have that kind of money," Bradden said. "Someone must be backing him. Who?"

Adrian gave him a pointed look.

"Zareck? That son-of-a-bitch." Bradden lowered the lasers and crossed the room to a bar. "Lucky for you I hate that bastard as much as you do." He set the lasers on the counter and took glasses from a cupboard mounted against the back wall. "What can I get you? Ale? Nectar for your lady friend?"

"Nothing, thanks. We're in a hurry, so if we could get down to business?"

Bradden finished pouring himself a drink from a decanter containing a bright blue liquid. He gave Adrian a considering look, then took a swallow of his drink and set it down.

"Sure, of course. Shall we step into the other room to discuss the terms?"

Adrian nodded and turned to Phoenix. "Wait here. This won't take long."

She would have rather gone with him, but the way Bradden kept looking at her made her uncomfortable, so she agreed to stay.

"Please make yourself comfortable," Bradden said coming toward her and lifting her hand in a gallant albeit archaic gesture, to his lips. "Major Bradden, at your service." His eyes sparkled with interest as he pressed his lips to her palm. A quiver of heat ran through her body, dispelling her earlier reservations. "And you are...?"

"Phoenix Eemin," she replied, charmed despite herself.

From the doorway, Adrian cleared his throat. Bradden gave her an apologetic smile. "My apologies, Ms. Eemin, but it would appear I must deny myself the pleasure of your company and attend to business."

The men disappeared into the other room and closed the door behind them, leaving Phoenix alone. She sat and couldn't stop the sigh that escaped her lips at the welcoming softness of the cushions as she sank into them. Once again, she felt her body relax and would have fallen asleep—except then she heard Adrian shouting from the other room. She couldn't make out his words, but he sounded mad.

The door opened a few minutes later and both men walked out. It was impossible to tell anything from their expressions.

She pushed herself off the couch and hurried over to join Adrian by the lift door. "Is everything okay?" she asked softly.

He gave a curt nod before addressing Bradden. "We'll wait for you downstairs."

Phoenix hardly noticed the ride down. "Did he give you the money?"

"Yes."

"That's good, then, right?"

"Depends on how you look at it," he grumbled as the lift reached the first floor and they stepped into the lobby.

"I heard yelling."

"You did."

He wasn't forthcoming with details, which irritated her. "What was the yelling about?"

"He wanted collateral."

Oh. "So you had to offer up your ship?"

"Bradden didn't want the ship; it's not here."

Oh, right. "Then what did he want?"

Adrian pulled one of his lasers from his holster and checked the charge. He spared her a quick look as he replaced it and pulled out the second one to check it. "You."

Phoenix was sure she'd heard wrong. "I'm sorry?"

"Bradden wanted you as collateral in the event I can't pay the money back."

"That's ridiculous. You talked him out of it, of course." She took a step closer, grabbing his arm to make him look at her. "You *did* talk him out of it."

He sighed. "I tried but Bradden wasn't interested in my lasers, which are the only other things I have to offer up."

"I am NOT a material possession to be bartered," she told him, her voice getting louder with her anger. "Tell

Bradden the deal is off. Better yet, I'll tell him myself as soon as he gets down here."

Adrian had finished checking the charge on his other laser. Holding it in one hand, he grabbed her arm with the other to keep her from storming over to the lift.

"You're right. You're not anyone's property and if you want me to tell Bradden the deal's off, I will, but you'd better make damn sure you can live with the consequences. Your father is running out of time and we need a way to pay for a ride to Previon. Black Hole is a chip-only city; there are no banks here and they don't accept credit transfers. I could borrow money from Bradden to pay Abe, but I'd have to leave you behind until I can pay Bradden back." She shook her head, letting him know that wasn't an option. "Right, so my only other option to get chips is gambling, but again, I have to borrow money to play. The only game in town that will pay out enough for me to pay back Bradden for staking my seat at the table plus pay Abe for a ride to Previon is Endgame." He sighed. "Look, I don't like it any more than you do—and I will burn a hole in Bradden's head before I ever let him touch you in a way you don't want. You have my word on that." He gave her a moment to let his words sink in. "It's your call, Phoenix. Do I tell Bradden the deal's off?"

Indignation and frustration burned inside her, but she knew she had no choice. With effort, she shook her head. He released her arm but only to grab her hand.

"Take this." He slapped the laser against her palm. "Don't let go of it but keep your hand in your pocket. We're going into a very bad part of town and I'll feel better knowing you've got a way to protect yourself."

"But I've never fired a laser before."

"It's simple. Aim and pull the trigger."

At that moment, the elevator doors opened and Bradden stepped out. Phoenix glared at him.

He gave a small laugh as he joined them. "I see you've told her about our arrangement. I'm sorry it displeases you. Given time, I think you'll find me a warm and generous benefactor."

"We won't be here that long," Adrian said.

Bradden merely shrugged. "For your sake, I hope that's true, but Endgame is as much a match of strategy as it is of chance. The big winners are never the inexperienced players."

He chuckled as he continued through the lobby to the front door.

Phoenix glared at Adrian. "You *have* played this before, haven't you?"

"Shall we go?" Adrian said, gesturing for her to follow after Bradden.

It wasn't until the three of them were sitting in the back of a shuttle flying to where the game was being played that Phoenix realized Adrian had never answered her question.

"Adrian, you do know how to play Endgame, right?"

He seemed to consider his answer before speaking. "I'm familiar with it."

Bradden, sitting on the other side of Adrian, chuckled softly. "I am so looking forward to this. Phoenix, love, did Adrian tell you how we met?"

Bradden talked throughout the ride, providing interesting bits of information about the city's history and recounting tales of several famous criminals and the bounty hunters who captured them. Adrian and Jack featured in more than one of these tales, which had been embellished more than a little, Adrian noticed. He didn't bother to correct Bradden. In part, because his thoughts were on remembering the finer points of playing Endgame and in part because Phoenix, despite her anger with both men, was listening avidly to Bradden's tales and her gaze, when she stole the occasional glance at Adrian, was filled with awe and admiration.

He wanted to savor those glances and how they made him feel for as long as possible. Soon enough, he was sure to disappoint her and those looks would change to ones of disgust and anger.

The shuttle eventually stopped in front of a non-descript two-story building set in the middle of what looked like a business district. Adrian made a quick visual inspection of the street and, seeing nothing to alarm him, stepped out after Bradden. Then he offered his hand to Phoenix, glad she wasn't too angry with him to accept his help. Her hand trembled ever so slightly when she placed it in his and he gave it a reassuring squeeze. If he seemed to hold onto it a little longer than necessary, she didn't object.

Bradden walked up to the door and knocked.

"Remember what I said," Adrian reminded her as they stood behind Bradden. "Keep the laser ready."

A section of the door opened above them and a small spybot flew out. It buzzed about them like an overgrown insect while its scanners ran visual, thermal and backscatter images.

Adrian wasn't worried that the scanners would detect their lasers. Weapons were expected at such high stakes matches. Players were less likely to cheat if they knew the other players were armed. Instead, the security scanners were used for profiling. They identified a player's race and affiliation. Known factions used Endgame matches to help fund their gang activities but if opposing gang members showed up at the same table, the game tended to end in violence. Such an occurrence was bad for business.

It took less than a minute for the spybot to finish its scan, then it flew back through door and the panel closed after it. The door then opened to admit them.

A hostess greeted them, exchanging a few private words with Bradden before leading them upstairs to the room where the match was to be played. In the center, a holographic image of a three-tiered game board floated in the center of the room. Each board was a different color – amber, violet and turquoise—and divided into sixty-four squares: eight columns and rows of alternating light and dark.

"This looks like a mosh game," Phoenix commented noting the thirty-two game pieces set up on opposite sides, sixteen dark grey versus sixteen pearly white. They stood at their stations docile and quiet, but the pieces would come to life as soon as the players put on the headband controllers. "I thought you'd be playing something a little less..." Mental is what she was going to say but thought better of it.

Adrian gave her a quizzical look. "What's mosh?"

"This." She gestured to the board, but felt confused. "Maybe I'm wrong. It looks like the game my father taught me to play."

"You played this with Skylar," Adrian clarified.

"If it's the same game, then yes. All the time."

"Are you any good?"

"I don't know. I only played against Skylar, but I beat him at least half the time."

"It's game time," Bradden said, rejoining them and herding them to one side of the room. When they reached the player's chair, Bradden held the headband controller out to Adrian. "Are you ready?"

Adrian took it, but instead of putting it on, he held it out to Phoenix. "I think you'd better play."

"What?" She stared at the thin silver metal band in horror. "Oh, no. I couldn't possibly. What if I lose?"

"If you lose, then you get to stay here with Bradden while I find another way to Previon—but that's going to delay things." He took her hands in his. "Phoenix. I've played this game exactly three times. Win or lose, you're our better bet.'

Without waiting for her to respond, he put the headband into her hands. Feeling like she was accepting the weight of the world, she closed her hand around it and nodded. She wished she could play a practice game but knew that was not possible.

"How many of the people in here will I be playing against?" She asked, trying to get a feel for how many games she was about to play.

"Just the quad in the chair over there," Adrian said slowly, like it should be obvious.

"Oh." So it wasn't a double-elimination tournament. That was unsettling, but not the end of the universe. "Are we playing best two out of three?"

"One game," Bradden told her. "Starting in five minutes so you'd better get ready. We won the credit toss and got white. First move is yours." He slapped Adrian on the shoulder. "We have to watch the game from over there." He pointed to the side of the room where the crowd of onlookers were gathering.

"I'll join you in a second."

"Good luck," Bradden said to Phoenix. Then he walked off, leaving her alone with Adrian.

She looked up at him, not bothering to mask her concern. She knew he saw it when he gave her upper arms a gentle squeeze.

"Forget about the money. Pretend you're back home, playing Skylar and just do the best you can, all right? Win or lose, you'll play a better game than I would have." With one final squeeze, he walked off to join Bradden and she was standing alone beside the game chair.

A buzzer sounded and the room fell silent. The lights in the room dimmed so that the only light in the room was on the game board. The dark grey game pieces stirred to life, indicating that her opponent was ready to begin.

Phoenix sensed all eyes on her so she sat in the game chair and put on the headband.

A familiar calm stole over her at seeing her game pieces come to life. She could do this.

The first thing both players did was position their game pieces. There were three stacked game boards, each named after a galaxy. Echelon Prime was the bottom level in amber light. The middle level, in violet light was the Elysian Rift and the top level, in turquoise light, was Solaris Dominus. Some game pieces were restricted to the board on which they started while other pieces could jump from one level to another.

Her opponent, Phoenix noted, had placed his pieces predominately on the Echelon Prime tier, suggesting he either wasn't comfortable with three-dimensional game play or wanted her to think he wasn't comfortable. She wasn't sure which.

It would be nice if she could use her abilities to sense the other player's intent but unfortunately, either because he wasn't human or because her skills were not well developed, she sensed nothing.

After second guessing the placement of two pawns and the king's knight, Phoenix pressed the button on the game chair to signal she was ready. The light over her opponent's chair dimmed. The game had begun and Phoenix sat beneath a spotlight considering her first move.

Too many bad openings in her early days of playing made this an easy decision and she moved the pawn sitting at Solaris Dominus E2 to E4. It was a common, but strong, opening.

Her opponent countered by moving his pawn on the same level from E7 to E5.

Wanting to test her theory about her opponent's comfort with playing on three levels, she made her next move on the Elysian Rift board, moving her king's knight from G1 to F3.

Instead of countering with a move on Elysian Rift or Echelon Prime, her opponent stayed on the Solaris Dominus level, moving a second pawn from D7 to D6.

Wondering if she'd correctly identified a reluctance to play on all three levels, Phoenix moved her second pawn on Solaris Dominus forward two spaces, from D2 to D4;

It was a surprise then, when her opponent jumped to Elysian Rift and moved his queen's bishop from its home position of C8 to G4. On the surface, this seemed to be a weak move—but was it?

She needed to counter with a strong move, so she moved her pawn at Solaris Dominus D4 to E5 where her opponent's pawn sat. When her piece moved into position, her opponent's pawn shattered into a million specks of grey light that twinkled and faded away.

From across the room, her opponent glowered at her and the feeling of hate nudged at her senses. Not from her opponent; she couldn't sense his emotions. So then from whom?

A bright shower of white lights on Elysian Rift snapped her attention back to the game. Her opponent had just taken her king's knight with his queen's bishop. She watched the last of the pearly white lights fade and considered her next move.

With a sense of satisfaction, Phoenix jumped her queen from Echelon Prime to Elysian Rift F3 and watched the shower of grey sparks as the dark queen's bishop vanished from the game field.

Her opponent went back to his Elysian Rift game piece and took one of her pawns with one of his.

In the next several moves, each player tested and probed the other's defenses.

When her opponent moved his fourth pawn on Solaris Dominus to B5, he triggered a Centauri black hole. The first piece sucked into oblivion was the dark pawn, quickly followed by the white queen's knight, which had been positioned on Echelon Prime in anticipation of a future move. Another dark pawn followed after it.

Game rules limited black hole elimination to three pieces so Phoenix prepped her king's bishop to jump from Echelon Prime to Solaris Dominus as soon as the hole closed, taking control of the level.

Her opponent had a different strategy in mind, though, and moved his queen's knight from Echelon Prime B8 to Elysian Rift D7. With his king now completely surrounded, Phoenix knew she had to lure her opponent's pieces away. The question was how.

She castled her king on the queen's side of Echelon Prime and waited for his next move.

The hatred that she'd been sensing intensified, becoming distracting. She tried to read her opponent's expression when it was his turn and the spotlight allowed her to see his face—but it told her nothing. Neither did his move—queen's rook to D8.

She jumped her queen's rook from Echelon Prime to Elysian Rift D7 and watched his queen's knight disappear in a shower of grey light. He countered by jumping his queen's rook from Echelon Prime to Elysian Rift, causing her piece to shatter.

With her king unprotected, she moved her king's rook into position beside it on Echelon Prime.

Her opponent moved his queen up a square in what seemed a wasted move. It didn't matter. She saw an opening and took it, moving her king's bishop from Solaris Dominus to Elysian Rift D7 where her opponent's queen's rook burst into pieces.

With her next move, she would take his king.

Of course, there were several moves he could make to avoid capture and he quickly made one by jumping his king's knight from Echelon Prime to Elysian Rift. Phoenix watched the pearly white shower of sparks that was once her king's bishop fade and disappear.

She looked up to see the smiling face of her opponent just before his spotlight faded. He liked taking her pieces, she realized. He probably thought the more pieces of hers he destroyed, the stronger his position – and he was feeling confident because his king was well protected.

It gave her an idea. In what she hoped would not be a mistake, she moved her queen to the opposite side of the board, jumping levels as she did, and landing on Solaris Dominus B8.

Gasps from the onlookers broke the silence. They knew what was coming.

Her opponent moved his king's knight with lightning speed to Solaris Dominus. Phoenix watched the pearly white queen burst into a brilliant shower of white lights and disappear.

Gales of laughter at her misfortune floated across the room, but her opponent was the only one laughing. Too late, he realized what she'd done, sacrificing her queen to lure his knight out of position.

As his spotlight dimmed and her spotlight came on, Phoenix moved her king's rook across the board to E8, where it stood beside the dark king.

"Endgame," she proclaimed, the echo of his laughter still hanging in the air.

They both stared at the board; she with satisfaction and he in disbelief. There was no move he could make to avoid capture and they both knew it.

"Endgame, white wins," a disembodied voice announced as the holographic game board flickered and disappeared. The lights in the room came up accompanied by the loud noise of many voices talking at once.

Someone pulled her from her chair and strong arms pulled her into a hug. At first, she thought it was Adrian, but then she saw him over Bradden's shoulder, looking on.

"That was fantastic!" Bradden said enthusiastically. "I had no idea you played so well." He let her go and she automatically stepped back, not comfortable being so close to him. He didn't seem to notice. "Let me go collect our winnings and then we can settle up."

"That was impressive," Adrian said, once they were alone. He gave a small chuckle. "Most of the people here bet on you to lose."

"Were you one of them?"

"Not a chance."

She smiled, warmed by his words. "Thanks. Did we make enough for us to get to Previon?"

"We made enough to book passage for two," he assured her.

"Good." As friendly and charming as Bradden might be, she didn't want to stay with him.

"Are you okay? You seem more nervous now than you did before the game."

"Yes, of course. I'm fine." But she wasn't. The feeling of anger and resentment that had been niggling at her earlier during the game were still there. She looked around the room.

"Yeah, you don't seem fine. What's bothering you?"

"I don't know," she admitted. "I feel like something's not right."

To his credit, Adrian didn't dismiss her feelings out of hand. He looked around the room. "I don't see anything to be alarmed about." Despite his assurance, his hand dropped to his side, close to where his laser was strapped.

"It's probably nothing," she hurried to assure him.

"Why don't we wait for Bradden downstairs," he suggested, guiding her toward the door. They'd just reached it when they heard Bradden call Adrian's name from across the room.

"Stay here," he told her. "I'll get our money and then we can leave."

She nodded, not trusting herself to speak.

What the hell was wrong with her? She focused all her energy on staying calm and almost instantly, the feelings of anger faded.

That's odd.

Experimentally, she focused on a man across the room that she recognized as one of her opponent's supporters. When their gazes met, disgust and disappointment filled her. He'd no doubt bet on her to lose, which explained why he'd feel disappointed.

More important, she realized she was picking up his emotions.

It was like what happened in Cloud City watching Mr. Zimmers be tortured and then later, on the ship, with Adrian's nightmare. She'd thought those had been anomalies—but what if they weren't?

She thought back to the bar when Adrian had been negotiating with that disgusting ship's captain. There had been a moment – oh, so brief – when she'd looked deep into Adrian's eyes and known that everything would be okay if she simply looked at the man in the red shirt. So she had – and he'd collapsed. Not dead, as Adrian later told her. Passed out from too much drink.

He irritated her, she thought with sudden and growing anger. She turned to watch him walking across the room to meet Bradden. Almost of its own accord, her hand strayed into her pocket where her fingers curled around the grip of Adrian's laser. She'd almost pulled the laser out before realizing the urge to shoot Adrian wasn't her own.

Someone in this room wanted to shoot him. But who?

She focused on each person, one at a time, but couldn't pinpoint the source of the hostility. Could it be coming from outside the room?

Searching the hallway behind her, she found it empty. She turned her attention back to the room where Adrian and Bradden stood talking. The urge to shoot him now was stronger than ever and she knew she needed to warn him.

She started walking toward him just as the door at the back of the room opened and a man stepped out.

With sudden clarity, she knew he had been the source of the homicidal feelings she was sensing.

Phoenix screamed out a warning to Adrian, but it came too late. The man pulled out his laser and open fired.

Two men near the back jerked backwards as if punched in the chest and fell to the floor. Those still standing pulled their lasers. Soon, laser bursts criss-crossed the room like security beams around a precious treasure.

One caught Bradden in the leg and he stumbled sideways into Adrian, knocking him off balance just as he fired his laser. His shot went wide, hitting the corner of the room.

The assailant was now striding forward, miraculously dodging laser fire; his whole attention fixed on Adrian, who was bent over Bradden now lying on the floor.

Phoenix knew that if she didn't do something, it would be too late. She pulled her laser, never doubting her ability to pull the trigger, and took aim.

Then, in horrifying slow motion, she saw Adrian jerk and crumple to the floor.

He lay still.

Dead.

Shock, mixed with an overwhelming sense of grief, filled her – and then transformed into a primal rage. She gave in to the sudden, deep need for vengeance and pulled the trigger of her laser.

Chapter 10

BURSTS OF LASER FIRE lit the room like the light display at the annual Unification Celebration. Adrian hugged the floor, mentally kicking himself for allowing that woman to carry a weapon.

Despite the erratic spray of laser fire, Adrian risked looking up. Phoenix was now the only one standing. Everyone else, like Adrian, had dropped to the floor to avoid getting hit. Judging from the way her body flinched every time the weapon discharged, and from her wild-eyed gaze, Adrian didn't think Phoenix was aware that she was still pulling the trigger.

It was too dangerous to approach her in this state. He might get shot. He considered calling out to her, but drawing her attention could have equally dire consequences. No, it was better to wait until she'd depleted the weapon's charge. At the rate she was firing, it should run out—

Suddenly, the room fell silent except for the muffled whine of the laser's trigger mechanism as it moved impotently back and forth.

Adrian jumped to his feet and rushed to Phoenix, pulling the weapon from her hand and shoving it into the back of his waistband. She didn't seem to notice.

Her wide-eyed gaze moved about the room until it settled on him. It took a moment before she recognized him but then her lower lip quivered and her eyes filled with unshed tears.

"Adrian?" Her voice was barely more than whisper.

"Yeah, sweetheart. It's me." He reached out to her, holding her steady so he could look into her face.

"It's all right," he whispered to her. "Everything's okay."

"I knew he was there." Her voice sounded far off and strained. "I felt him. I felt his emotions. He wanted to kill you, but I didn't know where he was to warn you." Her hand was shaky as she laid it against his chest. "I thought he'd shot you." Her voice sounded barely above a whisper. "I thought you were dead."

Her confession shot straight through him and he pulled her to him.

"Hush, sweetheart. You did warn me." The sound of her scream would haunt him for a long time. "What about you? Are you hurt?"

"No, I'm okay," she mumbled into his chest.

He gave silent thanks to whatever deities might be watching over them for her safety. After a few moments, he felt her breathing return to normal and reluctantly let her go when she finally eased herself out of his embrace to look around the room.

He saw her stiffen at the sight of the slain men.

"Oh, God. I killed them."

"No, you didn't."

Her head snapped around. "What do you mean?"

"The contract killer shot them when he was aiming for me."

"Oh." She continued her survey of the room until she spotted the killer, now laying on his side several feet away, his eyes wide and vacantly staring. The dark circle of charred flesh in the center of his forehead was the only sign of how he died. "Did I do that?" She sounded both pleased and surprised. He hated to disappoint her.

"No, I did that." With his forefinger under her chin, he tilted her head up so she could see the scorched holes in the ceiling and upper portions of the walls. "You did that. Good thing we're on the top floor."

He nearly smiled to see how crestfallen she looked. She was an enigma. On the one hand, she would have been horrified had she actually killed someone, but was now disappointed to learn that she hadn't. Adrian didn't think he'd ever understand her.

Without conscious thought, he pressed a kiss to the top of her head, then steered her across the room to where Bradden was struggling to his feet.

"Are you okay?" Adrian asked him, giving the charred mark on the loan shark's leg a closer look.

"Fortunately, it's just a burn," Bradden replied, wincing when he tried to put his full weight on the leg. "But it still hurts like hell." He looked around the room. "How many are dead?"

"Five, I think. We'll know shortly."

Now that the excitement was over, the survivors were getting to their feet. There was no local authority to call to report the incident, but there would still be questions: Who was the shooter? Who was his target? Why did he choose this forum for his attack? Who was paying for the damage?

Adrian knew if he and Phoenix didn't leave before the questions started, they wouldn't make their rendezvous with Abe.

"Is she all right?" Bradden asked, dipping his head in Phoenix's direction.

"Now that the crisis is over, she's in shock," he responded truthfully. "She'll recover."

"Please don't talk about me like I'm not standing here," Phoenix said in a sharp tone that lifted Adrian's spirits.

"See?" he said to Bradden. "She's practically back to her old self." He smiled at Phoenix to let her know he was teasing, then realized what he was doing. Five men had been shot—he'd nearly been one of them – and he was flirting with Skylar's daughter? What was wrong with him? Maybe he was in shock as well.

He shrugged it off, knowing he had bigger concerns. "Bradden—"

"I know," the loan shark interrupted. "You need to leave before things get messy." He quickly amended his words. "Messier." He reached beneath his duster into his hip pants pocket and pulled out a handful of credit chips. He counted out fifty and handed them to Adrian. "You know, I should be giving these to her. She played one hell of a game."

"I'll see that she gets her share," Adrian promised picking up one of the chips and handing it back. "This should cover the damage."

"You're doing it again," Phoenix muttered beside them. "I'm standing right here."

The men shared a smile as Bradden accepted the disc. "You should probably go out the back way. I'll call my driver and have him meet you. He'll fly you to the airfield."

"Aren't you leaving, too?" Adrian asked.

"Are you kidding? Look at this place. Even with your kind donation, the owner of this fine establishment doesn't have the funds to restore this place without taking out a loan. And if he's too smart for that, this might be the investment opportunity I've been looking for." Smiling, he held out his hand to Adrian. "Safe travels, my friend." He gestured to Phoenix. "Don't let that one get away." Releasing Adrian's hand, he turned to Phoenix. "It was a pleasure."

He turned and hobbled off, pulling his comm-unit as he went.

"Time to go," Adrian said, taking Phoenix by the hand. "We have a ship to catch."

Ten minutes later, they stood outside Abe Sansholox's ship. The big man and his first mate, Kohnner, were making last minute pre-flight systems checks. Adrian handed the big man two of the gold discs. He looked surprised to see them but quickly pocketed them.

"Kohnner will show you to a room."

The first mate was a burly man in desperate need of a haircut, shave and a bath. Phoenix worked hard not to wrinkle her nose at the offending odors wafting off the man as she followed him up the ramp and through the hatch. Within the narrow confines of the hallway, his odor became stronger. She could only imagine how bad it would be once the hatch doors closed.

"You'll stay in here," Kohnner said, stopping at a door. He palmed the control panel and the door slid open, disappearing into the wall. "We leave in fifteen minutes."

He left them standing in the open doorway, staring at the room. Obviously used as a storage room, it had stacks of various sized crates and packing containers creating an obstacle course for anyone who tried to enter. There was another door along the side wall—presumably to a bathroom—and once a few crates were moved out of the way, they'd actually be able to access it.

"Lovely," Phoenix muttered.

"Let's see if we can move some of this stuff out of the way," Adrian suggested.

Fortunately, most of the crates and containers were empty, leading Phoenix to wonder why Abe bothered to save them, but she was too tired to ask Adrian and in any event, wasn't sure she wanted to know the answer. Abe was, after all, a smuggler.

After some effort, they'd stacked the crates against the wall. In the process, they'd uncovered a bed. It was the only piece of furniture in the room but Phoenix wasn't going to complain. She was exhausted.

Risking a sideways glance at Adrian, she found him staring at the bed with a fierce scowl on his face.

Refusing to let the situation intimidate her, Phoenix walked over to the far side where she shrugged out of the duster. Then she climbed onto the bed, sitting with her back against the wall and her legs stretched out in front of her. She covered her legs with the duster.

"It's not completely horrible," she noted, patting the mattress. "A few lumps and who knows if the sheets are clean, but I'm so tired, I don't care. All I want to do is sleep."

Adrian only stared at the bed and she wondered if his thoughts, like hers, immediately went back to the safe house. For her, it had been reckless, but exciting. She'd be lying to herself if she didn't admit to being a little disappointed it had ended so quickly.

Afraid he might see the direction of her thoughts if she looked at him, she closed her eyes.

"As soon as we get underway," he said, "I'll find us something to eat in the galley. I imagine Abe and Kohnner aren't going to play the gracious hosts. We're pretty much on our own. Speaking of which, don't wander around the ship by yourself. I don't trust them."

"All I plan to do is sleep."

She felt her tension starting to slip away until Adrian's voice jerked her awake.

"Not yet. We need to talk."

She cracked open an eyelid to peek at him. "Can't it wait?"

"No." His serious tone made her wary.

"Okay. What about?"

"About what happened back there between us."

He sounded serious and not in a "let's do it again" kind of way. It was more of a "I'm not looking to get involved with anyone" tone. She'd been foolish to think there might have been more between them.

Her face heated with embarrassment but forced her tone to be light and matter-of-fact. "Don't worry about it. It was two adults reacting to stress; not a lifetime commitment." There, she'd let him off the hook.

When he didn't say anything, though, she felt compelled to look at him.

He stared at her blankly. "What the hell are you talking about?"

She suddenly realized that he wasn't talking about the kiss or what had nearly resulted from it. Here she was telling him it was no big deal and in fact, it had meant so little to him that he couldn't even remember it.

She didn't want to care, but the dull ache that sprang up in her chest said it was too late.

"Nevermind. What did you want to talk about?"

She prayed he'd leave it alone and save her any further humiliation, but then his eyes lit with understanding and he cleared his throat.

"That's not what I wanted to talk about."

She didn't think any more blood could rush to her face. "Oh."

"I meant back in the game room, right before that psycho came out of the closet. You apologized for not warning me and now I realize that you didn't call out."

Her head reeled from the sharp change in emotions. A moment ago, she'd been embarrassed. Now, she felt horribly guilty because it seemed he was blaming her.

"I'm so sorry. I meant to."

He waved aside her apology. "That's not what I'm getting at. I heard you scream my name – but I realize now it came from inside my head."

Her feelings of guilt turned to confusion. "You heard me?"

"Yes. Hell, my head is still ringing. And that wasn't the first time, either. Back in the alley, when I was fighting the chameleon, I heard your shout an instant before the second assassin jumped me—but you were standing at the far end. I shouldn't have heard you at all."

"I don't remember if I shouted out loud or not," she confessed.

"What do you know about your father?" His sudden change in topic threw her.

"Not much other than he's from Veridian Prime and works for the government."

"So he never told you he's telepathic?"

"What?" It wasn't possible. "He told me he was born on Veridian Prime."

"He was, but both his parents were HydroTerran. That makes you half HydroTerran." He gave her a moment to digest this news. "I think the reason I heard both your warnings is because you inherited Skylar's telepathic ability."

She leaned her head back against the headboard and considered what he'd told her. Receiving emotions and transmitting thoughts—she wasn't sure she could do either on purpose.

"You have to learn to control your abilities," Adrian said, startling her by voicing her very concern. He stood up and started pacing the room. "We can't have another incident like what happened at the Spacer's Den."

"The Spacer's Den?" What had happened there? She couldn't remember.

"How many drinks did you have?"

"Two glasses of Edenberry juice, honestly."

"And Jack?"

"The same," she answered, wondering where he was going with this.

"I've seen Jack put down half a bottle of Dead Man's Swill without blinking an eye and yet he got drunk off two glasses of juice? I don't think so."

"What are you suggesting?"

"I think because you're an empath, you picked up the drunken buzz from those in the room who really were drunk and then because you're a telepath, you broadcasted those emotions out to Jack—and maybe one or two others sitting close by."

His suggestion was ludicrous and she wanted to laugh, but couldn't. What if he was right?

When they'd first walked into the bar, she'd felt irritated, not drunk. And both Adrian and Jack had appeared to feel the same way. The longer she'd sat among the rowdy patrons of the bar, though, the better she'd felt. Drunk almost. From drinking juice?

She thought back to another incident; that time on the ship's bridge, right after her nightmare. She'd felt calm talking to Jack. Then Adrian had joined them and he'd obviously been agitated. Her sense of calm had quickly vanished until she'd become irritated. She'd been channeling his emotions, of course. She was an empath. It made sense.

What had happened next with Jack, though – had that been her fault?

Had his temper flared a little too quickly when Adrian appeared?

"Let's say, for argument's sake, that you're right," she ventured. "This could be a problem because I don't know how to control these abilities."

"You have about ten hours before we reach Previon to figure it out."

"Great." That was no help at all. "I'll get right on that." Her tone dripped with sarcasm as she leaned down and, undoing the fastenings of her boots, pushed them off her feet to fall onto the floor. Her eyes felt dry and itchy, and she was having trouble keeping them open. She eased herself down the bed until she was lying with her head on the pillow. Turning onto her side, she pulled the duster up until it covered her shoulders and closed her eyes.

Across the room, she heard a scuffling noise and cracked open an eyelid to see Adrian pushing the crates away from the bathroom door. She closed her eyes again, but a new noise caught her attention.

"What are you doing?"

"Nothing. I thought you were tired."

"I am, but I can't sleep with you making all that noise."

"I'm moving these crates around so I have enough space to stretch out."

"Don't be silly. You don't want to sleep on the floor. It's disgusting."

He stopped pushing a stack of crates and looked pointedly from her to the bed. "I don't *want* to sleep on the floor, but under the circumstances, I thought it might be better if I did."

She felt another blush heat her face as she remembered his nightmare. "I trust you, Adrian. Let's share the bed. It's the only way you'll get any decent sleep."

He gave her a dubious look and she thought he mumbled something under his breath about needing a cold shower, but he finally shrugged and turned off the overhead light, throwing the room into darkness. Only the emergency light in the corner provided any illumination with its warm, red glow.

She heard him take off his duster and for a breathless moment, wondered if she'd made a mistake. With a day's growth covering his face, his short brownish-blond hair glistening bronze under the red light, broad chest testing the fabric of his shirt and lasers holstered at his side – she found him irresistible and her pulse quickened.

Seemingly unaware of her, he removed the holster and draped it over the corner of the headboard where he could easily reach his weapon.

When he sat on the bed, Phoenix had to fight gravity to keep herself from falling toward him. She watched as he removed his boots, placing them neatly to one side on the floor. Then, giving her a final glance, he stretched out beside her, linking his hands behind his head.

"See," she said. "We fit."

Like fingers in a glove, she mentally added as she recalled their kiss. She felt the heat radiating off his body along every inch of hers. Trying to ignore him was like a drowning man trying to ignore the water.

She rolled onto her back and then onto her other side, searching for a position that would give her comfort.

"I thought you were tired."

"I am," she said, rolling onto her back again.

"Then stop fidgeting."

"I can't help it." They lay side by side, stiff and unnatural. Phoenix searched for something, anything to ease the tension. "Tell me about my father."

Adrian was quiet for a moment. "What do you want to know?"

"What does he look like? He uses an avatar in the chat room, so I've never seen him."

"You have his hair—and his stubborn streak." Adrian's tone was rich and comforting. She knew later she'd be upset that she didn't pay more attention, but she was so tired and his voice was soothing...

After several hours of peaceful sleep, Phoenix came suddenly awake. Something wasn't right, but it took her a moment to figure out what it was.

She was alone.

She placed her hand where Adrian had lain. His empty spot still felt warm. He couldn't have been gone long.

"Adrian?" She glanced at the closed door to the bathroom, but got no response. She got out of bed and knocked. When there was still no answer, she opened the door.

Empty.

Going back to the bed, she sat down. She wasn't worried. They were in space, after all, so how far could he go?

She resigned herself to waiting, but after a time, boredom set in – and then hunger. The more she tried not to think about how hungry she was, the hungrier she became until she knew she had to do something about it.

Putting on her boots and ignoring Adrian's order to stay in the room, she left in search of the galley.

The ship was substantially larger than Adrian's, easily accommodating a crew of ten, which meant there was plenty of ship to get lost in, but with only one wrong turn and a bit of backtracking, Phoenix found the galley. Finding it empty, she set about putting together something to eat for her and Adrian. With luck, she'd even beat Adrian back to the room.

With a little scrounging, she found bread, meat and cheese. She had just started making sandwiches when the sensation of being watched tickled the back of her neck.

Turning around, she found Kohnner's large hairy body filling the doorway; watching her. She didn't need to be an empath to know that food was not what he was hungry for.

Chapter 11

Kohnner's smile widened as he walked slowly, purposefully, toward her. Already standing against the counter, she couldn't back away and tried not to let him see her cringe in reaction to the way his gaze traveled along the length of her. Despite being fully clothed, she felt exposed and vulnerable.

"Adrian and I got hungry so we decided to make sandwiches." She forced a casual tone to hide her fear and, half turning, gestured to the unfinished sandwiches with the knife still clutched in her hand. She'd forgotten she had it and wondered if she had it in her to stab the man if he tried to rape her.

Oh, yeah.

The big man looked around the galley. "Where's Sun?"

"He just stepped out." She hoped he didn't hear the slight quaver in her voice. "You must have passed him in the corridor."

"No, I don't think so." His ravenous gaze traveled over her again, causing bile to rise up her throat. "I think you're here all by yourself."

He took a step closer and she realized just how massive he was. Before she realized what he meant to do, he'd grabbed the knife from her hand and set it on the counter, beyond her reach. She stared at it helplessly, realizing she was totally unprepared for this type of situation and had no way of defending herself.

Only, that wasn't true, was it? She had a skill. If only she knew how to control it.

Staring hard at Kohnner, she willed him to feel her fear. She visualized shooting a beam of raw terror straight into him.

His smile faltered and he blinked several times before shaking his head as if to clear it.

Elated by this small show of success, she increased her efforts—only to see Kohnner's alarmed expression fade and change to one of... excitement?

Uh oh! She hadn't meant to project that.

"I need to leave." She hadn't realized she'd spoken her thoughts out loud until he responded.

"No. Stay awhile. You and I are going to have some fun." His fetid breath nearly choked her when he laughed.

"Don't do it," Adrian's deep voice growled behind the large man.

Kohnner's smile wavered as he slowly turned to face Adrian. Phoenix wanted to run to him; take sanctuary in his embrace, but Kohnner stood in the way.

"This is my ship, Sun," the hairy man protested. "You don't get to tell me what to do."

"I wasn't talking to you. I was talking to her." Adrian gestured to Phoenix.

Me? Phoenix felt as confused as Kohnner looked.

"I'm surprised Abe didn't tell you. She's a Psychotran. Then again, maybe he's hoping you'll insult her and save him from having to split a million credits with you." Adrian spoke matter-of-factly.

Kohnner glowered. "A million credits? Abe said you paid him half that amount."

"Maybe you *are* too stupid to keep around if you believe that." He shrugged. "It's your funeral. I'll wait here." He gestured to the side counter as he walked toward it. "If you're lucky, it won't hurt." He gave Phoenix a speculative glance. "No, I think you're screwed. She looks angry to me. Does she look angry to you?"

Phoenix had just enough time to wipe the astonishment from her face before Kohnner turned to look at her. She glared at him and when the first hint of fear leaked into his emotions, she couldn't help but smile.

The big man's eyes grew wide and suddenly, he couldn't leave the galley fast enough. Phoenix knew her troubles weren't over, though.

"I woke up and you were gone. I waited, but you didn't come back and I got hungry."

His eyes narrowed. "Don't you dare blame this on me."

"You're right," she agreed. "I should have stayed in the room where it was safe. If you hadn't come when you did." She shuddered. "I thought he was going to rape me."

"No doubt. They don't get many women out here who look like you."

"What do you mean?" She hoped he wasn't about to suggest this was her fault. "How do I look?"

Now his gaze traveled over her body. "Innocent and clean. Strong, but soft in all the right places. Beautiful, like a precious gem." His gaze lifted to her face. "And right now, your hair looks like you just rolled out of bed after a long night of make-up sex." Phoenix sensed the shift in his emotions as anger turned to lust. "You'd tempt a saint; how do you expect a lesser man to resist?"

He crowded her against the back counter much as Kohnner had intended to, only Phoenix wasn't frightened. She waited in breathless anticipation, her heart racing.

His smoldering gaze captured hers, holding her mesmerized as he ran the palm of his hand across the curve of her hip and along the gentle indentation of her waist. She ached to feel his touch against her bare skin but contented herself with the sensation of his body pressed against hers.

When he lowered his head to kiss her, she didn't pull away. She wanted to feel his lips on hers.

His first touch was hesitant, as if he expected her to shy away or change her mind. When she didn't, his kiss grew bolder; more insistent. She wrapped her arms around him and kissed him with fevered eagerness; like she'd never get the chance to kiss him again.

Her reaction seemed to catch him by surprise because he hesitated for the briefest moment. Then it was a like she'd opened the flood gates. He pulled her against him, his mouth ravaging and plundering hers, their tongues coming together in a primitive mating dance. With the hard length of his desire pressing against her abdomen, Phoenix stopped thinking and let herself get lost in a tidal wave of emotions.

Adrian's iron-tight control evaporated in the heat of his need for her. He wanted to bury himself deep inside her. He didn't even think she was aware of the little moaning noises she made, but they were the most erotic sounds he'd ever heard. He considered carrying her back to the cabin; a more insistent part of him didn't want to wait that long.

About to reach for the waistband of his pants, he became aware of a new sound; a nasty, humorless chuckle from the doorway.

Abe.

Adrian reluctantly ended the kiss, pulling away from Phoenix despite her slight whimper of protest. Allowing his gaze to linger for a moment on her dazed expression, he knew she was unaware of their audience. It gave him a sense of satisfaction to know he'd dominated all her senses.

He turned, giving the man a cold hard stare. "Something I can do for you?"

"Yeah, you can get out of my damn galley. Use the cabin," Abe replied derisively. "This ain't no Pleasure Cruiser." He glared hard at Adrian. "We're four hours out. If there's someplace in particular you want to be dropped, you might want to tell me before we get there. Otherwise, I'm liable to drop you anywhere."

Abe walked off, but Adrian remained with his back to Phoenix until he was certain their visitor wasn't coming back. When he finally turned to look at her, she seemed suddenly shy, unable to look him in the face.

"Are you okay?"

When she didn't answer, he tipped up her chin with his finger and swore. Red marks lined her face where his fingers had held her too tightly; her lips were swollen from his kisses. If they hadn't been interrupted, what further injury would he have inflicted in a fit of lust? Cold reality grabbed him, reminding him of the type of man he was.

As gently as he could, he touched the side of her face, regret and shame rising like bile in his throat. "I'm sorry. I didn't mean to hurt you." His voice came out thick and hoarse.

She didn't respond, making him feel worse. The last thing he wanted was for her to be afraid of him. "I'll help you finish making the sandwiches. We can take them back to the cabin. After we eat, I'll take care of the landing arrangements—and this time, you'll stay in the room."

She nodded, too compliant and trusting. He knew he would protect her from the others but who would protect her from *him*? That was the question he asked himself.

Phoenix sat on the bed in the cabin, alone once again, with only her thoughts for company. It hadn't taken either of them long to finish their food and then Adrian had gone to the bridge to give Abe the coordinates where to land. That was all right. She was glad for a moment alone. She needed time to sort out her thoughts and emotions. What had happened between her and Adrian had been amazing—and amazingly stupid.

Her body still buzzed; her nerves wound tight with a desire she knew would not quickly abate. The memory of Adrian's hands caressing her caused her breasts to ache with need. Wanting—needing—to relieve the ache, she ran her hand across them.

It was a poor substitute for Adrian's hand and left her wanting more, which was where the "amazingly stupid" part came into play.

Why would she ever consider getting involved with Adrian? He was dangerous.

Dangerously attractive, she silently amended, then just as quickly chastised herself.

Adrian Sun was not the kind of man to settle down with a woman and have kids, so if that's what she wanted in life—and she did—then she needed to look elsewhere. After they found her father and returned him to Veridian Prime, she and Adrian would go their separate ways and she'd never see him again.

The thought was too depressing. She let her head fall back against the wall while she closed her eyes, letting the silence surround her. Eventually, her thoughts turned to her mother. So much had happened that she wanted to share with her. When she sensed her mother's familiar presence, she wrapped the feelings of maternal love around her like a warm blanket. She'd always been able to psychically connect to her mother. She'd always thought it was a one-sided communication from her mother to her, thanks to her mother's strong empath abilities.

This time, though, she'd initiated the link, unconsciously using her newly developing abilities. She reveled in the accomplishment. Then, realizing her mother was picking up her stress and sensing her worry, Phoenix tried to focus on feelings of love and reassurance, knowing her mother would feel them.

As she allowed the connection to end, she wondered if it would be possible to connect with her father in the same way.

She focused on him, knowing he would be harder to sense. Searching for him was like trying to pick out one star among the millions in the sky, nearly impossible – and it was exhausting. His essence wouldn't be as readily identifiable as her mother's. In fact, she wondered if she'd know it when she found it.

She thought of the times they spent playing mosh and her awareness of him during those times. With a jolt, she recognized that same awareness was with her now. She explored the feeling, hesitant at first and unsure if she was doing it correctly. It was like following a delicate strand of silk to the other end. She could tell she was getting closer, closer—

Suddenly, her entire body was awash in excruciating pain. She immediately shied away from it, throwing up mental walls to shield herself.

She'd found her father.

He was in such pain. She worried that he might not survive long enough for them to rescue him.

Knowing how destructive negative thoughts could be, she shut out her worries—but doing so gave her an idea.

She'd learned techniques for drawing strength from the positive energy around her. Could she use the telepathy to broadcast some of that energy to her father?

Back in the bar, she'd transmitted feelings of inebriation to Jack by accident but in the galley with Kohnner, she'd sent them intentionally—not that she'd been able to maintain her focus.

Still, it had worked.

Settling herself into a more comfortable position on the bed with her legs crossed and her hands resting lightly on her knees, she closed her eyes and visualized the positive energy all around her like beams of light. She drew them to her until she sat at the focal point; felt their heat beating down on her; filling her until she thought light must be radiating from her every pore.

When she could hold no more inside her, she visualized sending that beam of positive energy through the link to her father. When the link closed, she collapsed, exhausted, and fell asleep.

Deep in the bowels of Zarek's fortress, Skylar jerked awake from the stupor in which he'd existed for too long. Zarek's efforts to break him had been impressive and unrelenting. In fact, he was a little surprised to discover he was still alive. It would have been a depressing thought had he not at that moment been filled with a sense of renewed energy and hope.

He wasn't naive enough to believe he'd be rescued—no one knew where he was—but maybe he could resist giving Zarek the information he wanted until the capsule planted in his body released its deadly poison. Then, at least, he would no longer be a threat to his government and all who lived within it.

A vision of Serina appeared in his mind and he wished he could see her one last time to tell her how much he'd loved her all those years ago; how much he loved her still.

Chapter 12

ADRIAN AND PHOENIX STOOD on the outskirts of an immense forest located on one of the larger, more habitable, continents of Previon as they watched Abe's ship disappear into the clear blue sky. The surly ship's captain had left them with no food or water, and only the weapons they'd had on them, yet the knowledge that her father was nearby left Phoenix feeling optimistic.

"I don't suppose there's a path or road we could take, is there?" Phoenix asked, studying the thick foliage less than two meters away.

"This way." Adrian headed off to the right, away from the forest.

"Where are we going?" She asked after catching up to him.

He pointed to a small rise in the landscape. "Jack landed the ship just over that ridge. I spotted it during our descent."

"Do you think he's still there?"

"No. He'll have gone after Skylar." His tone was grim.

"Maybe he's already rescued him."

Adrian glanced at her as he kept walking with determined strides across the grassy field. "There's always a chance." His tone suggested otherwise.

Phoenix looked up at the cerulean blue sky above them and the dark, storm clouds gathering in the distance. The slight breeze smelled both of the ocean, to their right, and the forest, behind them. Over the sound of their footsteps, she heard the faint howl of an unseen animal. Its predatory sound sent a shiver down her spine. Back on Xenobia, there were no animals running wild. A person could walk through the forests and commune with nature without fear of being attacked, mauled—or eaten.

The animal howled again, this time sounding closer. Phoenix cast a nervous glance at Adrian, but he seemed unconcerned.

"You grew up here, right? Are the animals as dangerous as they sound?"

"Yes, but they're not the only danger here. The weather, the terrain—even the vegetation is deadly."

"And people live here voluntarily?" She couldn't believe it.

"Not initially. A couple hundred years ago, one of Veridian Prime's Ark-voyagers got lost and crashed here. Those living here now are descendants of the survivors."

They crested a small ridge and Phoenix spotted their ship. It was a welcomed sight.

When they reached it, Adrian punched a code into the keypad. The hatch door opened with a whoosh that echoed Phoenix's sigh of relief. Within moments, she was back in her cabin, slipping out of Adrian's too—big clothes and into the jumpsuit she'd worn before. Unfortunately, there were no smaller boots for her to wear, so she was stuck with the ones she had on.

In the decontamination unit, she washed her face and combed her hair, all the while wishing there was time to step into the bathroom's sani-mister because she felt dirty.

Adrian appeared in the doorway holding a backpack in one hand and a nasty looking machete in the other. It was time to go.

"I have food and supplies to last a couple of days."

"Will that be enough?"

"If we're not back in a couple of days, we aren't coming back."

With that grim pronouncement, they left the ship and headed toward the forest. Adrian stopped short of entering and bent to study the ground. Next, he studied the foliage. A minute passed before he moved half a meter to his right and repeated the actions.

"What are you doing?"

"Looking for the place where Jack entered. I want to follow his trail as much as possible on the chance he's still alive."

He said it so matter-of-factly, it made Phoenix shudder. He bent one last time to study the ground and the plants in front of him. "Okay, I think this is it."

She looked to where he indicated but couldn't see how it looked any different than the other areas he'd stopped to examine.

"Stay close behind me and only step where I step. And, for *krauk's* sake, don't touch anything." He waited until she nodded and then used the machete to clear away hanging limbs and vines.

Progress through the jungle was slow and it was quickly obvious to Phoenix why no one traveled through it on a regular basis. Several times, she tried to see past Adrian, looking for the supposed trail he followed in the knee-high undergrowth. Not finding it, she studied her surroundings instead.

The forest was filled with thin trees that stood about nineteen meters tall and had long branching limbs that wove a leafy tapestry high above their heads. Snaking in and out of the tapestry, with loops hanging down to the ground, were long, green and brown variegated vines

With so much vegetation blocking out the sun, Phoenix expected the forest to be pitch black, but enough sunlight filtered through to allow them to see – and what she saw surprised her.

The colors of this forest were beautiful—the tree leaves varied from the pale yellow of summer grass to a deeper Xenobian forest-green. The undergrowth, without the full benefit of the sun's rays, consisted of darker brown and greenish black leaves. Scattered throughout were plants with large, hand-sized blossoms made up of hundreds of thin, pink petals. What really caught her attention, though, were the vines with tiny purple flowers and opalescent leaves.

Intrigued, Phoenix moved in for a closer look, catching a whiff of its pleasant fragrance. The leaves swayed gently in the breeze, their surface changing color with each movement.

"What kind of vines are these?"

Adrian's hand closed over her wrist, pulling her away from the vine before she could touch it.

"What are you doing?" he snapped.

"I only wanted to see what it felt like." Still the sweet fragrance called to her and her eyes drifted from Adrian's stern face to stare longingly at the leaves. "I don't see what harm there is in one little touch, unless... " A thought occurred to her. "Are they poisonous?"

"No. They're carnivorous." He pointed to a clump of vines visible through a gap in some intersecting tree branches. She followed the direction of his finger and at first didn't see anything.

"What—oh."

Several strands of vine wrapped around the corpse of a small rodent-looking creature.

"The scent of the vine's flowers and the color of its leaves attract animals," Adrian explained. "When they come in contact with the vine, it wraps around them and begins constricting. For a plant, it moves pretty quickly. The smaller animals are usually squeezed to death before they can chew their way to freedom. Once the animal is dead, the leaves excrete an acid that promotes decomposition and as the body decays, the plant slowly absorbs it."

Phoenix shuddered. How could something so beautiful be so deadly?

"Shall we continue?" Adrian released her hand and went back to clearing a path through the trees.

"Wait." Phoenix stopped him mid-swing to get his attention. "Let me carry the pack," she suggested. "I want to help and there's no need for you to carry it on top of using the machete." He stared at her skeptically, but finally nodded and shrugged out of the backpack.

He held it while she slipped her arms through the straps, not releasing it until it was settled in place. It was heavier than she expected, but she didn't complain. Carrying it made her feel like she was contributing.

Adrian went back to swinging the machete, sending pieces of plants and tree limbs flying. They'd gone only a few steps when he paused to look back at her. "Thanks."

At first, she didn't know what he meant, but then he nodded toward the pack. She smiled and felt a small warm glow start deep inside. "You're welcome."

He returned to blazing a small path for them and she followed behind him, her thoughts wandering. She was no longer the same person who'd walked into The Abyss on Outer Fringe—had it only been a few days ago? That woman had been naïve and incapable of protecting herself.

She realized that some might still consider her naïve but she was no longer defenseless. She had a powerful weapon in her ability to both perceive and broadcast emotions, provided she learned how to control it.

Now seemed as good a time as any to experiment and she had the perfect target in front of her.

She stretched her awareness, feeling like she was reaching blindly into the dark with psychic hands outstretched. The harder she tried, the more worried and concerned she grew. She didn't see how this rescue mission could end well. If only she had done things differently; paid more attention, none of this would have happened—

She slammed into a hard, sweaty body.

"Why did you stop?" She growled. "We have to hurry." Didn't he realize they needed to keep moving? Time was of the essence.

"I don't know what you're up to, but I can't concentrate with you poking around inside my head like that."

Suddenly she understood the origin of her extreme anxiety and couldn't keep the smile from her face. "That was you?"

"Hell yes, it was me, and I'd appreciate you not feeding those same emotions back to me. It's distracting."

"Sorry." She hesitated, better understanding the heavy burden of guilt that he'd placed on himself but not knowing if he'd appreciate her trying to ease it. "It's not your fault, you know."

"What's that?"

"My father getting kidnapped; Jack going off on his own. None of it's your fault."

"Thank you for your psychoanalysis," he muttered. "Now stay out of my head."

"You're the one who told me to practice," she grumbled.

"Yeah, well I didn't mean while we're walking through a forest filled with things trying to kill us."

What? All thoughts of experimentation vanished as she looked around, not sure what she expected to see. When they resumed their trek, she kept her thoughts under tight rein and her attention on their surroundings.

Their progress was slow and they only stopped long enough to catch their breath or take a drink of water from one of the canteens. When they hit a particularly dense patch of growth, she had to wait for Adrian to hack through. A small four-winged insect flew into their area, catching her attention. Fascinated, she followed its flight, admiring the color of its rapidly beating red and orange wings.

It reminded her of the flutter-bugs that came out every spring back home. As a child, she would try to get one to land on her finger. This one, though, was easily three times larger. It flew to a nearby plant and hovered over one of the large pink blooms. Then it dived at the flower, mouth open revealing a set of tiny, razor-sharp teeth that it used to snap off the entire bloom. A soft crunching noise filled the air as the bug ate its meal.

Phoenix barely breathed, afraid it would decide it was still hungry. She wanted to get Adrian's attention, but was too afraid to take her eyes off the bug as it hovered in front of her. Then, in the blink of an eye, something long and skinny fell from the tree limbs above, wrapped around the insect and jerked it upward.

Behind her, she heard Adrian's grunt of satisfaction as he cleared the last obstacle from their path and moved forward. Phoenix hurried to follow him, but paused to look into the canopy above. Sitting on a limb was the largest tree-frog she'd ever seen, with a piece of red and orange wing sticking out of its mouth.

"Did you see that?" Phoenix asked as she caught up to Adrian.

He stopped in his tracks. "See what?"

The irritated expression on his face was enough to keep her quiet. "Nothing."

He gave her a curious look, but didn't press the matter and instead resumed his clearing of a path.

As the day wore on, heat and humidity penetrated the shade of the jungle. Soon, both Phoenix and Adrian were drenched in sweat; their clothes clinging to their bodies like a second layer of skin. Adrian had long since folded up his duster and placed it into the backpack. Now, he peeled off his shirt and stuffed it in with the duster. Phoenix wished she could do the same with her jumpsuit, but she couldn't – so she distracted herself by enjoying the view.

With each stroke of the machete, the muscles along Adrian's back and arms bulged and rippled. The sweat made his skin glisten and when he stepped forward, his pants, already plastered to his body, stretched, showing him off to definite advantage. She ached to let her fingers explore the contours of his body.

Three hours later, however, not even the spectacular view could distract her from her gnawing hunger or overwhelming fatigue.

"Do you think we could stop and sit somewhere?"

He looked back at her in mid-stroke of the machete. "Are you tired?"

She stared at him, dumbfounded. "Yes, I'm tired," she snapped. "I'm tired and hungry and I hurt everywhere, especially my feet ... " She paused and took a deep breath, then let it out slowly and tried again, in a calmer, less complaining tone. "Surely, you're tired, too?"

He stepped toward her, his eyes shining, sweat dripping, and then raised the machete in the air. She was pretty sure he wouldn't actually slice her in two with it, but when he brought his arm down, she couldn't help but flinch. She heard a thwacking sound next to her head as the machete sank, blade first, deep into the tree behind her.

Unable to take her eyes off Adrian, she held perfectly still as he put his hands on her shoulders. She waited, barely able to breathe, irrationally wondering if he might kiss her, inexplicably disappointed when all he did was turn her around so he could grab the pack.

Moving to the center of the small clearing, she watched as he used his boot to push aside some of the leaves and vines on the ground. When he'd cleared a small space, he dropped to his knees and opened the pack. After a moment of digging, he pulled out a vacuum sealed package. Removing a small knife from his boot, he sliced it open and pulled out four thick sticks made up of what looked like pressed nuts and fruit. He handed her two and then bit into one of the remaining two.

"What are these?"

"Food sticks," he said after swallowing a bite. "I suggest you eat them slowly because this is all we have for lunch."

She took a tentative bite at first, but was pleasantly surprised. The bar was both chewy and crunchy, and as hungry as she was, it was perhaps the best thing she'd ever tasted.

Neither spoke as they ate. When they finished, Adrian pulled out the canteen of water and offered her a drink.

"Ready?" Adrian asked after they'd both slaked their thirst and he'd put the canteen back in the bag.

Exhausted and sure she couldn't continue on much longer, she nevertheless got to her feet. Her father didn't have time for her to rest.

"Let's go."

The afternoon passed more slowly than the morning and Adrian had to keep reminding himself that they were making progress. He couldn't afford to move any faster and risk overlooking even the smallest danger.

Both his shoulder and back screamed in agony, but he forced himself to press onward, thinking of Skylar and Jack. Behind him, Phoenix emitted small huffs and groans of impatience that echoed the emotions seeping uncontrollably from her, washing over him.

"Why don't we go that way?" Phoenix asked as he cut away another small limb blocking their path. He paused to look where she pointed and saw the small opening he'd purposely avoided through the under-growth.

"Not a good idea."

"Why?"

Picking up a good-sized fallen limb, he walked over to the small, sandy stretch of path and tossed the limb onto it. For a moment, the limb lay there. Then the ground started moving in small rolling waves. As the grains of sand boiled and shifted, the limb slowly sank until it disappeared and the ground looked calm and peaceful once again.

Beside him, Phoenix gasped and clutched his arm.

"That's why it's important that you step where I do and stay on a path covered with undergrowth." He went back to where he'd left off and continued to cut a trail for them.

"Do you think Jack fell into one of those?" Her words were barely above a whisper as she voiced one of his gravest fears.

"I don't know," he replied honestly.

For another hour, they worked their way slowly through the jungle. Adrian had shifted the machete to his other hand some time ago and now that arm and shoulder ached as much as the other, further slowing their progress.

"Do you want me to do that?" Phoenix offered.

"No."

He could tell his blunt refusal irritated her, but frankly, he was too tired and in too much pain to be diplomatic. He hacked at another branch, feeling like his muscles moved in slow motion.

"Look, you can't even lift the machete anymore. I don't see how I'll do any worse."

He turned to glare at her and saw her chin lift a notch in defiance. Well, if she thought she could do it, he'd bloody-well let her try. Without saying a word, he handed her the machete and took the backpack. Then he switched places with her, letting her take the lead.

"Don't touch that," he said when he saw her reach out to grab the vines hanging in their path with her free hand. "You don't know if it's poisonous or not, and besides, if you hold that, you might cut off your arm. Make diagonal cuts and keep the blade out in front of you. Can't have you swing it down and accidentally cut off your leg."

She glared at him. "Do you mind? I think I know how to use one of these. Cutting away vines and under-growth is not a difficult concept to grasp."

He held out his arm for her to proceed and watched her lift the blade, this time without grabbing the bush with her other hand, and bring the blade down too lightly to do more than push the vines out of the way. When she glanced back at him, he raised an eyebrow, but otherwise kept his mouth shut.

She tried again, this time with more force. The vines fell to the ground and a path opened. They each stepped forward a few paces and then stopped as she tackled the next obstacle.

Adrian swallowed his own impatience. At this rate, they'd be dead of old age before they made it out of the jungle, but he let her continue. His shoulders needed the rest and besides, the view was nice.

Every time she lifted her leg to step forward, the fabric of her jumpsuit pulled taut, clearly outlining her form beneath it. When she turned slightly to get a bet-ter angle on slicing a vine and raised her arm, the front of the jumpsuit molded against her chest, allowing him to gaze on the perfect swell of her breasts. As she successfully hacked off a heavier limb, she turned to him, eyes alight with a happy glow, a smile on her face. He couldn't help but respond with his own smile.

When she turned back again, he let his gaze travel down the length of her slender form, hoping she was too focused on her work to sense his thoughts because they might embarrass her. The memory of those long legs wrapped around his waist was burned into his memory. He'd been right about her; about her passion. Unfortunately, she had no business being with a man whose own emotions were so volatile, he had to keep them under tight control. Although lately, he reflected ruefully, his control hadn't been all that great.

Lost in thought, he didn't at first notice the shimmering quality of the air in front of them. When he did, his shouted warning came too late.

Phoenix pushed her way past the illusion of light undergrowth and vanished. A second later, her scream filled the air.

It took every ounce of control not to rush after her. Instead, moving slowly, he tested the ground before stepping around Zarek's holographic projection. The largest sinkhole he'd ever seen was on the other side. Out of arm's reach, Phoenix fought against the sand sucking her downward.

"Hold still," he ordered, desperately looking around for something he could use to get her out. "Struggling makes you sink faster." Her panic washed over him in buckets, almost paralyzing him. "You've got to be calm, sweetheart." He tried again. "I'm not going to let you die, but I have to be able to think." He tamped down on his emotions, willing her to do the same.

Hands trapped at her sides, she'd already sunk up to her waist. Fear that he couldn't save her in time loomed over him.

Grabbing up the machete, he scrambled over undergrowth, skirting the sinkhole, to reach a vine hanging from a nearby tree. He ignored its pleasant fragrance and hacked through a length trailing along the ground. Taking up the freshly cut end, he let it curl tightly around his hand and wrist. The leaves pressed their poisonous surface to his skin, but he wasn't aware of the sting.

He pulled on the vine, testing how securely it was anchored to the tree. It would hold. With Phoenix unable to grab the vine and no time to think of a better solution, Adrian jumped into the sinkhole, landing beside her. She'd sunk deeper with the sand now closing around her chest. She hadn't uttered a word, but he saw the fear and terror in her eyes; heard her labored breathing as she fought for air.

Up to his calves, Adrian bent and plunged his free hand into the sand, wrapping his arm around her waist. Counting on the vine to keep him from sinking too fast, he tugged her up as high as he could. The effort caused him to sink a little deeper, but he didn't care. Her safety was his first priority.

He dragged her up, fear lending him added strength. As soon as her chest was free of the sand, he heard her suck in a lungful of air and cough.

"Can you pull your arms free?"

He held her as she struggled, trying to extract her hands from the unrelenting sand. It took precious seconds, but she finally succeeded. The moment her arms were free, she wrapped them around his neck in a deathlike grip.

"Not me, sweetheart. Grab the vine. Now just keep putting one hand in front of the other and pull yourself out of here, okay?" He tried to keep his voice calm and his feelings neutral. The last thing he needed was for her to feel his fear.

She nodded and did as he instructed. As she pulled herself up, he lifted from below. Each effort drove him down further. Soon, the roiling grains of sand closed around his waist. He prayed that she made it out before he sank too low to help.

It seemed to take forever, but finally he gave Phoenix that last shove she needed to climb out of the sinkhole. Already physically drained from hours of clearing brush, this final effort took the last of his strength. Now buried to his chest, he had nothing left to save himself.

"Go back the way we came," he instructed, breathless as the weight of the sand constricted his chest. "Get to the ship. Remember this sequence—five-one-six-nine—that'll open the hatch lock." He paused for another breath. "Activate the computer and type in the command 'LER.' That will send a signal to Lazureth." He glanced at her to make sure she understood, but she wasn't even looking at him. Desperate, he yelled – or at least he tried to, but he couldn't garner the breath and so it came out sounding like a cough. "Pay attention, damn it! Your life depends on it."

She turned to face him, a fierce light in her eyes. "I'm not leaving without you, so be quiet and save your breath."

She scrambled over the bushes to the machete lying on the ground. Then she followed the vine, still attached to Adrian's hand, up as high as she could reach.

As she raised the machete, he wondered if she was trying to kill him faster by cutting down the vine? Before he could shout at her to stop, she'd hacked it through with a single stroke. Immediately he sank another couple centimeters.

Adrian watched the freshly severed vine wrap itself around Phoenix's arm as it had his. With the vine stretched between them, Phoenix scrambled around a nearby tree.

Bracing her leg against the lower trunk, she hauled back on the vine. Adrian felt the tug on his arm along with a spark of hope. He watched her grab further up on the vine and pull back again.

The sand fought to keep him, but with Phoenix's refusal to give up, it had no choice. Tapping energy born of hope, he dragged himself hand over hand as he'd instructed her earlier.

Between their combined efforts, he eventually crawled out of the sinkhole—and collapsed on the ground, struggling to catch his breath. Nearby, he heard Phoenix's labored breathing as she rested against the tree. Forcing himself to his feet, he walked over to her. He picked up the machete and carefully sawed through the vine wrapped about her arm. Then he did the same with the end wrapped around his own. He needed to treat them both for the acid-burns, but that could wait another couple of minutes. First, he wanted to make sure that Phoenix was okay.

She didn't protest when he took her by the shoulders and held her in front of him, raking her from head to toe with a scrutinizing eye. Filthy, looking completely drained of energy and staring at him with those large, haunted eyes, she was the most beautiful sight he'd seen.

"You're one hell of a woman, you know that?"

Then he kissed her.

No doubt already a little in shock from nearly dying in the sinkhole, it took a full second before Phoenix responded. When she did, it wasn't to push him away, as she probably should have. Instead, she returned his kiss with a hunger and life-affirming intensity that matched his own.

After several minutes, Adrian wanted her so desperately that he was in danger of not caring they were in the middle of a dangerous forest or that Skyler was clinging precariously to life, so he forced himself to end the kiss.

He couldn't bring himself to release her, though, and so they stood, embraced in each other's arms, foreheads together and breathing heavily. After several minutes, Phoenix pulled away and, reluctantly, he let her go.

Her smile, when she looked at him, seemed shy. He found it endearing.

"I don't suppose you know where a girl might find a shower near-by?" She asked, her light tone sounding only slightly forced.

"I think the outdoorsy look suits you." He winked at her, and then went to retrieve the backpack. Taking out the canteen, he offered her a drink. She gratefully drank from it, trying to wash away the parched grittiness coating her throat.

After handing the canteen back so he could drink, she looked at the sinkhole that had almost claimed both their lives.

"How could I have missed something so large?"

"Very easily," he said, washing the lesions on her arm with the water before applying a first-aid salve. See the camera over there?" He pointed to a small stick-like object poking out of the ground. "Just one of Zerek's little deterrents to uninvited guests. It projects an image of the surrounding foliage over the sinkhole. It's almost impossible to tell the image from the real thing."

But he had detected it, she thought, taking the salve from him so she could dab the ointment on his freshly washed lesions. She remembered his shouted warning just before she stepped into the hole. This whole episode could have been avoided if she hadn't tried to prove she could lead them through the woods as well as he.

"Don't." Adrian placed a finger under her chin and tilted her face up until their eyes met. "I feel you blaming yourself. Don't. It could have happened to either one of us."

She nodded, unconvinced. Finished with the ointment, she gave it back to him to put away and walked over to stand next to the sinkhole again. The thought hit her that perhaps Xenobian empaths really couldn't handle the galaxy outside their small world, just as her mother had always argued. For years, Phoenix had considered that an excuse, but now she wasn't so sure. Suddenly she was very tired.

"How much further do we have to go?"

When Adrian didn't respond, Phoenix turned to see what he was doing. Only he wasn't there.

Trying not to panic, she looked around the area. The backpack was missing, also. Had he walked off, thinking she was behind him? Surely not. Her back had been turned. "Adrian?"

There was no answer.

She called a little louder. "Adrian?"

Heart pounding loudly, Phoenix felt the hairs on the back of her neck prickle.

Then suddenly, something wrapped around her chest, locking her arms down by her side, and snatched her into the air.

When she landed, she found herself high above the ground, stuck to a concentric pattern of thin threads stretched between the trees. The partial remains of something unidentifiable lay off to her left and to her right, Adrian lay cocooned in the same white fibrous substance now enveloping her.

Wondering what new danger threatened them, she spotted it instantly. A spider, twice the size of a person, with eight furry legs and huge pinchers stood over her. Its eyes glowed red in the fading light; its pinchers opening and closing, gooey spittle welling around its mouth.

Phoenix struggled against the webbing, but to no avail. It held her fast. Her heart pounded furiously and she couldn't catch her breath.

When the spider lowered its head, Phoenix felt her last shred of control snap. There was nothing left but blind terror and her own screams echoing in her mind.

Chapter 13

It happened so fast. One minute Adrian had been talking to Phoenix. The next, he was stuck to a Previon tree-spider's web, the upper part of his body cocooned in the spider's sticky silk. He knew the spider would eat him when it got hungry so he had until that moment to free himself from his sticky bonds. He'd been halfway to forming a plan when the spider had spun another length of silk and captured Phoenix.

No sooner had she landed on the web beside him than his every emotion and thought became dominated by fear. Now, he watched helplessly as the spider stood over Phoenix, too terrified to offer her comfort or caution her to silence.

The spider moved and another wave of terror hit him so forcefully, he cringed. At the same moment, the spider screeched and scrambled to the far side of its web, where it remained.

The small reprieve was enough for Adrian to grasp a tiny thread of rational thought and understand what was happening. Phoenix was telegraphing her fear to him and the spider. To the extent it kept the spider away, that was good – but he couldn't afford to lay there feeling terrified.

He fought against the web to turn his head in her direction. "Phoenix, sweetheart, it's okay."

"Oh, my God. Oh, my God. We're going to... we're going—"

"Phoenix!" Rising fear caused him to sound harsher than intended but it got her attention.

Her hair was so thick that while it was stuck to the web, she could still move her head a little. She swiveled it to look at him; her eyes appearing twice their normal size.

"Focus on the spider. Channel all those emotions to the spider. Can you do that?"

She stared at him blankly and he wondered if she was too frightened to understand him, but then she turned her head again, this time to face the spider.

In the short time he'd been talking to her, the spider had risen from its huddle and was moving toward them once more. It had only taken a step or two when once more it skittered back in fear. This time, the fear did not affect Adrian. He still felt it, but it wasn't as crippling as it had been moments before.

"That's it," he told her. "Keep it up."

He wasn't sure how long this tactic would work. At some point, either Phoenix would tire or the spider would grow immune to the fear. Struggling against the silk threads that bound him, he managed to loosen them enough to move his arm.

"Adrian!"

Phoenix's warning tone alerted him to the spider's movement. Shoving his arm downward as hard as he could, he was able to loosen the webbing enough to slip his hand around the grip of his laser. With the spider dangerously close to Phoenix, he was out of time. Pulling the laser from its holster and aiming blindly, he pulled the trigger.

The shot pierced the silk threads confining him and hit the spider high on its back. It reared up, emitting a high, keening wail. Now free, Adrian sat up and fired again.

A smoldering hole appeared in the spider's head just before it collapsed.

For precious seconds, Adrian didn't move, prepared to shoot again should the spider show signs of life. It didn't.

Satisfied the spider was really dead, he holstered the laser and reached for the knife in his boot. He'd cut through the remaining silk around his legs and crawled across the web to Phoenix, the knife held between gritted teeth.

She lay with her eyes closed, unmoving. Not even when he cut away the silk binding her did she stir. A fear more terrifying than the one he'd just experienced shot through him.

He placed a finger below her nose, hoping to feel an exhaled breath and nearly sagged with relief when he did. She'd only fainted.

He lifted her to a sitting position, so her head rested against his chest.

"Phoenix, sweetheart. Wake up."

"Wh... what?" Her eyelids fluttered open and she looked around until her gaze settled on him. "Adrian?"

"Yeah, sweetheart, it's me." He offered her a reassuring smile.

She started to return it but then frowned. "Where's the spider?"

He realized that in their current positions, he was blocking her view of the spider. He wasn't about to release her so instead he leaned to one side and gestured to the spider with his head. He enjoyed seeing the way her eyes grew wide.

"Is it dead?" Her voice sounded weak.

"Yeah."

"You're sure?"

He pulled his laser from its holster and fired another shot into the head of the motionless spider. It didn't move. "Pretty damn sure."

She jerked in his arms, staring wide-eyed first at the spider and then at him. Just when he thought he'd made matters worse with his action, she giggled. It was a stress reaction and he knew the giggles would likely give way to tears.

He didn't have to wait long before she was sobbing quietly into his chest. He was content to simply hold her, unsure whether he was doing it to comfort her or himself. It was the second time in an hour he'd thought he'd lost her. He never wanted to experience that again.

Eventually her crying subsided, but she didn't try to pull out of his arms.

"I don't know how much more of this I can take," he heard her mumble. "I thought we were dead—again. I was so scared."

"I know."

There must have been more sarcasm in his tone than he intended because she pushed away enough to look up into his face. Her own expression appeared puzzled.

It didn't take long for her to put it together. "I broadcasted my fear, didn't I?"

"Yes—and very clearly, I might add."

She winced. "Adrian, I'm so sorry. I wasn't even thinking... it never occurred to me that I... oh my."

"It made the situation challenging," he admitted. "But the good news is that the spider felt it, too – and that bought me the time I needed to get to my laser."

"I could have gotten us killed."

"But you didn't. We're alive." Wasn't he being all sunshine-and-flowers? It was definitely a departure from his usual frame-of-mind. He didn't have to wonder much what—or who—was responsible for the change.

"It's getting dark," she said, changing the subject. "How much further do we have to go?"

"Too far to go tonight. We'll stay here."

She looked around the web, her gaze settling on the dead spider. "Here?"

"Yeah. It's safer than down there. The web will stop anything that comes too close and the dead spider will act as a deterrent."

Phoenix wasn't thrilled about the idea of sleeping on the web next to the spider carcass, but Adrian made a good case—and she was so tired. She just wanted to rest.

"Okay," she agreed.

"Fortunately, I'd decided it was my turn to wear the backpack so when the spider grabbed me, I had it on."

The arms holding her fell away and she instantly missed their warmth and security. She watched Adrian remove the backpack and dig inside it. After a moment, he pulled out a small package that turned out to be an all-thermal blanket.

He spread it out next to them and the sticky web held it in place. With a little effort, they crawled onto it and sat in the middle. Beside her, Adrian dug into the backpack again and pulled out four food sticks. He handed her two.

Sitting side by side in a comfortable silence, they ate and watched the sun go down. Only the large corpse of the spider spoiled the view, until the forest all around them was cast into a vast expanse of endless black. With the adrenaline rush from the last couple of hours wearing off and the exertions of the day catching up to her, Phoenix felt her eyelids growing heavy.

She was startled awake by a miniature bolt of electricity flashing in the air not far from her head.

"What was that?" Another tiny bolt struck a leaf, sending a slim thread of smoke trailing upwards.

"Lightening bugs."

"Are they dangerous?" More of the bugs appeared around them.

"Only if we get struck." He reached into the backpack and removed a second thermal blanket. "This should protect us." He shook it out and spread it over them. "If you can, you should try to get some sleep."

"What about you?"

"I will, in a bit."

The web was comfortable and she was exhausted, but when she closed her eyes, the events of the day flickered through her mind, leaving her tense. She tossed and turned, unable to find a comfortable position.

After what seemed minutes, she heard Adrian sigh. He stretched out on his side, facing her, his head resting on the backpack. With a gentle shove, he rolled her away from him until she too was on her side. Then, he pulled her to him so they were lying together, spoon fashion, with her head on his lower arm while his other arm lay across her waist. Unable to resist, she nestled closer.

"*Krauk*. Hold still," he muttered, his warm breath brushing across her ear. She felt the hard ridge of him pressing into her bottom and instantly froze. Would he take advantage of the situation?

Did she want him to?

She waited in anticipation, but nothing happened.

After several minutes, she caught the sound of his steady breathing and realized he'd fallen asleep. Equal parts of relief and disappointment coursed through her. Then it occurred to her that he wouldn't have fallen asleep if there was even a remote threat to their safety. That thought allowed her to finally relax.

Feeling safe and warm in Adrian's arms, Phoenix watched the lightening bugs dart around above her, throwing off tiny bursts of light until her eyelids grew too heavy to stay open—and then she slept.

Dawn broke with muted sunlight filtering through the forest canopy above them. The breeze rustled through the leaves and plants, giving the place a deceptively peaceful feeling, while drawing Phoenix reluctantly from her pleasant dream. With the warmth of Adrian's body wrapped around her, she could easily have stayed there forever.

"I know you're awake," Adrian's whisper broke into her thoughts. His warm breath sent tingles running through her body and, not quite awake, she pressed herself closer. He placed a kiss on the spot just below her ear lobe and she arched her neck, loving the feel of his lips against her skin, sleepy enough to wonder if this were all part of her dream.

The arm cradling her head bent upward, bringing her face closer to his until he could lower his mouth and capture her lips with his own. They were firm and demanding, like the man himself. The hand at her waist traveled up to her swollen breasts and she moaned from the sheer pleasure of his touch.

Unable to resist the opportunity, she let her hand brush against his arm, reveling in the muscled strength of it. He still hadn't put on his shirt and she ravenously explored the hard planes of his chest just as she'd wanted to all yesterday afternoon. The reality of him was even better than the fantasy.

Then, almost as abruptly as it started, it was over. Adrian let the kiss end and moved his hand back to her waist.

"As much as I hate to end this, it's not the time or place." His voice sounded hoarse and he cleared his throat. "We need to find Jack."

She nodded. He folded up the all-thermal covering them and shoved it into the backpack. The other blanket was hopelessly stuck to the web and would have to be left behind.

They quickly ate two more food sticks before working their way across the web until they were perched on the edge, looking down.

"I don't suppose you're wearing your special boots?" Phoenix asked, thinking that the ground looked a long way down.

She glanced at Adrian, who stared at her with raised eyebrows.

"My what?"

"Those boots you had on at the cloud city when you jumped after me. Those would come in handy right about now."

Adrian rolled his eyes. "For some reason, I didn't think to recharge them after that incident. I must have been preoccupied with other things." His voice dripped with sarcasm.

"So how do we get down?"

He bent over, pulled a knife from his boot and then walked to the far edge of the web. "Just hang on to the web, okay? We're going for a little ride."

She grabbed on with both hands as Adrian bent down, grabbed a handful of webbing in his free hand and sliced through the threads anchoring the web to the tree.

Immediately, that edge of the web collapsed under Adrian's weight, startling a gasp out of her. Dangling precariously, he gripped the knife between his teeth and climbed up the web to the opposite side. Grabbing another handful of web in one hand, he took the knife and once again, sliced through the anchoring threads holding it to the tree. The web draped to the ground so all they had to do was climb down.

Once on the ground, they skirted the corpse of the spider, which had fallen in the process, and found the machete where Adrian had dropped it when the spider had first caught him. With a quick scan of their surroundings, Adrian led them past the sinkhole and once again, started clearing a path for them.

The morning passed slowly, but without incident since they managed to avoid the few poisonous plants and sinkholes they came across. During their trek, Phoenix worked hard to keep her fatigue and frustration to herself, not wanting it to affect Adrian in any way.

They stopped briefly for lunch and then continued on. As they walked, Phoenix occasionally caught glimpses through the tree branches of the fortress looming ahead of them in the distance.

The sight of it sent her thoughts turning toward her father and what they might find when they finally made it inside to rescue him. Distracted, she almost ran into Adrian when he stopped mid-stroke with the machete and stood very still.

"What—"

Before she could finish the question, he'd turned and covered her mouth with his hand. Confused, she looked around, but didn't see anything. Then she heard it—the faint murmur of voices – coming from somewhere ahead of them in the woods.

Excited to think they might have found Jack, she looked at Adrian with mounting excitement which died at the sight of his grim expression. Gesturing for her to be quiet and follow him, he moved through the woods, using the machete to push aside the brush, rather than make noise slashing through it.

It slowed their progress, but she didn't notice. She was curious about the voices.

As they drew closer, the woods seemed to thin out and she saw a large clearing up ahead. Instead of heading straight for it, though, Adrian led them around it, to a place where the surrounding growth provided more cover.

Stopping in a particularly dense section, they peeked through the vines and found they'd discovered a small encampment. There were eight or nine dark green tents pitched at one end and several men sitting on fallen logs at the other end, talking as casually as if they'd been sitting in someone's home. Phoenix was amazed. Why would anyone choose to live in the middle of the woods? Especially these woods.

Then she felt Adrian nudge her. Tearing her attention away from the small group of people, she followed the direction of his pointing finger and drew in a sudden breath. Sitting on the edge of the encampment was Jack!

Phoenix felt relief wash through her until she noticed his bound hands. These people had taken him prisoner.

Her first thought was that these people worked for Zarek. Her second was to wonder how they would free him without getting caught themselves.

Adrian touched her arm and gestured for her to follow him. She nodded but they'd only taken a step or two when the rustling of leaves caused them to stop. Phoenix turned to Adrian, bewildered, and saw his gaze was fixed on something behind her. She turned and saw that several armed men had materialized and were now surrounding them.

They were dressed in long sleeved green and brown camouflage shirts and pants, which explained why she hadn't noticed them sooner. Their expressions were stark and unfriendly.

Briefly, she wondered if Adrian thought the two of them could fight their way out, but he offered no resistance when one man pointed to the camp and ordered them to "start moving."

Almost immediately, the other men fell into place around them providing them no chance for escape. As they were escorted through the camp, people came out to stare. By the time they reached the spot where Jack was held, they'd drawn quite a crowd.

As soon as he saw them, Jack's eyes lit up. He stood, but the rope tethering him to the tree kept him from coming to meet them. Now that she was close enough to get a good look at him, she noticed he was dirty, had a black eye and there was bruising along his jaw.

By gesture, the men ordered Phoenix and Adrian to stand beside Jack and then proceeded to bind their hands with lengths of rope.

At least they were all tethered to the same tree, Phoenix thought.

After double-checking their restraints, the men walked off.

"I guess they don't care if we talk," Adrian said before turning to Phoenix. "You okay?"

She nodded.

"How about you?" he asked Jack.

"Better now. It's damn good to see you," Jack said.

Adrian gave him a rueful smile. "Nice to see they didn't kill you. It means I get to do the honors myself for leaving us stranded."

"Let's hope you get the chance," Jack replied, unfazed by his friend's anger.

"Have you ID'd our hosts?"

"Yeah. They call themselves Under Dwellers," Jack said. "Ever heard of them?"

Adrian looked thoughtful but then shook his head. "No. The name doesn't sound familiar. Do they work for Zarek?"

"No. As far as I can tell, they don't like him any more than we do. I thought our shared hatred might convince them we're on the same side, but they never gave me a chance to explain what I was doing here."

"Who's in charge?" Adrian asked.

"I don't know. I've not had the pleasure, but he's due to arrive any time now."

While the men talked, Phoenix allowed her gaze to wander around the campsite, studying what the various camp residents were doing. She was the first to notice, then, when several people started moving toward the opposite end. Intrigued, she continued to watch them.

Soon, it was more than a few people. It seemed everyone – everyone not tied to a tree that is – was moving to the far end of the campsite.

"Something's going on," she said, loud enough for Adrian and Jack to hear her.

Adrian and Jack glanced at her and she gestured with her head to the gathered crowd. They turned just as a small shuttle flew into camp and landed a short distance from the waiting people.

"*Krauk*," Adrian swore when the shuttle doors opened and man stepped out.

"You know him?" Jack asked.

"Yeah. That's Rheon Devson and I can assure you—he won't help us." Adrian spoke with a grim finality that Phoenix found terrifying.

"Why?" She was almost afraid to ask.

"Because I raped and murdered his sister."

Chapter 14

ADRIAN HEARD PHOENIX'S GASP and sensed her shock, along with Jack's, but he ignored them both. His gaze was locked on Rheon's cold, hard stare as the man walked toward them.

Rheon was a few years younger than Adrian and the last time Adrian had seen him had been the day of Trena's funeral. Rheon had been a scrawny lad of twelve, crushed under the loss of his only living relative. Adrian had ridden beside Zarek in the funeral parade through the streets of the nearby village, his self-loathing so great that he'd been unfazed by the horrified stares; horrified because Zarek, in his twisted sense of pride, had publicly broadcast Adrian's deed.

As he rode blindly through the streets, his attention had been caught by a movement off to the side. Turning, he'd found the young Rheon watching him, his face filled with despair and a hatred so intense, Adrian wondered how it didn't burn him there on the spot.

Even as he'd watched the boy duck back into the crowd and disappear, Adrian had been filled with resentment because, unlike himself, the boy was free to run away.

"So, you've finally come home." Rheon's leering voice broke into his thoughts.

"Rheon." Adrian kept his tone level as he struggled to stand, forcing Jack and Phoenix to join him.

Rheon gave a derisive laugh, shaking his head. "I've waited so long for this moment, hoping for the day our paths would cross so I could kill you. And here you walk right into my camp. How fortuitous—for me." His gaze traveled over Jack and Phoenix before returning to Adrian. "It's a shame that your friends will pay for your actions." He shrugged. "Oh, well. Kill them." He threw the command over his shoulder and the waiting men pulled their lasers.

"Wait!" Adrian shouted before the men could fire. "Please, Rheon. They're not part of this. They're innocent."

"As was my sister," Rheon bit out, his face turning red with anger.

Adrian had no defense. "You're right," he admitted. "She didn't deserve what happened to her—but I'm to blame for it, not them. They've done nothing wrong."

Rheon's stare was cold. "They chose the wrong friend."

"Then Zarek succeeds in making monsters of us both, doesn't he?" Adrian saw the shadow of doubt pass over the other's man face. Before he could press his advantage, a low-level buzzing started in his head, distracting him. He thought maybe Rheon heard it as well, because he blinked rapidly then shook his own head, as if to clear it.

"Any last words?" Rheon asked, raising his hand to signal the men to aim their lasers.

"At least your sister had the courage to fight her own battles." Adrian challenged as the buzzing in his head grew to a painful level. Beside him, Phoenix gasped as Jack muttered something unintelligible beneath his breath.

Adrian's attention was on Rheon whose eyes narrowed in anger. Clearly, Adrian's taunt had hit its mark.

"Cut him free," Rheon ordered one of the men. "You're right. Killing you with my bare hands would be more satisfying."

With a quick flick of the knife, Adrian's bindings fell away. Rheon didn't give him a chance to straighten before he tackled Adrian to the ground. Whether because of his own sense of guilt or because the circulation had not yet returned to his hands, Adrian's movements were sluggish and the other man landed several well-placed blows.

But for Adrian, for whom Zarek's torture chamber was home and the Outer Fringe, his playground, violence came naturally and fighting had long ago become a survival skill. Within moments, Adrian had pinned Rheon to the ground.

The pain was nearly unbearable and he'd hit Rheon in the face several times before he thought to stop. While the other man was too dazed to move, Adrian got to his feet and hauled him up, holding him like a shield against a possible attack from the rest of the Under Dwellers.

With his arm around Rheon's neck in a chokehold, he confronted Rheon's men. "Stay back or I'll kill him. You... " He nodded to the front man. "Release my friends—now." Rheon suddenly weighed heavy in his arms, like he'd lost consciousness, but it could just as easily be a trick so Adrian didn't loosen his hold.

As soon as he was free, Jack relieved the Under Dweller of both his knife and laser, using the first to cut Phoenix's bonds and then aiming the second at the group of men.

"Now what?" he asked.

"Hold him," Adrian barely managed to order. He shoved the unconscious Rheon at Jack as the pain in his head overwhelmed him. He squinted across the group, trying to see past the shards of glass that were surely piercing his brain. He recognized this agony and wanted to know who the hell was wielding the discipline wand.

"What's the matter?"

Jack's words sounded faint, as if coming from a great distance. Almost totally consumed now by the pain, Adrian forced himself to check on Phoenix.

When he saw her face, he knew she was picking up his pain. He tried to go to her, but his feet felt leaden. "Phoenix?"

She looked over at the sound of his voice. Her gaze briefly met his, beseeching him for help. Then her eyes rolled back in her head. He caught her as she slumped to the ground and eased her down, grateful for the excuse to kneel before his own legs gave out.

He looked out across the crowd, searching again for the wand and whoever wielded it. To his surprise, all of the dwellers were lying on the ground, some uncon-scious while others writhed in agony.

He knew there was significance in this, but his own agony was too great for him to think clearly. With one hand clutching his head and the other holding Phoenix to his chest, he couldn't take much more.

Then, miraculously, the pain stopped. Adrian waited to see if it started again, but after a full minute of noth-ing, Adrian knew the episode was over. He glanced down at the woman in his arms and stroked the damp tendrils of auburn hair from her face. Her breathing seemed normal and after a moment, her eyelids fluttered as she regained consciousness.

"Are you okay?"

When she nodded, he helped her to sit, but kept his arm around her for support. Around them, the fallen dwellers were slowly coming to, many of them muttering obscenities as they struggled to their feet.

Adrian turned to see Rheon, also conscious now, staring at him with eyes opened wide in apparent surprise.

"You have a chip?" He sounded surprised.

Adrian studied Rheon's haggard face and that of the other men. He knew his own surprise must be showing in his expression. "All of you have one as well?"

"Yeah."

In that moment, Adrian made a decision he hoped he and his friend wouldn't live to regret. He nodded at Jack to let Rheon go.

Jack didn't look convinced, but made sure the other man was solidly on his feet before releasing him and stepping back. Rheon looked surprised but didn't take advantage of the situation.

"How is it that so many of you have the chips?" Adrian asked.

Rheon's voice was grim when he spoke. "Several years back, Zarek implanted chips in all the male servants who worked inside the fortress as part of his security measures. Same thing to any male villager who had business at the stronghold—or was unlucky enough to be caught on the premises without one. Zarek forced us to serve him in a wide capacity of ways. His perverse pleasure knows no bounds."

Adrian felt a chill run down his spine. He knew how Zarek must have used the men.

"A fortunate few," Rheon continued, rubbing his forehead as he nodded toward his group, "managed to escape into these woods. As you can imagine, we are no real threat to Zarek, who can destroy us with the flip of a switch. These little episodes are merely his way of reminding us that he still controls us." Rheon gave his men a quick visual inspection before turning his attention back to Adrian. "How long have you had the chip?"

"Fourteen years."

The news seemed to shock Rheon. "I wouldn't have thought Zarek would do that to you."

"I was a difficult child." Adrian didn't want to elaborate. He released Phoenix and after exchanging a quick look with Jack, climbed to his feet, feeling more confident now that he could stay standing. "Now, where were we? Ah yes, I remember." Jack stepped forward at his nod and pressed the end of the laser to Rheon's temple. "Tell your men to toss their weapons aside."

Adrian was tired and the need to find and rescue Skylar weighed heavily on him. Rheon and his men were a complication he didn't have time for. Something of his thoughts must have shown in his eyes.

"Do as he says," Rheon ordered.

"Now the way I see it, we can do one of two things. I can kill you all now so I don't have to worry about you interfering with my plans, or I can spare your lives out of respect for Trena and we call a truce."

"How can I trust you?"

"You can't—any more than I can trust you."

"Then we have a problem," Rheon said.

Adrian crossed over to Jack and took the laser from him. He wouldn't ask his friend to do his dirty work. "Remember, it was your decision."

"Wait!"

Adrian relaxed his finger and waited for Rheon to continue.

"Perhaps we *could* agree to a truce," he said.

"I don't know," Adrian said, purposely sounding tentative. "You don't sound sure and I'm not big on the idea of getting shot in my sleep."

"That won't happen."

"So you say." Adrian wasn't convinced, but maybe there was a way they could agree. "A common goal would give us both the reassurance we seek."

Rheon cocked his head to one side. "I'm listening."

"There's only one way that Zarek can project the frequency of the discipline wand this far from the fortress and that's through the tower amplifier. If we take that out, Zarek's range of influence is dramatically lessened."

"Why didn't I think of that?" Rheon sneered, his tone full of sarcasm. "Unfortunately, the front gates are heavily guarded. No one gets in without being searched. The only other way in is to scale the face of the cliff and there's a mountain of bones at the base attesting to the numbers of people who have tried that and failed."

"I know another way in." Adrian waited a heartbeat before continuing. "And I know the layout of the fortress well enough to get us to the tower without being noticed."

"Your information is a decade old. How reliable can it be?"

"Most of the fortress is inside the mountain; carved out of stone. It's not that easy to change the layout."

The two men studied each other for some time. "Go on," Rheon finally said.

"Zarek is holding a friend of mine prisoner. I'm here to get him out. Blowing up the tower will provide the perfect distraction."

"You know Zarek will kill you if he catches you."

"That's a risk I'm willing to take."

Rheon was quiet for several seconds before he nodded. "Okay. I'm in."

For the first time since starting on this journey, Adrian felt a glimmer of hope. He'd come to Previon with
no real plan. Now he had a plan and allies to help
execute it.

Adrian holstered his laser and shook hands with
Rheon. The atmosphere around the camp relaxed
and at Rheon's gesture, his men returned to their daily
routines.

"We can go to my tent and talk," Rheon offered,
leading the way.

Adrian waited for Phoenix to join him before following after the Under Dwellers' leader.

"Are you okay?" she whispered, reaching out to place
her hand on his arm.

That simple action, along with the question, had
more impact on him than he'd anticipated. After his
confession to raping and killing Rheon's sister, he'd
expected Phoenix to shy away from him out of fear
or disgust. He wouldn't have blamed her. He was
disgusted with himself but he'd had ten years to learn to
live with it. She hadn't. Perhaps she refused to believe
him capable of such heinous acts.

No. That was wishful thinking. It was more likely
that she hadn't even heard his confession. He thought
back to the moment when he'd made it. His head had

been turned away from her. He'd been shocked to see Rheon. Yes, it's possible neither she nor Jack had heard his confession.

He hated to think how they'd react when they discovered the truth.

"Adrian?" Phoenix whispered urgently, pulling him from his thoughts. He realized he hadn't answered her.

"I'm okay. You?"

She attempted a smile. It was weak. "I'm scared."

He reached for her hand before he thought through his actions, grateful, once again, when she allowed him to take it instead of pulling it away.

"I won't let anything happen to you," he reassured her.

"It's not me I'm scared for."

Of course. She was worried about her father. "We'll find Skylar and get him out."

She squeezed his hand. "I'm scared for you and Jack. That man really hates you. Please don't trust him."

"Right now, I don't see that we have much choice."

Once they were inside Rheon's tent, the three men sat on crates around a table, making their plans. Phoenix watched them from her position a short distance away where she sat on the edge of a cot by herself. She was okay not sitting with the men. She needed a chance to think about everything, but especially about Adrian's confession.

She had little doubt he'd told the truth. The intensity of guilt that radiated from him left little doubt – but that was the problem, wasn't it? The kind of person who rapes and murders a young woman isn't likely to feel guilty about it afterwards. Maybe it was naiveté on her part, wanting to believe he hadn't really committed those acts, but she'd seen the dream hadn't she? So she knew it was true—but it didn't fit. Adrian wasn't the kind of man who raped women. Of that, she was certain—so there was more to the story. She just needed to find out what it was.

She turned her attention to the men's conversation.

"The fewer of us to go in, the better," Adrian was saying. He turned to Jack. "Do you still have the explosives?"

Rheon, whose men had undoubtedly searched Jack when they'd captured him, looked as surprised by the question as Phoenix felt. Adrian hadn't mentioned anything to her about explosive.

Jack, however, merely smiled and reached down to pull off his left boot. Turning it over, he pressed the side of the heel. The top panel slid back. From inside, he removed two large flat discs.

"Are you crazy?" Rheon demanded, leaning as far away from Jack as he could without actually getting up to leave the table. "Aside from blowing yourself up, you could have blown up my entire camp walking around on those."

Jack glared at him. "You took me prisoner and threatened to kill me. If I'm dead already, what do I care if I take you and a few of your men with me?"

Adrian scowled at them both and plucked the discs from Jack's hand. "They're not active without the control chip," he told Rheon. Then to Jack, "I assume you've got those?"

"In my other boot heel."

Adrian held them up for inspection. "Two explosives, strategically planted and remotely denoted after we've located Skylar. Zarek's men will be deployed to the bomb sites. We'll rescue Skylar and walk out the front entrance, right under their noses, concealed in the crush of people hurrying to get out. One of your men can be waiting a short distance off with a shuttle to fly us to our ship."

Jack and Rheon fell silent as they considered Adrian's plan.

"No, I can't let you do this," Phoenix said, drawing their attention. "It's too dangerous. My father wouldn't want you risking your lives for his anymore than I do. I don't know what I was thinking when I came to you," she said to Adrian. "I guess I was hoping he was just stuck somewhere without transportation—not that he was being held prisoner by a sadistic monster. I won't let you do this."

All three men stared at her in silence. She felt the weight of their thoughts pressing in on her as they considered her words. They would realize she was right and abandon their plans; they would... turn away and ignore her completely?

"That explains how we get out," Jack said, turning back to Adrian and Rheon as if she'd never spoken. "But how do we get in if the only entrance is heavily guarded?"

"That's the part I want to know as well," Rheon agreed. "I've been all over that cliff and never found another way in."

"You won't see it unless you know where to look for it," Adrian said. "Because it's underwater."

Phoenix wasn't sure she'd heard him correctly. From Jack's and Rheon's expressions, she saw they were also startled.

"You're suggesting we swim to an underwater entrance?" Rheon asked.

"No. There's a cave at the base of the cliff. It used to be an old entrance complete with a door into the fortress. The cave is underwater most of the time, now, thanks to centuries of settling, except for twice a day, at low tide. Then the cave—and the door into the fortress—are above water level and accessible by boat."

Jack and Rheon stared at Adrian as if they found his plan absurd, but then smiles broke across their faces.

"Genius," Jack stated.

"It could work," Rheon agreed.

"Won't the door be locked?" Phoenix asked.

Once again, the three men fell silent as they turned to stare at her.

She shrugged. "If it used to be an entrance, even if it's underwater most of the time, it makes sense Zarek would keep it locked, don't you think?"

"She's right," Rheon agreed, his expression turning grim.

"I'm pretty good with computers," Jack said. "There aren't many security systems I can't hack."

Adrian shook his head. "This one predates modern technology, I'm afraid. Impossible to open from the outside, but easy enough from the inside." He turned to Rheon. "Who do you have on the inside working for you?"

"No one."

"What?" Adrian sounded shocked.

"We are not a band of rebels trying to fight Zarek," Rheon said defensively. "We're a group of escaped prisoners and slaves trying to avoid recapture. The only way to do that is to keep our distance and make sure no one on the inside knows where we are. Zarek can be very persuasive when he's trying to get information."

"I'll go," Jack volunteered. "A single person, alone, has a good chance of slipping in unnoticed."

"Right, but not you," Adrian said with conviction. "Did you forget that Juarez is working with Zarek now? All of his men know you by sight."

"Well, *you* can't go," Jack pointed out. "You're probably the most recognizable—and you have the chip in your head. All Zarek would have to do is turn on the discipline wand and it's game over—same for Rheon and all of his men."

"I'll go."

Phoenix realized she'd spoken her thoughts out loud when all the men turned to stare at her.

"Absolutely not," Adrian said, turning away from her; dismissing her suggestion.

Jack and Rheon, however, continued to study her; appearing speculative.

"Zarek and his men don't know me," she continued, starting to embrace the idea.

"She has a point," Rheon said.

"No," Adrian said with finality.

"Why not?" It irritated her that he wouldn't even consider it.

"There are so many reasons why sending you is a bad idea, it's not worth getting into."

"Humor me," she challenged, getting mad.

"I'd like to know as well," said Rheon, offering his support.

Adrian looked at them both as if they'd just stuck the hot end of a laser in their mouths.

"First, you're a woman—"

"Come up with something original, Adrian. That argument got old about five hundred years ago." She crossed her arms and glared at him.

"Okay," Adrian bit out. "You can't fight. You can't shoot. You have no idea what type of people Zarek surrounds himself with or how to deal with them. And if that's not enough, do you—do any of you," he looked around the room, "really think it's a good idea to send a female empath into a place run by a sadistic letch?" He turned back to face Phoenix. "How long do you think you'll last if you get caught?"

His words scared her, but she didn't want him to know it so she gritted her teeth until she could barely speak. "I'll last as long as I need to."

"How brave of you." Sarcasm dripped from his every word. "So instead of planning one rescue, we'll need to plan two." He offered her a wicked smile. "Only you won't be kept in the same place as Skylar, I can assure you of that. Zarek will have special plans for such a lovely prize. He'll want to keep you close."

Phoenix raised her chin, hoping he wouldn't see the way it trembled. "Then rescue my father and leave me there."

Adrian stood so abruptly, he knocked his chair over. Then he closed the space separating them. When he spoke, all sarcasm and ridicule was gone from his voice. "I would never leave you there. Do you understand me? Never." His tone was genuine; his words for her alone.

"Yes," she said softly so only he would hear it. "Everything you said it right. I don't know how to fight or shoot—and going in there scares me to death, but we don't have a choice. We're out of options—and we're out of time."

Adrian's jaw tightened in a clear attempt to control his anger. "I don't like this."

"I know," she said again, understanding.

"And what if the door isn't locked?" Jack asked. "What if it's welded shut?"

"Then I walk out the same way I came in," she said.

"There are a lot of 'ifs' in this plan," Jack said. "But I don't see that we have any other choice." He looked around and after a moment's hesitation, Adrian and Rheon both nodded their agreement.

Instead of leaving her behind, they were going to trust her to play a pivotal role in her father's rescue. It was a huge victory, but her moment of elation was immediately dampened by the grim thoughts of all the things that could go wrong.

Phoenix spent the rest of the night memorizing floor plans and learning self-defense moves. Adrian was a relentless instructor, never once slowing down or going easy on her. Though she didn't say anything, she was pretty sure that all this training was a waste of time because should she actually run into trouble, she'd probably be too scared to remember any of it.

When the first light of dawn slipped through the forest ceiling, Phoenix knew it was time to leave. They had to coordinate her infiltration of the fortress with the ocean's tides.

Adrian walked with her to the beach where Rheon waited with a boat to take her to the village. She was wearing clothes that Rheon had secured from one of the women in his camp. They were a little large for her and she had to roll up the sleeves to keep them from hanging below her hands.

Once in the village, the plan was for Rheon to purchase bolts of fabric that she would carry to the fortress and pretend to sell.

The morning temperature was cool and a slight breeze blew her hair about as she stood with Adrian. He brushed away a strand that strayed across her face.

"Be careful."

She nodded and suddenly the self-doubt that she'd kept at bay for so long, surfaced. She swallowed, fighting not to show her fear.

Adrian placed his finger under her chin, lifting it until she was looking into his eyes. He lowered his head and kissed her briefly, but with such intensity, she knew she'd remember it for a long time.

"If something happens, I will come for you," he whispered. "As long as I draw breath, I will come for you."

It was time to leave. He helped her into the boat and as Rheon guided it out into the ocean, Phoenix kept her gaze focused on Adrian, watching until he was nothing more than a speck on the beach. She hoped she hadn't just kissed him good-bye for the last time.

Chapter 15

Two hours later, Phoenix sat in a shuttle as it made its final descent to the landing pad outside the fortress entrance. She was suffering with a fatigue headache, upset stomach and a nearly debilitating case of nerves. What madness had possessed her that she thought she could do this?

That morning, she and Rheon had arrived at the village to a whirlwind of activity. Apparently, it was Zarek's birthday and he had requested entertainers for the day's festivities. It had given Rheon an idea. The male leader of an all-female dance troupe was a childhood friend of Rheon's. He had also been friends with Trena and blamed Zarek for her death. While he would never openly defy Zarek, out of fear for his own safety and that of his dancers, he was willing to include Phoenix in his troupe to sneak her into the fortress. After that, she was on her own.

She was provided a costume to wear that consisted of brightly colored scarves tied to a ribbon strategically wound around her body. The end result provided the illusion, if not the reality, of being covered. When she moved, the scarves floated about her body, separating to provide interested onlookers glimpses of her bare skin. She doubted if anyone even bothered to look at her face, which she supposed was good.

Once the shuttle landed, Phoenix followed the other dancers across the large flat stretch of rock that made up the fortress' landing pad. The fortress itself looked like a massive stone box built into the side of a mountain; flat on top and solid all-around with a set of large double metal doors in front. Perched on top was the amplifier tower.

Another wave of uneasiness washed over Phoenix. How did Adrian think they could possibly get close enough to plant a bomb when there were fortress guards standing out front, well within visual range of the tower? They were intimidating figures, to be sure; tall and solidly built, each holding a pulsar rifle in their hands.

She was tempted to abort the mission but turning back now would only attract more attention. The troupe had reached the entrance and even now were under a guard's close scrutiny as he compared what he saw to the information on his digital tablet. Her uneasiness grew worse when she noticed the guard's furrowed brow.

"According to my information, there should only be ten dancers," the guard said to the troupe leader. "You have eleven. One of your dancers will have to remain outside."

The troupe leader shook his head. "Impossible. The number we are performing requires eleven dancers. If one of my dancers can't be admitted, then there's no point in any of us being here. We might as well go."

The guard shrugged, clearly not caring. Phoenix wondered what she should do. Should she slip away and try to sneak in later by herself?

"Ladies, we are returning to our shuttle," the troupe leader called out. Then, turning back to the guard, he asked, "May I have your name?"

"Why?"

"Zarek specifically requested we perform for him on his birthday, so when he contacts me later, upset that we failed to deliver his present, I will give him your name." When the guard remained silent, the troupe leader gave a dismissive wave of his hand. "Never mind, I'm sure Zarek has his own means of finding out who turned us away. Who knows, maybe he won't even be upset."

They were half-way to the ship when—

"Wait," the guard called after them. "You're cleared to enter."

"Hurry, ladies," the troupe leader said, ushering them back towards the entrance. "You've made a wise decision," he told the guard as they passed. "This will be a birthday Zarek will never forget."

As the group of them passed through the front doors, Phoenix heard the sound of the shuttle's thrusters firing and knew it was leaving. It would return later to pick up the dancers and take them back to the village. If everything went according to plan, she would be with them, having successfully found and opened the door.

She raised her hand to her throat to touch the necklace Rheon had given her before he'd left. His parting words replayed in her mind.

"You have two hours. If you need to abort, press the middle stone on the necklace and it will transmit a signal to us. Return to the village with the performers and I'll come get you.

"After two hours, we'll be inside the cave where the signal won't reach and after two and a half hours, the entrance to the cave will be underwater, trapping us inside the cave. At the end of three hours, if you haven't opened the door, the entire cave will be underwater and we'll be dead."

Phoenix shuddered at the memory and calculated how much time had already elapsed. The shuttle ride had taken about thirty minutes, so she had ninety minutes to find the door and open it.

No problem, she lied to herself.

Inside the fortress, a stern-faced male servant wearing a simple tunic and pants greeted the troupe. He led them through the corridors and Phoenix couldn't help but be impressed. If this had been any place other than Zarek's fortress and she was there for any reason other than to rescue her father, she would have found this place fascinating.

Instead of dark and gloomy like a cave, the arched ceilings of the corridors were painted to look like a clear sky on a summer's day. There were no lamps mounted to the walls, yet it was bright enough that had she not known they were underground, she would have thought she was standing outside—especially when she felt a gentle breeze ruffle the scarves of her outfit.

The number of people about also surprised her. She'd thought this was Zarek's private residence, but it was more like a small city. Or maybe it was more like a prison since the residents all wore the same beige tunic and pants outfits and no one was allowed in or out without being first cleared by the guards.

A wave of guilt hit her. Many of these people would be hurt when the bombs went off. Collateral damage in the rescue of her father. How many innocent lives — for there was no doubt in Phoenix's mind that the servants were as much prisoners as her father—had to be lost before the price paid was too great?

She tried to push the thought from her mind as the servant led them down the main corridor. They passed several open doorways to rooms in which people seemed to be busy. In one room, desk jockeys worked at computers while in another, workers tended rows of plants. In yet another, heavy machinery was being operated.

No one seemed particularly happy. The servants shuffled along with heads bent and eyes cast downward, showing no interest in anything going on around them. Wondering what empathic impression she might get, Phoenix opened her mind and focused on one, but picked up nothing. It was as if they kept their emotions carefully guarded – or maybe they had endured so much pain and suffering, they were no longer capable of feeling anything.

It was a disturbing thought.

Phoenix realized she hadn't been paying attention to where the servant was leading them and looked around for a landmark feature that might tell her where they were. According to Adrian, the fortress was designed so no single set of stairs led to all five levels—a precaution designed to slow invaders should the fortress ever be breached.

Just up ahead was the first staircase leading down. She looked around to see if anyone was paying attention to her and when the troupe passed it, she stepped out of line and ran down the stairs. She stopped near the bottom and listened for sounds of pursuit. Hearing none, she mentally checked off the second phase of her plan and stepped out into the corridor, nearly bumping into a passing servant.

It was unclear who was more startled, Phoenix or the man. As her frazzled mind fought for a plausible explanation for her presence, the man muttered under his breath and scurried away. A passing woman on the opposite side of the corridor never even glanced at them.

They didn't care that she was there.

Feeling bold, Phoenix turned left and walked purposefully down the corridor. This level wasn't as nice as the one above. The walls and ceilings were painted a dingy white which, along with the slightly stale air and harsh lighting, gave it an institutional atmosphere.

When she reached an intersection, following Adrian's instructions, she turned left. At the next intersection, she turned right.

When she reached the end of the corridor, she stopped and frowned. There was supposed to be a staircase here. Instead, there was a solid wall.

The corridors all looked the same and in her fatigue, maybe she turned down the wrong one.

There was nothing left to do but go back the way she'd come and retrace her steps, paying closer attention this time as she went. When she ended up back at the same dead-end, she knew she hadn't made a mistake. The staircase that had once led down to the next level had been sealed.

It wasn't the end of her mission; just a minor set-back, she told herself in an attempt to stay calm. There was another staircase. All she had to do was find it.

Returning the way she'd come, she took a right at the first intersection instead of a left and kept walking, trying to remember the floor plan Adrian had drawn for her.

As she walked, she thought of her father. It hurt to know she was this close and couldn't do anything to help him. Almost without thinking, her mind reached out to him.

Pain and agony hit her. She stumbled and would have fallen had she not reached out to steady herself against the wall. The emotions were strong; like he was nearby.

Maybe he was.

Once the idea took root, she couldn't ignore it. What if her father was on this level, behind one of these closed doors? Could rescuing him be as simple as opening a door and letting him out?

No, of course not, she reasoned. *Stick to the plan.*

Even as she made up her mind, her guard slipped and the pain came through, stronger than before. She hurried through the next intersection of corridors and felt the pain subside. It didn't go away. It simply grew fainter.

Experimentally, she backtracked to the intersection and turned. When the pain started to grow faint, she did a one-eighty and headed in the opposite direction. The pain grew stronger.

She stopped when the intensity felt the strongest and looked around. She was standing in front of a closed door. So positive was she that her father was on the other side, she'd pushed the door open and stepped inside before she'd even thought about what she was doing.

Twenty or more men sitting around the U-shaped table all stopping talking or eating to stare at her. Phoenix stared back in shock. What had she walked into?

The man sitting at the head of the table caught her attention. He was an older man; perhaps in his late fifties, but well-preserved. He was handsome and his blond hair was graying at the temples giving him a distinguished look, but it was his cold grey eyes that really held her attention. They looked at her like a hungry cat eyed a mouse; predatory and calculating. It sent shivers down her spine.

"I see the entertainment has arrived." The man's voice sounded as cold as his gaze. He smiled at her. "And she is especially lovely. Happy birthday to me."

Damnit, she thought. *I just can't seem to stay out of trouble.*

Chapter 16

"SHE'S OVERWHELMED TO BE in your presence, Zarek," the man sitting to the right said with a snort of laughter. "See how she trembles?"

Zarek smiled as he picked up a chunk of roast with his greasy fingers. "It's nice to be appreciated."

He tossed the meat against the far wall and Phoenix's gaze followed its path. For the first time, she noticed the three men chained to the floor. Filthy and emaciated, they lunged for the meat, fighting one another for possession of it. Phoenix realized then it had been their suffering she'd mistaken for her father's.

She turned back to face Zarek and saw the cruel, excited gleam in his eyes as he watched the men battle. Finally, one prevailed and the other two lay beaten while the winner devoured the meat.

Zarek smiled and turned his attention to her. "You may begin your dance."

He wanted her to dance? Then she remembered her disguise. He didn't know who she was. A modicum of relief swept through her, quickly dispelled by a new concern.

She didn't know how to dance. Rheon had assured her it wouldn't be necessary.

She looked about for a musical group, hoping for music to inspire her, but found she was alone. Feeling the weight of Zarek's gaze on her, she knew she couldn't stall any longer.

Slowly raising her arms out to her sides, she lifted her right leg and, pointing her toes, gracefully stepped forward. She stepped forward again, then with the next step, spun on the ball of her foot in a pirouette. On and on she went, putting herself through the dance-like steps of the *Illuma Vidra Kata*, a floor exercise designed to promote balance and harmony. Each step brought her a deeper sense of calm.

She glided into the second of the Kata's seven levels. The fabric of her dress floating about her body seductively. The men in the room seemed mesmerized by her performance and as she finished the second level and stepped into the third, she wondered how long they expected her to continue; how long before she could make her escape?

She swayed about the room, exaggerating her steps as she took inventory of possible exits. The only doors were the one she'd come in through and the one behind the table.

She moved to the next level of the Kata and considered her options. By the time she moved into the seventh level, still having no plan, she was feeling desperate.

All too soon, she finished the seventh level and ended her dance. The clapping started slowly, but soon everyone applauded. She bowed and took a step back, and then another, hoping to ease her way over to the door through which she'd entered.

Zarek raised his hand and immediately the clapping stopped.

"You have not been dismissed. Come here."

She forced her feet forward despite every fiber of her being urging her to run in the opposite direction. At least the table separated them and she wouldn't have to stand too close.

Zarek stood and, at the wave of his hand, two men pulled the table apart creating a gap in the center through which Zarek stepped.

He slowly circled her, raking his gaze over her. This close to him, Phoenix didn't need her empathic abilities to sense his arrogance and conceit.

"You're new," he remarked. "I don't remember seeing you before."

"Yes. I'm from Gorth," she said, repeating the story Rheon had made up for her just in case she was questioned. She kept her eyes cast downward in a clear show of subservience, remembering Rheon's and Adrian's descriptions of the villagers' behaviors.

When Zarek reached out to stroke her cheek, she shied away, realizing her fear wasn't an act. It was the wrong move to make because he gripped her jaw and forced her to look at him.

She clinched her teeth tightly to keep from crying out and endured his inspection. After a moment, he released her – but only so he could take a closer look at her necklace.

"This is an interesting piece. I don't believe I've seen work like this before."

What should she say? "A man in our village makes these."

She held her breath as he lifted it to take a closer look, afraid he would detect the special stone that wasn't a stone at all. He was in the process of turning it over when the door to the room burst open. The rest of the dancing troupe, followed by musicians, rushed in. As the musicians struck up a lively tune, the dancers began twirling about the room, the scarves of their costumes fanning out around them.

Zarek turned to watch and when three of the dancers twirled past, Phoenix let them sweep her into their group. As they continued to move around the room, she did her best to mimic the other dancers' moves.

When she passed the open doorway, she slipped out.

Thankfully, the corridor was empty. She ran for the corner, turned but then had to slow to a walk so as not to draw attention to herself.

She walked with purpose, trying to give the impression that she had a destination and a legitimate reason for being there. She continued through the corridors, taking whatever turns would make it the most difficult to find her. When she felt sure Zarek had sent no one to follow her, she finally stopped to catch her breath. That had been too close.

Remembering Adrian's comment about time pieces mounted in the corridors, she looked around and finally found one.

The shock was like a physical blow. She'd had no idea she'd been in the dining hall so long. Her two hours was nearly up and she hadn't even found the stairwell to the third level.

She fought back disappointment and accepted her failure. There was nothing left but to signal the men and abort the mission.

Reaching for her necklace, she touched only the bare skin of her throat. Alarmed, she felt around for the chain. It wasn't there.

The necklace was gone.

Phoenix ran her hands over the length of her body, checking the folds of her outfit, hoping the necklace had caught on the material when it had come loose.

When she didn't find it, she retraced her steps along the corridors, hoping to spot it on the floor. Finally, she was forced to conclude that it had come off in the dining hall while she was dancing. Knowing she couldn't go back for it, she forced herself to take a deep breath and forget the necklace. It was time to find the door to the underwater cave.

Mentally reviewing the floor plans Adrian had drawn her, she started back down the corridor. If she was correct, there was a set of steps located at the opposite end of this level that led downstairs. The fortress was wide and it would take time to reach it, but it seemed her only option.

Again, she walked with purpose but with her head down.

Reaching the far end, she spotted another time piece and noted the time. The entrance to the cave would be underwater now, trapping the men inside. She quickened her pace as she rounded the next corner, expecting to find the stairwell. Instead, she encountered a dead end.

Not again! She wanted to scream.

The steps were supposed to be there. Now what?

She mentally reviewed the floor plans, looking for where she'd taken a wrong turn, but came to the same conclusion. The stairs should be here. She studied the walls as if the opening might magically appear—and nearly overlooked the dark shadow near the corner. She moved toward it, noticing as she did how it widened.

She nearly cried with relief when the shadow turned into a narrow opening with a set of stone steps leading downward. She hurried down them not even stopping on the third level, but continuing down to the fourth.

According to Adrian, this was primarily a maintenance level; a poorly lit one.

Heading toward the source of a loud, thundering sound, she found the generator and from there, located the small opening that contained one last final narrow set of steps which she took to what Adrian had said was once the dungeon level. It was later abandoned in favor of the modern virtual chambers on the upper levels where Zarek could more easily reach them.

When she eventually reached the bottom, she turned left and moved cautiously along the darkened passageway. Sporadically placed low-glow lamps cast eerie shadows on walls that felt slimy and damp to the touch.

She was close. All she had to do was find the door and turn the lock. Adrian would be waiting for her on the other side.

She picked up her pace, almost running, heedless of the noise she made. When she sprinted around the last corner, she came to an abrupt stop.

The two guards sitting in front of the door glanced up in surprise.

Phoenix stood dumbfounded. She was so close; she could see the door. She could hear the sound of the ocean on the other side of it. Yet, with the two massively built guards standing in her way, it seemed impossible to reach.

"No one's allowed down here," the bald guard with the nose-ring growled as he rose from his seat.

She felt the barest hint of interest and curiosity coming from him. An idea came to her.

"I was sent down here by one of the upstairs guards," she said, forcing a smile. She stepped closer, making sure to sway her hips so the fabric of her skirt parted, giving the men a peek at her legs.

"Why?" The seated guard with the black mustache asked though his attention was clearly on her legs.

She smoothed the fabric over her hips, emphasizing their shape. "He said you might be...lonely."

The guard stood and the two exchanged looks, clearly not expecting this. As if cued by a silent signal, they pulled their lasers and pointed them at her.

"You stay right where I can see you," the guard with the nose-ring ordered. Then to the other guard, he said, "go check it out. It might be a trick."

The guard with the mustache walked past her, moving quietly. With his laser held ready to fire, he approached the end of the short corridor, leaned into the wall so he could look around the corner and then stepped out into the open. "All clear."

He came back to stand beside Phoenix and she felt his warm breath across the back of her neck. When he trailed a hand across her shoulder, she nearly shuddered in revulsion.

"Guess she's legit. So, how do you want us?" he asked, leering at her. "Together or one at a time?"

She wanted to vomit, but instead managed to coo. "Ohhh, one at a time, but who goes first?" She tried to broadcast waves of possessive anger at both men in the hopes of starting a fight.

"You got it," the guard standing beside her said. To his friend, he said, "We'll be right back."

Instead of protesting as she'd hoped, the other guard only nodded. Her broadcasting wasn't working. She had to feel an emotion before she could broadcast it. The problem was, the only emotion she felt was terror.

Starting to panic, she wished Adrian was there. If he knew what she was doing, he'd be furious and then she could tap into that rage.

It was as if thinking of him created a link between them, because suddenly, she felt him; felt his dawning realization that she was reaching out to him and then his understanding of why she was afraid.

When the blast of primitive, raw anger hit her, she nearly forgot about her plan, too overwhelmed with rage to think clearly. As she was being led down the corridor, she struggled to reign in the anger and then directed all of the emotion to the guard being left behind.

"Hold it there," the guard with the nose-ring shouted. "Why do you get to go first?"

The guard beside her kept walking. "Because I don't want your sloppy seconds."

"Well, maybe I don't want yours."

The guard holding her released her arm, turning to face his friend. "I think she'll want a real man first."

The other guard emitted a low growl as he quickly strode forward and shoved his friend, causing him to stumble back. He quickly recovered and tackled the first guard to the ground. His laser skittered across the floor though he didn't seem to notice.

Phoenix took advantage of their distraction to move toward the door. Now, how to open it?

The men's emotions were making it difficult for her to think clearly. She took a deep breath, forced herself to be calm and really studied the door. Two large inset dials on either side of the door had radial lines pointing outward.

Could it be that simple? She placed a hand on each dial, ready to turn them until the lines pointed inward.

"Stop! What do you think you're doing?"

The guards had stopped fighting.

Her time was up. Even as a hand grabbed her shoulder, she twisted the dials and sent forth a silent prayer.

To her amazement, the door swung open. Adrian, looking like he could kill, barged in, lasers drawn, Jack hot on his heels.

The two guards fell back, dragging her with them, clearly surprised at the turn of events. While the first guard wrapped an arm about her throat, the other let out a yell and charged forward, scrambling to draw his laser and aim it at the intruders.

Adrian never missed a step. He smashed the guard coming at him with in the face with his fist while shooting the other guard with his laser. As the man crumpled to the ground, Adrian reached Phoenix and pulled her to him. She went willingly, savoring the feel of his arms wrapping around her; grateful beyond measure that he was alive.

"I didn't think I'd see you again," she babbled. "I didn't think I'd make it in time."

"But you did. We're safe." He hugged her a little tighter, then, taking her by the arms, he set her away from him just far enough for him to see her face. "Are you okay?"

She shuddered, thinking about what had nearly happened, but nodded. Adrian seemed to accept this answer but his expression swiftly turned into a frown as his gaze traveled over her entire body.

"What the hell are you wearing?"

She looked down at herself, wondering why he was so angry.

"Dancer's costume." She thought it should be obvious. Maybe she was still broadcasting anger without realizing it.

"Where'd you get it?"

"Rheon. He arranged for me to sneak in with a dance troupe."

"She looks good, doesn't she?" Rheon said stepping up to join them.

Adrian's fist snapped out to the side, making contact with Rheon's face. The man folded to the ground. "An outfit like that only invites trouble."

Jack glanced at Rheon's unconscious form but didn't seem too concerned as he spoke to Adrian. "Just thought I'd point out that we still need him."

Phoenix glared up at Adrian. "How about—thank you, Phoenix, for infiltrating Zarek's fortress and saving our butts?"

For a moment, his expression changed; softened a bit. Then the cold, hard mask of the bounty hunter was back.

"Let's get that door closed," he said, "before the tide gets any higher."

As Jack hurried to comply, Adrian looked back down at her, the corners of his mouth lifting ever so slightly. "Good job, Phoenix. Thanks for saving our butts."

She smiled back. "You're welcome. Now, what are we going to do about him?" She pointed to unconscious body of the guard.

"I'm going to drag him through that door and let the tide take him," Adrian said.

Though she held no affection for the guard, she wasn't cold-blooded enough to let him drown. Adrian must have sensed her distress because he heaved a sigh of exasperation, closed his eyes and lifted his free hand to rub his temples. "Fine. Around the corner are a couple of storage rooms. I don't think they're used anymore. We'll put him in there."

"But what if no one finds him. He'll starve to death."

"Don't push it, Phoenix. Those men were about to rape you. If you don't want him to suffer, I can kill him now."

"No, you're right," she agreed.

Together, Jack and Adrian dragged both bodies into a nearby cell. Phoenix was surprised when, a few minutes later, Jack returned alone.

"He's securing the cell door," Jack said, seeing her questioning look. He knelt beside a slowly recovering Rheon and helped the man to a sitting position. When Rheon waved him away, Jack joined her.

"Is he okay?" she asked.

"If you mean Rheon, he'll be fine. If you mean Adri-an, well, this is a new experience for him and he's not dealing well with it."

"Killing?"

"What? No. Being in love."

"Love?" She stared at him in utter confusion.

"Yeah. You see, he doesn't usually care about—," he shrugged, "about anything, really. The fact that he cares about you so intensely can only mean he's in love and, well, I guess you could say it irritates him."

She tried to think back, wondering what Jack saw that she didn't. "You think he's in love with—me?"

"Yep—and, not that you asked, but I think you're in love with him, too." He winked before walking off, muttering something about checking on Adrian.

Chapter 17

"WHAT ARE YOU DOING?"

Adrian looked up at the sound of Jack's voice. "Are you alone?"

"If you mean, is Phoenix with me, the answer is no."

"Good." Adrian released his grip around the former-ly unconscious guard's throat and let the now lifeless body fall back to the floor. He knew Phoenix would be upset if she found out he'd killed the guard but he couldn't afford to leave the man alive. Too much was at stake.

Jack, on the other hand, was a pragmatist. He might not like the necessity of killing the guard, but he un-derstood it.

Adrian stood and crossed to the doorway, stopping when Jack didn't move out of his way but continued staring at the bodies. He hoped he hadn't been wrong about Jack's attitude.

"Is there a problem?"

His tone held a sharp edge and caused Jack to give him a startled look. He shook his head.

"No problem. Just thinking it might not hurt to put on their shirts. We're less likely to be stopped if we look like guards."

"Good idea." Together, they removed both guards' shirts.

"What do you think?" Jack asked, holding one of the shirts up against himself. It was a little large.

"Yeah, definitely your color," Adrian deadpanned.

Jack rolled his eyes, but pulled the shirt on over his own. Adrian did the same. Then they left the cell.

Adrian wasn't sure whether Phoenix even noticed he was wearing the guard's shirt when he joined her. Not that he wasn't grateful to be spared her inevitable condemnation for his actions, but it wasn't like her not to notice. She seemed distracted.

"Everything okay?"

There was a pause before she answered. "I'm fine."

Her tone told a different story as did the fact that she wouldn't meet his gaze. If they'd had the time, he might have pressed for the truth. There wasn't, so he went to check on Rheon but noticed that Phoenix kept sneaking peaks at him when she thought he wasn't looking.

Assuring himself Rheon was fully conscious and not planning to exact payback for being knocked out, Adrian led the group through the lower level and up the long stone staircase to the maintenance level. When they reached the landing, he and Jack went first, lasers drawn in case they ran into problems. They didn't.

Slowly, they crept along the perimeter of the room, keeping as much as possible to the deeper shadows. It took a lot of machines to keep an underground fortress running and most were located on this level. The noise from all those engines masked the sound of their footsteps, but it also masked the sound of anyone else's footsteps, so they had to stay alert. Only once did they have to hide behind cooling equipment when two maintenance workers passed.

It didn't take long to find the Luminite crystal generator used to power the broadcast tower. They had decided to plant one of the bombs here. It would be the easiest to plant and should they be unable to plant the other, at least the broadcast tower would be out of commission for a short time. This explosion wouldn't be strong enough to cause a cave in – after all, this wasn't a suicide mission.

Jack removed a bomb and activation chip from his boot heels. He inserted the latter into the former and then tapped a couple of commands into the comm-unit strapped to his wrist. Adrian watched him, always impressed with Jack's computer skills. He wondered where Jack had obtained these skills but the one time he'd asked, Jack made it clear he didn't want to talk about it, so Adrian let it rest. He understood wanting to leave one's past in the past.

"Done," Jack announced, bringing Adrian's attention back to the moment. He nodded and started to lead the group toward the East stairwell.

"We can't go that way," Phoenix said, placing her hand on his arm. "That staircase is sealed off at the top. I came down the one at the opposite end."

So Zarek had finally completed the West staircase and closed off the East one, Adrian thought. It explained why it had taken Phoenix longer than expected to get to the door.

When they reached the West staircase, Phoenix stopped him when he would have started up.

"What's the matter now?" he asked as his gaze inadvertently strayed to catch glimpses of creamy skin peeking out between one of several openings in her skirt.

"I should go first," she explained, seemingly unaware of the way his eyes devoured her. "When I was walking around earlier, no one paid attention to me, so I should go up first—in case there are people there. I can signal you when it's clear."

Dressed only in a couple of scarves, there was no way she'd gone unnoticed, he thought. He felt an almost uncontrollable urge to batter every man who'd laid eyes on her. At least Jack and Rheon were smart enough not to ogle her in his presence.

"Not happening," he told her, firmly but gently. "Just because the guards and servants know better than to look twice at one of Zarek's play things, which is what you look like, it's too dangerous."

He heard Rheon give a snort and realized this had been the man's intent all along and, damn it, it had been a good idea much as he might personally hate to admit it.

He led the way up the stairs and, encountering no one, gestured for the others to follow. They continued down the corridor until Adrian drew them to a halt at the first intersection.

"We'll split up here," Adrian said. "Jack and Rheon, to get to the tower, take the second right and then the third left. The stairs there will take you to the main level. From there—"

"Yeah, yeah," Jack interrupted. "We know. You made us memorize the plans. We've got this." He gave Rheon a push to start walking. Over his shoulder, he added, "Meet you at the holding cell after we've planted the last bomb on the tower."

"Roger that." After they'd disappeared around the next corner, Adrian turned to Phoenix. "You doing okay?"

She nodded and though she met his gaze, she quickly looked away. Puzzled, he stared a moment longer and noticed something he hadn't before.

"Where's the necklace?"

Phoenix lifted her hand to her throat and shivered.

"I lost it. I don't know if it came off while I was looking for the staircase or," she paused and sneaked a glance up at him. "Or when Zarek was looking at it—"

"You ran into Zarek?" He was so stunned, he wasn't sure he'd heard her correctly.

She sighed. "I thought I sensed my father nearby. There was so much pain and suffering coming from the room, I just knew he was behind the door. I couldn't walk past and leave him there." Her eyes seemed to beg him to understand. "So I opened the door and went inside—only my father wasn't in the room. Zarek and several of his men were. They were eating—and torturing these poor men chained to the floor."

She told him the rest of it. Of how she'd been mistaken for a dancer and Zarek's interest in the necklace. Adrian didn't know how to react. He was beyond angry with her for taking such a risk and putting her life in danger, while at the same time immeasurably relieved no harm had come to her. Or had it?

"Did he hurt you?" Adrian demanded, ready to add one more offense to Zarek's already long list. Zarek's day of reckoning was coming sooner than he realized.

"No, he didn't have time. The other dancers arrived and I slipped out while they were performing." Only now that she was safe with Adrian did she allow herself to remember how truly frightened she had been at the time.

"It was a stupid thing to do," she admitted. "And I may have put the entire mission in jeopardy."

Adrian shook his head. "Even if Zarek found it odd that a dancer was walking around on her own, he'll soon be too distracted to remember her or her unusual necklace. Now, let's go find Skylar, shall we?"

She nodded and fell into step beside him as they continued down the corridor. The closer they got to the holding cells, the stronger his memories became.

The endless hours of solitude, of feeling abandoned by everyone who might have cared for him; of wishing he could die just to end his loneliness and suffering.

Adrian guided Phoenix past the turnoff leading to the holding area, stopping before a set of metal doors. A quick glance showed no one was around to see them, so Adrian opened one of the two doors and ushered Phoenix inside. He stepped in after her and closed the door behind him.

It was a small, dark room with barely enough space for the two of them to stand side-by-side. The only illumination came from the small lights of the various pieces of equipment.

"It's better if we wait here for Jack and Rheon," Adrian whispered to Phoenix, hoping his matter-of-fact tone would reassure her.

"What is this place?" Her whisper came from close beside him. "I can't see a thing.

"Utility closet. Each wing has a bank of small Luminite crystal generators to power computers and other small equipment."

They fell silent so only the gentle hum of machinery and the sound of their breathing was audible. Usually a man of action, the inactivity wore on him. It left him too much time to think about the woman standing next to him. Was there even a chance for them to have a real relationship? If he asked, would she consider staying with him? Would he be willing to give up bounty hunting to go live with her on her home planet?

The more he thought about it, the more anxious he got because he didn't know the answers to any of his questions – and now was not the time to ask Phoenix.

It seemed like they'd been in there forever when Adrian finally heard the sound of footsteps outside the door. He pulled his laser and had his finger was on the trigger when a familiar voice said, "It's us."

Adrian opened the door and guided Phoenix out into the corridor. "Any problems?"

"None," Jack said. "Most of the people are so miserable here, they only care about themselves. The only person who gave us a second look was a guard and he was too new to know if I was legit or not."

"They're not expecting to be attacked from the inside," Rheon added. "What now?"

"Now, we get what we came for," Adrian said.

He led the group to the holding area, stopping outside the door.

"There won't be much time," he told them. "There's a main control desk from which all the rooms are monitored and the only way in or out is through this door."

"How many guards," Jack asked.

"At least two; but there could be as many as five, depending on the number of prisoners they have."

"These shirts will buy us enough time to see what we're up against and take them by surprise. I'll take right. Jack, you take left and Rheon, you take center." He looked at each man in turn until they nodded. "Any questions?"

"What should I do?" Phoenix asked.

"Wait out here until I call you," Adrian said.

"Don't I need a laser?"

He ignored her. After the episode at the Endgame competition, he thought they were safer if she was unarmed. Instead, he placed his hand on the door's control panel. The door slid open and the two guards behind the desk looked up. Their momentary confusion at seeing two fellow guards pointing lasers at them was all the advantage Jack, Adrian and Rheon needed.

The guards fell to the floor in twin heaps. Behind him, Adrian heard Phoenix gasp.

"He's here," she whispered, coming through the door. "I can feel him."

Before he could stop her, she rushed behind the desk and down the short hallway leading to the cells, looking through the small window in each door as she passed.

"Pull those bodies behind the desk where they can't be seen," he ordered Jack and Rheon before charging after her.

He glanced into each cell as he hurried past, double-checking they were empty. He caught up to Phoenix outside the fourth cell. With her hand pressed to the door, she stared inside, tears running down her cheeks.

Skylar was there, battered and pale, suspended from the ceiling by tethers around his head, back, wrists and ankles. Fifty or more wireless electrodes were attached to his head and body. They were used, Adrian knew from personal experience, to deliver a variety of mental and physical abuses.

Intravenous tubes ran nutrients to his body, prolonging his life; prolonging his suffering.

"We have to get him down," Phoenix pleaded, reaching out to touch the control panel that would open the door.

"Wait." Adrian grabbed her hand as Jack and Rheon joined them. "Something's not right." A myriad of thoughts raced through his head—guards watching the long unused underground entrance—the ease they had getting to the holding level—Skylar left under the watch of only two guards. It didn't make sense. Zarek knew when he kidnapped Skylar that Adrian would come after him.

Of course, he'd known. In fact, he'd counted on it, hadn't he?

"It's a trap. Don't go into the cell." Adrian ran back to the desk and studied the control panel. It had been upgraded since he left, but everything appeared normal. Adrian ducked down to look under the desk and that's when he saw the blinking green light.

Krauk.

He grabbed one of the dead guards by the legs and hauled the body down the short corridor to where the others waited. "The silent alarm has been activated. We don't have much time."

"Then let's grab Skylar and get out of here," Jack said vehemently.

"I don't think that's Skylar," Adrian replied. "In fact, I think this whole thing is a trap. Help me stand this body up."

Together, they heaved the guard to an upright position. Palming open the door, Adrian shoved the guard's body inside, letting it fall forward.

As soon as it hit the floor, Skylar's body vanished, the cell door slammed shut and a yellowish-green gas billowed out from the floor and ceiling vents, filling the room.

"Dy-ruline acid," Rheon said slowly. "I'd say not only were they expecting you; they want you dead."

"But I'm sure I sensed my father close by," Phoenix said, sounding anxious.

"I don't think you were wrong," Adrian assured her, starting toward the far end of the corridor, peaking through the door windows of each cell as he passed. "The source of that holographic image is close."

He found Skylar in the last cell and hesitated only a moment before opening the door to go inside. Zarek wouldn't waste the resources to set up two identical traps. If the first failed, he would be counting on it slowing them down long enough for the guards summoned by the silent alarm to arrive. Adrian was counting on the bombs to soon keep those guards too occupied to respond.

Still, one couldn't be too careful when dealing with Zarek.

"Stay back," Adrian warned Phoenix. Then to Jack and Rheon, "help me carry that last body down here."

A short time later, Adrian palmed open the door and let the dead guard's body topple forward.

Nothing happened.

"All right," he said. "Let's get him out of here."

"His link is faint," Phoenix said in a shaky voice, watching as Adrian placed two fingers against her father's neck.

"So's his pulse."

He went to the side wall and pressed a button. The tethers supporting Skylar lengthened, lowering him until he lay on the floor. All four of his rescuers began working to undo the cuffs binding him.

"What about these electrodes?" Jack asked. "Is it safe to remove them?"

"Yes, just pull them off. The intra-venous tube, though, will need to be removed more slowly."

They removed it last and Adrian felt like it took forever.

"Skylar," he said, leaning over the prone figure. "Can you hear me, old man?" As if in response, the old man's body started to twitch. "What's going on here?" Adrian asked to no one in particular.

"He's in pain."

Phoenix's voice sounded weak and Adrian immediately turned to her. Kneeling with eyes closed, she leaned forward on arms braced against the floor.

Adrian reached out, putting a hand on her shoulder. "Are you okay?" Then it hit him. Skylar was a telepath; Phoenix was an empath. He was unconsciously broadcasting his pain and she was feeling it.

Damn it. He should have anticipated this. "We need to get you away from him." He started to get to his feet, but she waved him back down.

"I'm fine."

"Yeah, you sound fine," he muttered sarcastically, hearing the weak and shaky sound of her voice. He looked back down at Skylar, wondering what he could do to ease both their suffering, but even as he was considering options, Skylar's shaking stopped and his breathing came easier. The attack, it seemed, had subsided.

Relieved, he looked at Phoenix. To his surprise, she looked worse. Something wasn't right. "Phoenix?"

"I'm fine. Let's get my father out of here."

"I didn't know you could do that." Jack said. Then, to Adrian, he added, "She's easing his pain – I'm not sure how." He shook his head in awe. "I've heard of this but never seen anything like it before."

Less impressed, Adrian scowled. He didn't like anything that put Phoenix at greater risk. One look at her face, though, and he knew it was pointless to ask her to stop. He was about to give the order to blow the bombs, when the old man's eyelids fluttered open.

"Adrian?" The voice was scratchy and weak; Adrian could barely make out his words. "Are you really here?"

"I'm really here." He patted the old man's shoulder. "And it's damned good to find you alive. We're going to get you out of here."

"We?" Skylar blinked several times, like he was trying to clear his vision, and he turned his head to see who else might be there.

When his gaze fell on Phoenix, she smiled, giving his shoulder a reassuring squeeze, pleased when his eyes lit with recognition

"You came." He lifted his hand like he wanted to touch her; make sure she was real. She took it in hers, feeling elated.

"Of course, I—"

"Serina," he sighed. "I missed you."

It was hard not to feel disappointed, but it's not like he'd ever seen her. She supposed she did look like her mother had twenty-five years ago.

"Skylar, this isn't Serina; it's Ph—"

She shook her head. "Not now," she mouthed. If these were her father's last moments of life, then let him think she was her mother.

"I missed you, too." *If only you knew how much.*

"My one regret," he whispered, obviously growing weary from his exertions. "Agreeing to leave."

Those simple words told such a story. Neither her mother nor Skylar ever married. Could it be that they never stopped loving one another?

As if in answer, a profound sadness with a touch of heartache welled up inside her. The emotions were coming from her father.

"Don't you dare give up," she told him with conviction. She looked over at Adrian and saw in his gaze the same resolve to keep her father alive.

"Rheon, help me get him up," Adrian ordered. "Jack—blow the bombs."

Jack raised his wrist to his mouth. "Security protocol voice rec: Jack Marsden. Initiate three second count down." Jack looked at each of them in turn. "Brace yourselves."

Phoenix wasn't sure what she expected—a distant rumble and maybe a slight vibration of the floor? Instead, the explosions were so loud it sounded like ships had crashed into the side of the cliff. She was knocked to the floor despite having braced her hand against the wall. Dust and ceiling debris rained down on them, leaving Phoenix to wonder whether they'd get out alive or be buried along with everyone else.

"Phoenix," Adrian shouted, struggling to hold up her father while reaching for her.

"I'm fine." She assured him, getting to her feet. "Let's go."

They hurried down the short hallway to the command center. Rheon went ahead of them to open the door. Outside the holding area, the corridors were in a state of chaos. Panicked shouts filled the air as people hurried for the stairwells.

Rheon pushed his way into the crowd with Jack and Adrian, supporting her father, following close behind him and Phoenix close behind them. Soon, the corridor was packed with people trying to escape the fortress before it collapsed. Phoenix became less worried about being caught helping a prisoner escape and more worried about getting separated from the others. She focused on staying close to Adrian and more than once used her elbow to discourage someone from getting between them.

The stairwell, being narrower than the corridor, created a bottle-neck. As the crowd surged upward, the challenge became keeping one's footing on the stairs as they were pushed along.

Phoenix thought things would get better once they reached the first level but that proved not to be the case. If possible, this level was even more crowded with everyone pushing to reach the exit. Adrian turned to shout something to her, but the noise in the hallway was too great for her to hear him. She supposed he was advising her to stay close, like that wasn't exactly what she was trying to do.

When she caught a glimmer of light up ahead, she felt a rush of excitement. Just a few more meters and they'd be outside.

So caught up in the thought of escaping Zarek's fortress, she didn't notice the fallen body hidden beneath the swarming crowd of people until her foot hit it. With the crowd of people pushing her forward, she had no chance to recover her footing and went down. She had only a moment to register that she'd fallen over a dead man when people started stumbling over her.

She tried to push them away; tried to force them to give her enough room to climb back to her feet, but it was useless. There were just so many of them. Booted feet stepped on her legs; knees knocked her in the head hard enough to leave her stunned. Her cries for help couldn't be heard above the noise of the crowd. If she didn't get to her feet soon, she was at risk of getting trampled to death—not, she realized, unlike the man whose body she'd tripped over.

Chapter 18

PHOENIX KNEW SHE HAD to do something fast before it was too late.

She twisted so her back was to the oncoming crowd and tried to grab someone's hand hoping their forward momentum would pull her up. Her first attempt failed as the person pulled free of her grasp. She reached for another and then another, all with the same results. She was growing desperate when someone grabbed her beneath her arms and lifted to her feet.

At first, she thought Adrian or Jack had come back for her, but when she turned to her savior, she saw it was one of Zarek's servants. He didn't wait for her to thank him, but pushed her forward before the crowd knocked them both down.

She realized then that even if Adrian or the others knew she'd gotten separated from them, they wouldn't have been able to stop and come back for her. One of them would surely be waiting for her just outside the fortress. All she had to do was stay with the crowd until she was out.

She continued shuffling forward and eventually reached the doors. For a moment, she enjoyed the fresh air, then turned her thoughts to finding Adrian. One look around and she knew finding him wouldn't be easy.

There were a hundred or more people milling about outside.

Phoenix wandered around, looking for two men supporting a third, thinking such a triplet would stand out. It turned out to be a more prevalent image than she'd expected thanks to the number of injuries caused by the explosions. Then it occurred to her that she was wasting time. She knew where the shuttle was waiting for them. She would meet them there.

She started through the crowd, trying to reach the path leading away from the fortress. She was almost there when a motion overhead made her look up in time to see a shuttle flying overhead, the pilot's face just barely visible through the front windshield. It was Jack.

She was too late. They had left without her.

Too stunned to move, she stared stupidly into the sky. Logically, she understood the urgency around getting her father to Veridian Prime before the capsule containing its deadly poison opened—but they'd left her behind!

It took a second before she remembered the dance troupe's shuttle. She would take it back to the village and worry about finding Adrian later.

She studied the crowd and finally caught sight of one of the dancers. She tracked her progress to the landing pad where a shuttle waited. She must have overlooked it when she'd been searching earlier for Adrian and Jack because she felt certain she would have noticed it.

She headed for it and when she climbed aboard, the troupe leader merely raised his eyebrow and then nodded. She took that as permission to hitch a ride and walked to the back where she grabbed a window seat.

Only about half the dancers were on board, so they had to wait. Phoenix watched the crowd of people going back into the fortress now that the danger was over, but her thoughts were working on the problem of how to let Adrian know she'd escaped. She saw him so clearly in her mind, that when she spotted him in the crowd outside the fortress, it didn't click at first that he was actually there. By the time it did, he'd wandered off, leaving her to wonder if she'd really seen him at all.

Then his words floated back to her. *I will never leave you behind.* Her heart leapt with joy. He'd come for her.

She hurried to the front of the shuttle. "I'll be right back," she told the troupe leader. "Please don't leave without me."

"I can't promise that," he said, sounding genuinely sorry. "It's too dangerous. It won't be long before Zarek suspects we had something to do with what happened and comes after us. You have until the last of my girls is on board and then we're leaving."

Knowing she couldn't ask for more than that, she nodded and left.

Back among the crowd, it was harder to see. Phoenix went to the place where she last saw Adrian and looked around. Of course, he wasn't there.

She stood on her toes, trying to see over the crowd and caught a glimpse of him just inside the fortress entrance. Relieved, she pushed her way through, noticing as she did four more dancers hurrying past. She hoped they weren't the last.

Suppressing a shudder as she stepped through the fortress entrance, she started down the corridor. Where had he gone?

She was passing the first stairwell when an arm reached out and grabbed her. A hand clamped over her mouth, effectively cutting off her scream.

"It's me."

At the sound of the familiar voice, she relaxed.

"Adrian?" She was so glad to see him, she threw her arms around his neck, holding him tight.

"Are you hurt?"

"No, I'm okay," she assured him, her face pressed against his neck. She filled her lungs with the scent of him; reassured by it. "I thought you'd left me. I tripped and fell. By the time I made it outside, I'd lost track of you. Then I saw the shuttle fly off." She paused. "I thought you'd left me," she admitted.

"Not a chance," Adrian whispered. His embrace grew tighter. "I've never been so afraid as I was when I realized you weren't with us. I assumed the worst, but I had to make sure Skylar made it to the shuttle. Once they took off, I came back for you. Now, we need to get out of here."

That reminded her. "The dance troupe's shuttle is outside, but we have to hurry. They're not going to wait."

He nodded and, taking her by the hand, led her back out into the corridor. As they hurried toward the entrance, Phoenix kept her attention focused on the shuttle, just visible over the heads of the people in front of them. When she saw the hatch start to close, she gripped Adrian's hand tighter to get his attention.

They were fighting against a returning stream of people and making little headway. Disheartened, she watched as the shuttle lifted into the air. There seemed no point in hurrying now. The shuttle was gone.

She didn't think she could feel worse until the sound of grating metal and rattling chains told her she was wrong. The guards were closing the fortress's large metal doors.

Adrian didn't break stride but immediately changed directions, leading her back the way they'd come, down the stairs to the second level.

Only once did Adrian stop and that was when they happened across the solitary body of a dead guard. Phoenix watched in horror as Adrian pulled out a knife, cut off the man's thumb and placed the severed digit in his pocket. Then he hauled the guard's body to the nearest closet and placed him inside.

Before she could recover enough to demand an explanation, they were once again hurrying down the corridor to the next stairwell.

The third level had sustained the least amount of damage from the bombs and subsequently, was less populated as everyone else was tending to disaster recovery matters elsewhere. Adrian guided her along the corridor, making first one turn and then another. He finally came to a stop at the head of a very long corridor lined with doors.

"What are you doing?" Phoenix asked, when he touched the interactive computer screen embedded in the wall, bringing it to life.

"Finding us a place to hide." He scrolled through several screens before finding the one he wanted. When he was done, he tapped the power icon and the screen went blank. "This way."

They continued down the corridor and Phoenix noticed numbers mounted above each door. They stopped before the one numbered 3-23. There was no handle on the door and no obvious way to open it.

"How are we going to get in?" she asked.

Adrian didn't bother with an answer. Instead, he pulled the severed thumb from his pocket and pressed the pad of it against a small panel that Phoenix hadn't realized was there. The door slid open.

Adrian and Phoenix shared a glance, then Adrian stepped inside with Phoenix following after him. The door slid shut with a resounding snap that left Phoenix feeling a bit trapped.

"This is that guard's residence?" she asked, noting the lounger and chairs sitting in front of the entertainment module mounted on the wall. There was a small kitchenette off to the side and a door that, presumably, led to a bedroom.

"It is," Adrian answered, walking around, taking stock of the area. "He won't be needing it. We'll hide here for a couple of hours then sneak out through the cave at low tide—and let's hope our boat is still tied off."

"Oh." It was a good plan; better than she'd hoped for. "I assume you looked up that guard's name on the panel down the hall? That's how you knew which room was his?"

"Yeah." Adrian had finished his check of the main area.

"How'd you know the guard's name? I didn't see him wearing a name badge."

Adrian paused his inspection to look at her. "I recognized him from my time here before. Hardt was one of the guards Zarek had watching me. Son-of-a-bitch liked to beat up women and kids so don't waste any time feeling sorry for him."

There was no comment she could make to this and he didn't seem to expect one. Instead, he disappeared through the far doorway into the bedroom to finish his inspection. Wanting to make herself useful, she went into the kitchenette and looked through the cooler and pantries, finding enough food for several meals.

She sensed Adrian's return from the back room before she heard his footsteps. His presence filled the room.

"All clear."

She turned at the sound of his voice, her pulse racing. She couldn't help it. He just had that effect on her.

The kisses they'd shared in the safe house had awakened something in her and now that they were alone again...she hoped he couldn't read the direction of her thoughts in her expression.

"You're hurt."

"Oh, no... wait. What?" Startled, it took a moment for his words to register. When they did, she followed the direction of his gaze. The material of her skirt, now torn and stained with dirt, was stuck to her equally dirty leg.

"You're bleeding."

She took a closer look. He was right. Rivulets of blood, not dirt, ran down the length of her leg.

"It must have happened when I fell. People kept stepping on me." Her voice faded as she remembered being trampled. Now that she was no longer in immediate danger and the adrenaline rush had passed, she grew conscious of just how bruised her hips and legs felt.

She twisted, trying to get a better look at her injury but it was high on back of her thigh. She tentatively probed the area with her fingertips, but with the costume matted to her skin, it was impossible to tell anything.

"Let me look."

Heat rushed to her face. "I don't think so." She had little on beneath the costume and the thought of him getting that up close and personal was too unsettling.

"You could be seriously hurt."

"I'm not," she argued. "If it was serious, it would hurt – and it doesn't so I'm sure it's only a scratch."

"Still, it needs to be cleaned and I'm not sure you can reach back there."

"I can do it." She turned and headed for the bedroom, feeling the burn of his gaze on her as she went.

"Be sure you do a thorough job, otherwise I'll just end up doing it anyway—and enjoy every second."

Blood rushed to her face at the image his words conjured. He winked to let her know he was teasing but made no move to follow her into the bedroom, for which she was grateful. Once inside, she closed the door behind her, as a precaution.

It was a modest room with a bed and a single dresser in the way of furnishings. She'd expected to feel uncomfortable there, but the bed was made and the room looked clean. There were two doors besides the one through which she'd entered. One led to a bathroom and the other to a surprisingly large closet. The bathroom, like the bedroom, was clean and neat. The closet, on the other hand, looked more like what she'd expected of a single man's room, with as many clothes piled on the floor as hanging up.

Going into the bathroom, she was relieved to find it was fully functional, complete with shower and running water.

There was even a mirror over the sink and one look at her reflection left her horrified. Her hair was a tangled mess. Her skirt was ripped in several places in addition to the back being matted to her leg. Her top wasn't in much better shape and if it hung any lower, she'd be exposing a lot more than cleavage.

Behind her, the shower stall beckoned invitingly and before she'd made the conscious decision to shower, she was turning on the water. She found a fresh bar of soap in the pantry because she couldn't bring herself to use the old soap already in the shower.

She considered disrobing, but there was no way to take off the costume without ripping open her wound, so she stepped beneath the hot stream of water without bothering to undress. The outfit was quickly soaked and when it had softened enough that she could pull it away from her wound without too much pain, she peeled it off and left it piled in the corner of the stall. The hot water felt heavenly – until it hit her wound. Then it stung, bringing tears to her eyes.

Maybe she was hurt worse than she'd thought.

Bloody water circled the drain. She watched it for several long seconds but when the water soon cleared, she sighed with relief. If the bleeding had already stopped, she couldn't be hurt too bad.

She lost track of how long she stood there but when she finally shut off the water and stepped out, she felt immensely better.

There were no towels to dry herself but there was a heated sani-blower. She stepped into the unit and jets of warm air buffeted her hair and body until she was completely dry. Opening the door to the bedroom a crack, she peeked out. The room was empty.

Stepping out, she looked around. She had nothing to wear. The idea of putting on the guard's clothes was revolting, but what choice did she have?

She was about to search for an outfit when Adrian chose that moment to knock on the door.

"Phoenix, are you all right? Can I come in?"

"Just a moment," she replied nervously. With a frantic look about, her gaze fell on the bed. The top cover was too thick so she grabbed the white sheet beneath it and, pulling it off the bed, wrapped herself in it.

"Come in."

"You were in there for a while," Adrian said, stepping into the room. "I just wanted to make sure you were... okay." He swallowed hard, suddenly at a loss for words. He was sure he'd never seen anything as breathtakingly sexy as Phoenix standing before him wearing nothing but a sheet, looking nervous and a little lost as she gazed up at him through twin auburn curtains of her freshly washed hair. For a moment, all he could do was admire how lovely she looked.

He should be commended for the self-discipline he demonstrated in remaining where he was, because every fiber of his being yearned to gather her into his arms and taste again the sweetness of her lips. He knew if he gave into the temptation, he wouldn't be able to stop – not with a bed so readily available and nothing but time on their hands.

When she started biting her lip, he realized he was making her even more nervous with his silence, so he cleared his throat and asked, "How was your shower?"

That made her smile. "The hot water felt wonderful. I strongly recommend it."

Suddenly self-conscious, he looked down at his clothes wondering how bad he smelled. He couldn't remember the last time he'd taken a showered.

"Yeah, I could probably stand to get cleaned up." Not hot water, though. A nice cold shower was what he needed. He raised his head again to meet her gaze. "How's your leg?"

"It's sore," she admitted, "but I think it's fine."

He would have felt better checking it himself, but the image of her bent over the bed with the sheet pulled high to reveal her bared lush posterior to his inspection nearly made him groan aloud.

"I think I'll take that shower, now," he said, hurrying for the bathroom.

She said something about towels but he wasn't really paying attention. His entire focus was on getting to the bathroom and closing the door before she noticed the quickly rising evidence of his arousal.

Once inside the bathroom, he leaned against the closed door and glanced down at himself, shaking his head. It was the normal reaction of a man standing too close to a nearly naked woman, he mentally argued. There was nothing special about this particular woman. It didn't mean anything.

He knew it was a lie.

His self-control was legendary, thanks to his father's abuse. Yet, when he was around Phoenix, it was like he had no control at all. Why was that?

He pondered the question throughout a long, cold shower, but when he finally shut off the water, he wasn't any closer to an answer than when he'd started.

Or maybe he just didn't want to accept the answer.

By the time he stepped out of the sani-blower, warm and dry, he was willing to accept that he cared for Phoenix. A lot.

Admitting it wasn't as horrible as he'd imagined—and unless he was wrong about all the looks she'd sneaked at him and the way she'd responded earlier to his kiss, she might just like him back.

Thinking of all the ways he could find out for sure brought a smile to his lips—which wavered only slightly when he realized there were no towels in the bathroom. Nor was there a robe. Phoenix's words belatedly registered. He disliked the idea of putting his dirty clothes back on but, as tempting as it might be to walk out of the bathroom naked just to see the expression on her face, he decided against it. Now really wasn't the time for fun and games; they were hiding from a very dangerous man and should remain ever diligent until they were safely back on board his ship.

Reluctantly, he put his pants on. The shirt had a blood stain on it, so he searched the cabinet for stain remover and after not finding any, used soap and water to get as much out as he could before laying the shirt across the counter to dry. He'd put it on later.

Opening the bathroom door, he was greeted by a vision that sent his blood rushing once again to his nether regions.

Phoenix lay on the bed facing away from him, fast asleep. The sheet that had so completely covered her before had fallen open, exposing a length of her leg and the gentle swell of a nicely shaped butt. The only thing marring the erotic picture was the cut at the base of that lush posterior. The flesh on either side was red with new infection and the wound itself had started to bleed again.

"Damnit," he muttered under his breath as he stepped back into the bathroom. In his earlier search of the cabinets, he'd come across a first aid kit. Getting it out, he searched it for a mini-reparator which would completely heal the wound. Apparently, though, the modern advances in medical science hadn't reached Previon, so he had to make do with a bio-patch. At least, it would keep the wound sealed and facilitate healing.

Taking it into the bedroom along with a damp cloth, he knelt before the bed. He had to close his eyes for a moment and remind himself that he was rendering aid—but damn she had a nice ass!

A sound roused Phoenix from her sleep, though not enough to bring her fully awake. She was just too tired to open her eyes. Feeling a cool breeze across her rear, she reached for the sheet to pull it over her.

"Hold still."

The male voice sounded much too close, bringing Phoenix instantly awake.

"What are you doing?" she yelped, grabbing at the sheet because Adrian was kneeling before her exposed posterior.

"Nothing—yet," he growled, pushing her back over onto her stomach so her bare butt was up in the air. "That cut on your leg is bleeding again. I'm going to bandage it."

"I told you, it's not that bad." She tried once again to roll onto her side, but he easily stopped her.

"I'm not asking permission," he said in a stern tone. "Now lie still or I'm going to use the sheet to tie you up."

"You wouldn't." She glared at him over her shoulder.

"Don't tempt me."

Chapter 19

Burying her face in the mattress, Phoenix thought she would die. In part from embarrassment, but mostly from the sheer pleasure of Adrian's touch. His hand was warm against the back of her thigh and the cool rag he used to clean her wound did little to cool her heated flesh. He moved with excruciating thoroughness, slowly working from the outside of her leg inward. When his hand brushed against the juncture of her legs, she shuddered and groaned.

No male had ever touched her so intimately.

She was about to combust and the worst thing was that he seemed wholly unaffected by their situation. His fingers worked with impersonal precision to clean her wound and then apply the bio-patch.

Finally, he was done. "How does that feel?"

How did what feel? His hands on her body? The warmth of his breath against the back of her leg when he leaned forward to inspect his work?

It felt erotic.

Stimulating.

"Great...I mean, fine. My leg, that is. It feels fine." She stumbled over her words, knowing he must think her an idiot. "Thank you."

He covered her with the sheet, so she rolled to her side in order to look up at him as he stood. Her pulse quickened at the sight of his bare chest; well-muscled and covered with a light matting of dark brown hair. He was so virile, her breath caught in her throat. He projected an energy and power that undeniably attracted her.

Feeling like he could read her every thought by looking at her face, she still dared to meet his gaze.

"You are so damn beautiful, Phoenix." There was a primal tone to his words that made her shiver much as the feel of his hand against her bare leg had moments before. "I want to make love to you so badly, it scares me."

Phoenix waited with breathless anticipation, but he didn't move towards her. He looked like he was struggling to decide what to do. Perhaps it was a misplaced sense of honor that was stopping him. The yearning in his gaze and the tenting of his pants told her it wasn't a lack of desire.

Then she remembered his nightmare and subsequent confession. She didn't need her abilities to know he was filled with doubt. Doubt that she could be as attracted to him as he was to her. Doubt as to whether he could avoid hurting her.

Her heart ached for him. She wasn't naïve but she'd never made love to anyone before; never seduced anyone, so she acted on instinct.

Tossing the sheet aside, she climbed out of the bed and crossed the short distance separating them. His breath caught when she raised her arms to link her hands behind his head, pressing herself against him as fully as she could.

"You're killing me," he whispered hoarsely. "Instead of tempting me, you should tell me to leave."

"Enough talk," she whispered, rising up on her toes to press her lips against his.

He grasped her hips and pulled her tightly against him, enveloping her in his embrace. Then his lips descended on hers, capturing her mouth with fervent intensity. She surrendered completely to a kiss that felt like molten steel binding them together.

When his hand found her side, she lost all coherent thought. His touch awakened every nerve, sending electric shivers through her. She thought her knees might buckle and was grateful when he lifted her into his arms and carried her to the bed, gently laying her down.

She had only a moment to notice the absence of his warmth before he joined her. The closeness of their bodies sent her senses spiraling. He gave her no time to dwell on uncertainties, reclaiming her lips with passion, his touch a gentle exploration that promised new discoveries. She shuddered at the sweetness of his presence, embracing the connection that transcended words.

Adrian's kiss deepened, becoming more urgent and demanding. His tongue danced with hers in a sensual tango as his hands roamed her curves, igniting trails of fire everywhere they touched. Phoenix arched into him, craving more contact, needing to be as close as possible.

He broke the kiss to trail his lips along her jaw and down the column of her throat. She gasped when he found the sensitive spot just above her collarbone, her fingers threading through his hair to hold him there. His talented mouth and tongue worked their magic, sending pulses of pleasure radiating through her body.

"Phoenix," he breathed, his voice rough with emotion. "If we don't stop now, I won't be able to control myself. Tell me to leave before it's too late."

She silenced him with a searing kiss, pouring all of her desire and longing into it. Pulling back slightly to meet his heated gaze, her eyes shimmered with emotion and conviction.

She reached up to cup his face, her thumb brushing across his sculpted cheekbone. "I don't want you to stop, Adrian. I trust you completely. I...I need you."

With a low growl, he captured her mouth once more in a consuming kiss. Phoenix lost herself to the fire raging between them, their bodies moving together in a timeless dance as old as creation itself. Adrian worshipped every inch of her with his hands and lips, his reverent touches stoking the flames higher.

As he settled his weight over her, fitting their bodies together like matching puzzle pieces, Phoenix knew there would be no going back. But here in Adrian's embrace, joined with him in the most profound of ways, she had never felt more complete. Tonight, they would cross the threshold into a newer, deeper connection, one that would bind their hearts forevermore.

Adrian woke hours later feeling better than...well better than he'd ever felt in his entire life, as far as he could recall. Phoenix still lay nestled in his arms and he hated to wake her. What he wouldn't give to stop time so they could just stay like that, forever. Unfortunately, they didn't have forever. So long as he had this chip in his head and Zarek was alive, Adrian was on borrowed time.

"Phoenix, sweetheart, wake up." Unable to stop himself, he kissed her forehead.

"Hmm, Adrian." She sighed his name and her lips lifted in a smile. He hated seeing the smile fade as she came more fully awake. "Is everything ok?"

"Yeah, sweetheart, for now. It's almost time, though, so we need to get dressed."

They maneuvered themselves off the bed, Adrian making sure Phoenix had the sheet around her. He wasn't sure if she'd be shy around him now without clothes, but he knew he didn't need the distraction.

Without facing her, he pulled on his pants. The shirt he'd left in the bathroom was mostly dried, so he put it back on. When he returned to the bedroom, Phoenix was still standing wrapped in the sheet. A blood stain at the bottom was a fresh reminder of what had passed between them.

"I think there's time for a quick shower if you want one," he told her. "And I can probably find something in the closet for you to wear."

"I can look when I get out of the shower. What I'd really like is something to eat. I'm starving."

"Okay, I'll see what I can find in the kitchen." He gave her a quick kiss and walked out.

He found it ironic that he felt happier and more carefree stuck in Zarek's fortress under the constant threat of discovery than he had a week ago when his only concern was which bounty to track down next. A part of him couldn't help but wonder if he was feeling his own emotions or receiving emotions Phoenix might be projecting.

Not particularly liking the direction of his thoughts, he pushed them aside and searched the pantries for food. By his calculation, they had only about two hours before low tide. He didn't know how much time it would take them to sneak downstairs or what they'd find once they got there. He'd just as soon not wait until the last minute to find out.

Selecting several items of food, he had just carried them to the table when the apartment door suddenly opened and a boy walked in. He looked about ten years old though Adrian was not a great judge of age, and seemed familiar with his blond hair and golden brown eyes. For a prolonged moment, they stared at each other in shocked silence while Adrian considered what to do.

His mistake was thinking a child wouldn't be dangerous.

Smiling, the boy raised his hand. Adrian recognized the discipline wand nano-seconds before crippling pain ripped through his head, driving him to his knees.

Zarek had found him after all—and had used a boy to do his dirty work.

Blinded by the pain but desperate to protect Phoenix at all costs, Adrian crawled toward the boy. If he could only reach him before Zarek's men arrived—

Another nauseating wave of pain had him writhing on the floor, clutching his head.

"Hello, Sun. Did you really think we wouldn't find you?" Juarez's voice dripped with mock politeness as he and several guards walked into the apartment. "Hit him again." He said to the boy.

As the next wave of pain coursed through him, Adrian was helpless to fight off the guards who roughly secured his wrists and ankles together with cuffs.

"Check the bedroom," Juarez then ordered. "Make sure he's alone."

It was too much to hope Phoenix had figured out what was going on and hidden herself. No, Juarez's guards were going to take her by surprise and the thought of what they'd do to her had Adrian praying for a miracle like he'd never prayed before.

"How?" Adrian gasped, trying to distract Juarez and maybe find an opening to attack.

"We found Hardt's body. Missing thumb was a dead give-away, pardon the pun." He laughed at his own joke.

The appearance of the guards in the bedroom doorway drew Adrian's attention.

"Room's empty," one reported. "He's alone."

Adrian managed to school his expression to not look surprised—or worried—though he was both. Where was she?

"Let me guess—Marsden is flying O'Mallen to safety? Well, congratulations on breaking the old man out." Juarez's tone dripped with sarcasm. "It might come as a surprise to you that Zarek doesn't give a shit about O'Mallen. It's you he wanted all along. Beats the hell out of me why, but there you have it. Bring him," he said to the guards as he headed for the doorway.

They reached down to grab him, but Adrian reared back, twisting his body, making it difficult for them to hold on to him.

"Petrof, would you mind?" Juarez asked.

As the feel of red-hot pokers ripped through his brain, Adrian fell onto his side. The pain continued and Adrian knew he was going to pass out. He focused on the boy's face for as long as he could as the darkness stole up to take him.

Just before he passed out, it hit him who the boy looked like.

The boy looked like him.

Chapter 20

JACK'S KNUCKLES TIGHTENED ON the controls as the Black Jack shuddered, the wormhole spitting them out into the swirling cosmic gases of the Outer Fringe. Beside him, Skylar gasped, clutching the armrest.

"Easy, old timer. We made it." Jack glanced at the SDIA agent, noting the sheen of sweat on his forehead, the ashen pallor of his skin. It was a miracle the agent had survived everything Zarek had put him through.

A blinking red light on the control panel told Jack the last wormhole jump had depleted the Luminite crystals powering his ship. They'd never make it to Veridian Prime without stopping to let the crystals recharge.

"We're going to have to stop," he told Skylar, guiding his ship to the space station. "Recharging the crystals shouldn't take too long."

He hoped he was telling the truth. The capsule inside of Skylar was a ticking bomb and Jack didn't know how much time they had.

Pulling into the closest open docking bay, he set the ship down and switched off the engines. Almost immediately, the recharging drones appeared and got to work.

Jack helped Skylar to the airlock. "What do you say we get some grub while we wait?"

They made their way to The Abyss and found seats at the bar. Jack nodded at Kylix, in her female form, behind the bar, her chestnut hair glinting under the holographic murals.

"Jack. Skylar. It's good to see you both!" Kylix slid two Galaxian Ales across the smooth surface of the bar's countertop. "Staying long?"

"No. We're just passing through, on our way to Veridian Prime. We needed to recharge and grab a bite." Jack took a swig, savoring the cold bite. If Kylix sensed his urgency, she didn't let on.

"Tell me again about my daughter," Skylar urged him, for the third or fourth time since leaving Previon.

"Like I said. She's brave, and smart. And as stubborn as you, old man," Jack told him with a smile. "I can't say she has the best taste in men, though, considering I'm pretty sure she has a thing for Adrian." Skylar frowned when Jack chuckled. "What was her mother like?"

"Serina?" Skylar said the name wistfully. "She was perfect. Beautiful, strong. I was so in love with her." He raised his glass to his lips. "Still am," Jack thought he heard him mumble. Then Skylar shifted on the stool, his face pinched. "Jack... we may have a problem."

"What is it?" Jack's eyes narrowed. There wasn't time for problems.

With a shaking hand, Skylar set his drink back down and pulled his sleeve up to reveal purple lines snaking across his skin, pulsing faintly.

"What the hell is that?" Jack asked, feeling shocked.

"It's the capsule's early warning sign. It's starting to degrade."

Jack's gut clenched. He knew what that meant. Once the capsule ruptured, the poison would flood Skylar's system. Game over.

Jack raised his hand to get Kylix's attention at the other end of the bar. "We need your help," he told her as soon as she walked over. "Please tell me there's someone in the station who can disable a biomechanical capsule before it kills my friend here?"

Kylix leaned over the bar, her ice blue eyes studying the rash. Jack could practically see the gears turning behind her ancient gaze and he prayed for a miracle.

When she straightened, a glimmer of hope lit her eyes. "Talk to Lena. She's your best shot."

"Lena Alvarez? The engineer?" Jack's brow furrowed. He'd heard stories about the half-Lyran engineer and the marvels she could work with large engines, but couldn't fathom how she could help with a biomechanical problem.

"Trust me, Jack. If anyone can crack this, it's her. You'll find her down in the lower levels, probably hustling some poor saps at the gaming tables." Kylix's tone left no room for doubt.

Jack hesitated for a split second, then nodded. Kylix had an uncanny way of knowing things. "I'm on it. Keep an eye on Skylar for me, will you?"

"Of course," she said. "But hurry. Time is not on your side."

Jack bolted from the bar, his boots pounding against the metal grating as he raced towards the lifts. The lower levels of Outer Fringe were a labyrinth of dimly lit corridors and seedy establishments, a haven for the station's less savory elements.

Where the hell am I supposed to find her in this maze? Jack's mind raced as he moved past gaming tables and tattoo parlors, searching for any sign of the elusive engineer. Unlike the upper levels of the station, the air on this level was thick wit the stench of sweat and desperation.

A sudden commotion caught his attention, with raised voices and the telltale clink of credit chips. Jack pushed his way through the throng, following the sound to a cramped alcove tucked away in the shadows.

There, amidst a ring of onlookers, stood Lena Alvarez. Petite and fierce, her purple hair gleaming under the flickering lights, she faced off against a group of snarling gamblers, their faces twisted with rage.

"You cheated, you little bitch!" The largest of the bunch jabbed a meaty finger in her face. "No one's that lucky, not even a freak like you."

Lena smirked, unruffled by the man's bulk or insult. "It's called skill, sweetheart. Not my fault you don't have any."

The brute lunged, but Lena was faster. She side-stepped with inhuman grace, using his own momentum to send him sprawling. Infuriated to see their friend go down, the others closed in.

Knowing there was no way Lena could take on all those men, Jack didn't hesitate. He charged into the fray, fists flying. Shouted curses and the crunch of bones shattering filled the air as he laid into the attackers, clearing a path to Lena's side. Soon, the majority of the attackers not laying unconscious on the floor decided to cut their losses and ran off, leaving Lena and Jack alone, standing back-to-back; both breathing hard.

Finally, Lena turned to face him and flashed him a grin, her black eyes sparkling with mischief. "I had it under control, but thanks for the assist."

"Actually, I came down here looking for you," he said with a smile, adrenaline singing in his veins. "I'm Jack, by the way. Jack Marsden."

"You came down here looking for me?" She cocked her head, curiosity plain on her delicate features. "Color me intrigued."

"Kylix said you might be the only one who might be able to save my friend," he told her, the urgency of his mission crashing back.

Lena's eyes widened; surprise quickly replaced by a steely determination. "Kylix said that, huh? " She appeared thoughtful for a moment, but then shrugged. "Okay." She pinned the last still-standing attacker with her glare. "Are we done here?"

He hesitated for a moment but then nodded glumly and backed away.

She turned to Jack. "One second." She moved over to the card table in the alcove, collected the winnings piled in the center and stuffed them into her pockets. Then she rejoined Jack. "Lead the way."

As they raced back to The Abyss, Jack could only pray they weren't too late. Inside the bar, Kylix told them she'd had Skylar taken to the Black Jack, which is where Jack and Lena found him, his pale form stretched out on one of the ship's beds. Purple lines snaked across his skin, a stark contrast to the sickly pallor of his face.

"Damn," Lena breathed, hurrying to his side. She examined the rash, her brow furrowed in concentration. "This looks like a medical issue. I'm no doctor What do you think I can do?"

Jack quickly told her about the poison capsule and then waited, fear a leaden weight in his gut. "Can you help him?"

She didn't answer right away. "You said the capsule is biomechanical?"

Hope surged through him. "Yes."

She sighed. "I have an idea that might just buy your friend some time, but it's no guarantee. I don't want you to blame me if this doesn't work."

Jack thought Skylar was unconscious, but he opened his eyes then. "You won't be blamed," he assured her.

She nodded and then reached into her pocket, withdrawing a case no bigger than the tip of her smallest finger. From inside her jacket, she retrieved a small computer and turned it on.

"What is that?" Jack asked, eyeing the case warily.

"An experimental nanobot. First of its kind."

"No shit!" he exclaimed, moving closer to examine it. Nanobot technology had been around for eons, but they were almost prohibitively expensive, and their use was strictly regulated. Jack was beyond intrigued that Lena had one. "How'd you get it?"

She gave him a sly smile. "Won it off a Zorian tech mogul in a game of Nebula Poker."

Amazed, Jack shook his head. He was finding Lena more and more intriguing. "And you think it can help Skylar?"

"I'm better with machines than coding, but if I can program it to interface with the capsule's clock, there may be a way to reverse the countdown or at least, stop it temporarily." Lena's fingers flew over the computer's holographic keyboard, inputting commands. "It should buy us some time."

Jack watched the code scroll across the holographic feed, impressed with Lena's computer skills. Only once did he suggest alternate coding which, after studying it, she conceded was better than what she'd originally had. "You know your way around coding," she noted.

Jack shrugged. "It's kind of my thing. That and hunting down criminals."

Lena gave a soft chuckle, but continued to work. Then, with a final keystroke, her hands grew still. "I think that's it. Ready to see if it works?"

He nodded and she removed the nanobot, which was no larger than a freckle, from its case.

"Okay, Skylar. Deep breath out." When he complied, she held the nanobot below his nose. "Now, big inhale through your nose," she told him.

Immediately, the nanobot shot up into Skylar's nostril.

"Here goes nothing," she muttered, turning back to the computer and pressing a button to activate the nanobot.

Jack's gaze went to the purple lines on Skylar's arms, still pulsing as if with a life of their own.

"The nanobot has reached the capsule," Lena, still watching the computer screen, informed him. "Okay," she continued slowly. "Interface initiated. Fingers crossed."

It took a minute or two, but then, gradually, the purple lines began to slow their pulsing.

Jack let out a breath he hadn't realized he'd been holding. "I think it's working." As the rash continued to retreat, he felt a wave of gratitude wash over him. He turned to Lena, ready to express his thanks, but she was already moving towards the exit.

"Wait," he called after her. "How much do I owe you for this? You gave up your nanobot; I know that wasn't cheap. Name your price."

She stopped suddenly, catching sight of something beyond the ship's viewport. "How about a ride off this station?"

Jack followed her gaze, his stomach dropping as he recognized the disgruntled gamblers from earlier. They were gathered at the entrance to the docking bay, armed and looking for blood.

"Strap in," he said grimly, sliding into the pilot's seat. "Things are about to get bumpy."

Seconds later, the Black Jack shuddered as it tore away from the Outer Fringe space station, its engines straining against the sudden acceleration. Jack's hands flew over the controls, coaxing every last bit of speed from the aging vessel.

Beside him, Lena had already strapped herself into the co-pilot's seat. Her fingers danced across the console, eyes scanning the readouts with practiced ease. "Approaching the wormhole," she reported. "Ready to jump on your mark."

Jack nodded, his jaw set with determination. They entered the wormhole and outside the viewport, stars blurred into streaks of light. He couldn't help but feel a surge of exhilaration. This was what he lived for—the thrill of the ride, the rush of adrenaline.

Several hours later, barely out of the wormhole, a shrill alarm pierced the silence of the cockpit. Jack's heart sank as he recognized the telltale signs of an engine malfunction.

"Damnit," he muttered, his eyes scanning the flashing indicators. "The engine is overheating. We need to drop our speed before it burns out completely."

Lena was already out of her seat, grabbing a toolbox from a nearby storage compartment. "I'm on it," she said, her tone steady despite the urgency of the situation. "Just keep us flying straight."

Minutes stretched into an eternity as he waited, his eyes fixed on the star scape outside. When Lena finally reappeared, her face smudged with grease but triumphant, he felt a wave of relief wash over him.

"That should hold us for now," she said, wiping her hands on her jumpsuit. "But we'll need to make some more permanent repairs once we reach Veridian Prime."

"Thanks," Jack said, a newfound respect for his impromptu passenger taking root. "I'm better with computers than engines. I don't know what I would have done if you hadn't been here," he admitted.

Lena flashed him a grin, her black eyes sparkling with mischief. "Probably would have ended up as space dust," she teased, but there was a warmth beneath her words, a sense of camaraderie that normally only came with years of flying together.

As they settled into a comfortable silence, the Black Jack hurtling through the void once more, Jack found his thoughts turning to Adrian.

"What's on your mind?" Lena asked softly, as if sensing his introspection.

He hesitated, unsure how much to reveal, but something about Lena's presence was disarming, inviting honesty. "I had to leave my partner behind on Previon. That's where we found Skylar being held hostage. I agreed to fly Skylar back to Veridian Prime while Adrian stayed behind to rescue Skylar's daughter. I'm hoping they're both okay."

"I understand why you'd be worried," she told him. "Maybe once Skylar is safe, we can go back and check on them."

We.

He wondered if she was aware of what she'd said and was about to ask her when the alarm went off, letting them know they were approaching a planet.

"Veridian Prime, dead ahead," Lena said, reading the screen.

Finally, Jack thought. He only hoped for Skylar's sake, they weren't too late.

Chapter 21

Phoenix's head ached like it had been smashed between two compactor plates. She considered checking her skull for cracks and oozing gray matter, but it hurt too much to move.

She wasn't sure what happened. She'd found clothes that fit in the back of the closet and had just finished dressing when an excruciating pain filled her head. She'd lost consciousness and fallen, fortunately landing on one of the many piles of clothes on the floor.

Now that she was conscious, she noticed that most of the pain was gone. All except for her cheek. Something hard, and smelly, was poking her. She felt around and pulled out a well-worn shoe. Wrinkling her nose, she tossed it aside and knew she couldn't keep lying there.

Pushing herself to her knees, she had to wait for a wave of nausea to pass before getting slowly to her feet. About to step out of the closet, she hesitated. Why hadn't Adrian come to check on her?

Something was wrong, that was obvious but what was the right move to make? Should she race into the outer room to see if Adrian was hurt and needed her help? Or stay hidden because Zarek's men had found them.

She opted for action; albeit cautiously.

Moving to the open doorway, she stood and listened. Hearing nothing, she peeked out.

The room was empty.

Pressing herself against the wall, she side-stepped her way to the bathroom and then leaned to the side until she could see inside.

Empty.

That left only the outer room.

Crossing the room, she placed her ear against the bedroom door. There was nothing but silence. She reached for the handle but stopped, afraid. She was alone and unarmed. The door was thick and just because she couldn't hear anything didn't mean the room was empty. How would she know for sure?

Then she remembered that she wasn't without resources.

Opening her senses, she reached out, trying to detect nearby emotions. When she felt nothing, she grew concerned. Not even Adrian's familiar presence was there.

She opened herself further and sought him specifically.

At first, there was nothing and the disappointment was nearly crushing. She hadn't realized how quickly she'd grown used to him being there.

Then she felt him—faint and unsteady, like he was a long way off. She pushed a wave of love toward him and for a moment, their link grew stronger. Then abruptly, the connection was gone, as if a wall had been erected between them but not before she felt his fear—not for himself, but for her.

She opened the door and stepped into the room, not surprised when she found it empty. Food lay where Adrian had no doubt placed it, but he was gone. What had happened to him? She knew he'd never leave her alone voluntarily, so that meant he'd left involuntarily.

Why?

How?

What should she do?

Adrian's instructions came back to her. She supposed she should go to the underground entrance as they'd originally planned - as she'd promised him she would if something happened to him. Low tide had to be soon, she only hoped she hadn't missed it. She could take the boat back to Rheon's campsite where hopefully she'd find Rheon already preparing a second rescue mission. They'd slip in, find Adrian and rescue him just as they had her father.

Except Zarek would be expecting that.

Maybe Rheon would have a better idea. She'd rather have Jack to help her, but he was off saving her father.

Going back to the closet, she searched for a pair of shoes, but they were all too large, so she resigned herself with putting back on the dance slippers.

Then, after taking a deep breath to calm herself, she left the apartment and headed for the lower levels of the fortress.

There was a noticeable absence of guards roaming the halls and Phoenix wondered about it. Perhaps Zarek and his men felt that only Adrian had posed a threat and now that he had been captured, they need not worry about other attacks. It didn't really matter to Phoenix, as longas it made her trip to the lower levels easier.

There was more activity on the maintenance level, as crews cleared away debris from the explosion, but it worked to her advantage as everyone was too distracted to notice her. She made it to the underground cave with little trouble. This time, as she approached the final stretch of corridor, she remembered to peek around the corner first. Her luck held - the door was not guarded.

She hurried to it and turned the dials that would unlock it. The tide was low. Elated, she stepped out and found the boat right where Adrian said it would be. Judging from the level of water in the cave, she still had time to row out before the tide sealed off the entrance. She wasn't sure which way to go after she left the cave, but hoped she would be able to see the beach once she was far enough out. The rough waters might pose a problem, but she was determined.

She prepared to step into the boat, her thoughts turning to Adrian, testing their link to see if she could reach him. The wall was still up but when she pushed against it, she felt it give. She sent waves of positive energy and reassurance to him, hoping he'd know she'd followed his advice and had safely reached the cave.

She received an impression of relief just before a horrible pain hit her. The wall slammed into place and the pain vanished, but in that brief moment, she knew without a doubt that Adrian was being tortured and wouldn't survive long enough for her to escape and bring back reinforcements.

Stepping out of the boat, she headed back into the fortress. She wasn't sure how she'd do it, but she was going to save Adrian.

The Black Jack shuddered as it dropped out of hyperdrive, the swirling vortex of Solaris Dominus filling the viewscreen. Jack's hands flew over the controls, guiding the ship towards the glittering capital city of Galathea.

In the co-pilot's seat, Lena leaned forward, her eyes wide with wonder. "I've never seen anything like it," she breathed.

Jack allowed himself a small smile. "Welcome to the heart of the Solaris Dominus galaxy," he said.

As they descended through the atmosphere, the ship was hailed by the Galactic Air Control. Jack transmitted their clearance codes, his jaw tightening as he explained the nature of their mission. "We have a critically ill SDIA agent on board," he said, giving them Skylar's name and SDIA number. "Requesting immediate medical assistance upon landing."

The response was swift and efficient. "Clearance granted, Black Jack. Proceed to the roof top pad of the SDIA building. A medical team will be standing by. Sending you the coordinates now."

Jack glanced over his shoulder, his gaze falling on Skylar's unconscious form. The agent's skin was ashen between the purple lines now covering most of his body. *Hang on a little longer, old man,* he thought.

With a deftness born of years of experience, Jack guided the ship across the city to the coordinates provided by the GAC and deftly set the ship down on the roof top pad. As the engines powered down, he was already on his feet, moving to Skylar's side.

Lena joined him, her expression tight with concern. "Will he make it?" she asked softly.

Jack's response was cut off by the hiss of the airlock. A team of medics rushed in, their expressions grim as they assessed Skylar's condition.

"We need to get him into surgery immediately," one of them said. "The capsule is on the verge of rupturing."

As they loaded Skylar onto a stretcher, Jack felt a wave of helplessness wash over him. He had gotten the agent this far, but now his fate was in the hands of others.

He felt Lena's hand on his shoulder. "You did everything you could," she murmured.

He nodded, not trusting himself to speak as he watched the medics carry Skylar across the roof to the lift. They disappeared from view as the doors closed, leaving Jack with an unsettling feeling. He wondered if he'd ever see the agent alive again.

He thought of Phoenix then, who had gone through so much to rescue her father only to possibly lose him. He wondered if Adrian had found her and if they were safe. He couldn't shake the sense of urgency to get back to Previon and check on them. Two things kept him from setting off immediately. First, he needed to wait to see if Skylar survived the surgery. When he next saw Phoenix, she would want to know if he was alive or not. And second...

"I've got to get my ship's engine repaired," he said, turning to Lena. "Where can I drop you?"

She shrugged. "I'm kind of between jobs at the moment. How about you take me to the nearest maintenance bay and I'll take care of the engine? And I'll do a hell of a lot better job than any commercial mechanic."

He considered her offer. "Yeah, but how much will that cost me? I'm kind of strapped for credits at the moment."

She simply smiled. "My fees are negotiable."

He studied her for a long moment, unable to shake the feeling that he was on the brink of change. For the better or the worse, he couldn't say. Then he shrugged. "Sure. Why not?"

Chapter 22

ADRIAN HUNG SUSPENDED IN the middle of the very holding cell from which they'd rescued Skylar. Caught in a black void of pain and despair, he'd long since lost all sense of time. With the various electrodes attached to his head and body, he was made to live through horrifying experiences. He fought to separate virtual events from reality, holding onto to the thread of his humanity as tightly as he could.

He'd felt Phoenix reaching out to him; had felt her love and concern. He'd grasped at it like a drowning man would a life raft. He longed to hold her in his arms one last time. Then Juarez had activated the discipline wand and he'd had to block his feelings to spare her from the pain.

A buzzing noise started and Adrian tensed. The sound always preceded another virtual episode of horror. Adrian knew that whatever he was about to endure, it wasn't real—no matter how real it felt.

In the blink of an eye, he was standing before men gathered behind a glass wall. They watched him with gazes full of hate and fear. They were here to die and he was their executioner.

He knew the men were innocent and what he was doing was wrong. He stared at his hand, hovering above the control panel and tried to force it back down to his side. It wouldn't move, reminding him that a force stronger than his own will power compelled him.

A familiar voice whisper into his ear, urging him to press the button that would release the deadly poison into the sealed chamber.

"No," he protested even as his hand moved to comply.

The green gas began to seep out of the walls. Inside, the men cried out in terror. One by one, they fell. Dead.

Guilty of no crime other than they were there for Zarek's amusement.

With that small part of him that held onto reality, he recognized this was only a fabrication, not that it lessened his feelings of guilt, which was what his tormentor intended.

Adrian had no idea how many times he relived the nightmare. When the guards came to remove him from the holding cell, he no longer cared what they might do to him. Binding his hands behind his back like he might actually have the strength to attack them and escape, they practically dragged him down the stairs to Zarek's private audience chamber. Deposited in the center of the room, he managed to stay on his feet, but just barely.

Zarek sat on his raised dais at the head of the room, much like a king presiding over his court. Juarez stood beside him wearing a condescending smile. At the foot of the platform sat the boy who'd entered the apartment. The family resemblance he'd noticed before was more pronounced.

"Hello, Adrian." Zarek's voice sounded hard and cold, just as Adrian remembered it. "Welcome home. It's been a long time."

"Not long enough."

Zarek raised his hand to his heart. "You wound me."

"I doubt it." Adrian couldn't keep his eyes from straying to the boy who held the discipline wand in his hand.

"I understand you've met Petrof." Zarek nodded his head to the boy, whose gaze never left Adrian's face. "You no doubt remember his mother, Trena Devson? I believe at one time, you two were—close."

Adrian struggled to understand what Zarek was implying. He'd only been with Trena that one day and it had ended with her death. There was no way Petrof could be his son.

Zarek must have understood because he smiled and patted the boy's head. "Petrof is *my* son; born the day before you raped and murdered his mother."

Adrian barely had time for the information to register before Zarek waved his hand and the boy activated the wand, sending Adrian to the floor in agony.

"That's enough for now, Petrof." Zarek reached over and took the discipline wand from the boy. "We don't want to kill him—yet. He'd miss the big surprise we have for him."

The door to the chamber opened, but Adrian kept his head bent, not interested in any surprises Zarek had for him.

The sound of his name, whispered in a too familiar voice, proved him wrong.

Looking up from where he knelt on the floor, Adrian watched two guards drag Phoenix into the room.

Their gazes met; hers full of fear and apology; his full of impotent rage.

"Look who we found sneaking through the containment center?" Zarek laughed. "Why, I actually think she was planning to rescue you."

"Let her go," Adrian demanded, struggling to rise to his feet.

"I hardly think so," Zarek replied.

"You don't need her; you have me."

Zarek laughed. "It's not about need; it's about want. And you're in no position to negotiate. Why, I do believe you care for her. That alone is reason enough to keep her around for a little while." He looked over at Phoenix. "I see she cares for you, too. Do you think she still will once she knows the truth about you?"

"I already know about Trena. Adrian told me everything." Phoenix's voice sounded strong and defiant, filling Adrian with pride.

Zarek chuckled as he looked over at Adrian. "I can see why you like her. This one has spirit. How long do you think it will take to break her? Well, no mind." He turned to Phoenix. "I doubt Adrian told you everything. For instance, did he tell you his real name?"

Adrian swallowed his cry of protest and fixed his gaze on Phoenix. He would have given anything to spare her—to spare himself—what was coming. He hadn't thought Zarek could hurt him any worse than he already had. He'd been wrong.

Zarek chuckled. "No? I guess he wouldn't have. Well, his real name is Anthony David. A.D. for short. A.D. Rianson. He rearranged the letters and became Adrian Sun, but it doesn't change the fact that he's my son."

"I know."

She sounded so matter-of-fact, Adrian wasn't sure who was more surprised; him or his father.

Zarek recovered quickly, looking from Adrian to Petrof. "Well, yes. I guess it's obvious, isn't it? Appearances can be so revealing." Then his tone changed and Adrian saw his gaze travel the length of her body in an assessing way. "You look familiar. Have we met before?" Then he smiled. "Yes, I remember. You danced for me earlier. Isn't that right, Juarez?"

Juarez crossed the room to stand before her. As the two guards held her, he ran his hand down her cheek in a kind of caress. "Yes, she danced for us." He looked at Adrian. "What about you? Has she danced for you, Sun? Was it sweet? Was it worth dying for?"

Juarez grabbed the back of Phoenix's head and roughly pulled it forward, kissing her in a brutal taking of lips. She fought against the assault, but the guards' hold rendered her helpless.

While his father watched the struggle with obvious delight, rage filled Adrian. Catching the guards by surprise, he raced for the dais.

Zarek's reaction was faster and he activated the wand.

Adrian stumbled and fell under the assault, immobilized. With Zarek laughing at his failed attempt, the guards hauled him back to the center of the room.

"I think it's time to end our little game. I might not have been the father you wanted, but as a son, you were certainly a disappointment." He shrugged. "If at first you don't succeed..." He let the sentence hang as he turned a fond glance on Petrof. "Finish him off," he ordered, handing Petrof the wand.

"No!" Phoenix screamed, fighting against the guards. Adrian felt her fear and sense of helplessness.

"You want me to kill him?" Petrof spoke for the first time and his child's voice sounded uncertain.

"Of course," Zarek said. "He killed your mother. He deserves to die."

"No, Petrof," Phoenix shouted. "Adrian didn't kill your mother."

Petrof cast an uncertain look at his father.

"Just do it!" Zarek exploded, sounding like the mad man he was.

"I—I can't." Petrof threw down the wand and ran from the room. The guards moved to stop him, but Zarek waved them aside. "Let him go."

"He'll never be like you," Adrian said.

Zarek looked at him sharply. "You think not?"

"No. He's refusing you, just as I did."

Zarek looked thoughtful for a moment, then shrugged. "You may be right about Petrof. But I assure you, he's not like you. He said he couldn't do it, not wouldn't do it. I always knew you had it in you to kill; my challenge was to figure out how to control that ability."

"I thought that's what the chip was for."

"Well, yes. At first, but you proved stronger than I expected and learned to resist it, didn't you? Not like the virtual manipulations."

Adrian felt the tingling start at the base of his spine. "What do you mean?"

Zarek chuckled. "You believed you tortured prisoners, abused children—even raped and murdered an innocent woman."

Why hadn't he considered it before? Adrian wondered. He knew why, at sixteen, he hadn't thought of it. The technology was too new and he hadn't known it existed. Later, though, after he'd grown up and knew such things existed, why had it not occurred to him that Zarek had used such manipulations on him as part of his "training"?

"You killed her," he gasped as the pieces fell together.

Zarek clapped his hands together. "Well done," he muttered, sarcastically. "After ten years, he finally figured it out," he said to no one in particular. "Really, Anthony. You are a disappointment."

Zarek leaned over to retrieve the discipline wand from the floor. Adrian only had a moment to prepare himself before the agony ripped through his skull, sending him once more to the floor.

When he felt Phoenix's soft, probing emotions, he struggled to push her aside, but his efforts were weak as he fought to remain conscious. She pushed past his barrier as if it was nothing and her essence brushed against him. He tried one last time to erect his mental barriers, but his heart wasn't in it. He craved her touch, in any way possible. She was the light to his dark; the warmth to his cold.

Her love enveloped him, holding him close and slowly his pain subsided. At first, he thought Zarek had let up on the wand, but then he understood what was happening. As she had done with Skylar, she was easing his pain by taking it on herself.

Adrian knew that if he allowed her to continue, she would die and his life would not be worth living. With that single thought, he shoved her out of his mind and welcomed his own death.

Phoenix felt the severing of their link on an almost physical level. She'd glimpsed his acceptance of death and knew he felt he was protecting her by giving up. How he thought she'd want to go on without him, she didn't know, but she planned to make him understand—she couldn't lose him.

Knowing she was risking death, she focused her thoughts and threw all her energy into one last effort to reach him. When she found the link, she shoved herself through it until she found his pain and drew it into herself, letting it fester and build until it consumed her. Her head felt like it would explode. Her vision faded to gray, but she maintained the link. When her legs buckled, she didn't try to stand but let the guards support her weight.

Just when she thought she might actually die from the agony and never see Adrian again, she felt his love flow into her, bolstering her. Then she felt the link to her mother snap into place and the collective psychic energy of hundreds of Xenobian friends. She'd never felt anything like it before in her life.

Their positive emotions buoyed her; gave her the strength to take control of the pain and like gentle hands molding clay, gather it into a single, narrow funnel.

When the damn burst and the pain and agony spewed forth, Zarek was the sole recipient.

Adrian watched in fascination as his father collapsed, clutching his head. The guards rushed forward, their prisoners forgotten, as they tried to figure out what to do.

"What's the matter?" Juarez demanded, sounding nervous and wary at the sound of Zarek's shrill cry of agony.

Across the room, Adrian's gaze met his fathers. He felt no sympathy for the man; only loathing.

A slight breeze behind him made Adrian turn. Petrof had returned and was holding Adrian's knife. Ironic, Adrian thought, that he'd survived a sadistic father only to be murdered by his own half-brother. He braced for the attack, but the boy surprised him and used the knife to cut through the bonds holding his wrists together.

The boy's gaze jumped to something over Adrian's shoulder, alerting him to danger. Grabbing the knife, he turned to see Juarez charging. Adrian threw the knife with deadly accuracy. Juarez stumbled to a stop and looked down at the knife sunk deep into his chest. When he looked up at Adrian, his expression registered shock and disbelief.

"That's for touching her," Adrian bit out and watched the man fall to the floor, dead.

Then Adrian crossed the room to check on Zarek. Miraculously, the man still lived. Pulling the knife from Juarez's chest, he kicked the discipline wand beyond the man's reach and placed the sharp edge of his knife blade against his throat.

"You were a lousy father, but an effective teacher. I *do* have it in me to kill." He drew the blade lightly across the surface of the skin, leaving behind a thin line of blood. "Are you proud of me now, Father?"

Then Phoenix was kneeling beside him, placing her hand over his. He gave her a questioning look and noticed Petrof holding her other hand, watching him with a combination of fear and awe. The boy looked so much like Adrian had at that age.

He took a deep breath. Maybe he wasn't quite the monster he thought he was after all. While he had no compunction about killing his own father, he couldn't bring himself to kill Petrof's father in front of the boy.

He wiped the blade on Zarek's shirt and returned it to his boot.

"We're leaving," he announced. "But first." He walked over to where the discipline wand lay and smashed it beneath the heel of his boot.

At that moment, the door of the chamber burst open and Rheon barged in, followed by twenty or more armed dwellers. They came to an abrupt halt at seeing Juarez dead and Zarek on the floor.

"You seem to have everything under control," Rheon observed.

Adrian smiled. "I'm still glad to see you."

"Rheon, how is my father?" Phoenix asked.

Rheon gave her a sympathetic look. "I don't know. We've not heard from Jack since they left."

Adrian felt concern for Skylar course through him and didn't know if it was his own or Phoenix's. The man had been more of a father to him than his own and of the two, Skylar's death would be the one he'd mourn.

"I'll see if I can arrange for a ship to come and..."

Rheon stopped speaking when his gaze fell on Petrof. Adrian realized then that while boy looked like him; he also looked like his mother.

"Rheon, this is—"

"Trena's son," Rheon said with stunned disbelief. He turned a steely gaze on Adrian. "Your son?"

Adrian shook his head. "He's my half-brother."

Rheon's gaze flickered to Zarek and then back to Adrian for confirmation.

"I was never with Trena," Adrian said and the sound of the words were liberating—even if Rheon didn't look convinced.

"What do you plan to do with my nephew," he demanded.

"I plan to take care of *my* brother," Adrian said, not liking Rheon's tone. Rheon opened his mouth to argue, but Adrian held up his hand to forestall further argument. "We'll work it out."

A scraping sound behind him caught his ear. Adrian turned to see Zarek rising to his feet, a laser in his hand. He pushed Phoenix out of the line of fire just as the laser went off.

The shot went high, grazing Adrian's shoulder. He pulled his knife from his boot and let it fly.

The knife found its mark in Zarek's chest—next to a laser hole that suddenly appeared. Beside him, Rheon stood, laser in hand and a grim look of satisfaction on his face.

Zarek was dead and Adrian realized that he was finally free. There were no more demons from his past left to haunt him. There was only his future ahead of him—and Phoenix, if she would have him.

When she stepped to his side and slipped her arms around him, he decided not to waste one more second before letting her know how he felt.

"Phoenix, I love you."

She smiled. "Empath, remember? And in case I'm not telegraphing it loud enough for you to understand, I love you, too."

Then, surrounded by onlookers, he kissed her thoroughly and with a promise of more to come.

Chapter 23

Though the rays of the early morning sunlight streamed through the curtains, Adrian was in no hurry to get out of bed. He rolled to his side and propped himself up on his elbow, looking down into Phoenix's face, still flushed from their lovemaking. He brushed a strand of hair from her cheek, then ran a finger gently across her lips, savoring their texture.

"Have I thanked you yet for saving me?"

She smiled. "I thought that's what you were just doing."

"No. That was strictly recreational."

"Really?"

He loved the way her eyes lit up when she was happy; the way she smiled at him; the way she made him laugh. The truth was, he loved everything about her. He wanted to spend the rest of his life with her.

He bent his head to kiss her, enjoying the taste of her lips. Then he trailed kisses along the column of her neck and would have gone further if she hadn't grabbed his head.

"Are you sure no one will walk in on us?"

"In Zarek's apartment? I'm sure. No one ever voluntarily came here." He pushed her back down as a look of horror crossed her face and she tried to get out of bed. "Relax. I'm kidding. This was never Zarek's apartment. It was empty and several of Zarek's grateful servants were happy to clean it. It's ours to use for as long as we want it. Now, where was I? Oh, yeah." He lightly kissed the spot between her breasts.

He felt her tremble and out of the corner of his eye, watched her nipples harden with her arousal.

Then her whole body stiffened and he felt her alarm hit him like a freighter.

"Oh, no. Hurry. Get up." She pushed him aside, kicking at the sheets as she tried to climb out of bed.

"Phoenix, sweetheart, what's wrong?"

She turned wide horrified eyes on him. "He's here."

Oh, krauk. Adrian scrambled out of the bed. Finding his pants, he hopped toward the bedroom door, first on one foot and then the other as he struggled to pull them on. Once in the living room, he shut the bedroom door behind him and started for the door. The security systems were off while repairs were being made. Until they came back online, there were no door locks and anyone could—

Whoosh.

"Skylar!" Adrian hurried to the older man as he stepped through the door. "Damn, it's good to see you again," he added, giving the man a hearty embrace.

"Adrian, my boy. I don't know how to thank you for coming after me. I owe you."

"No, you don't."

"Yes, I do."

Adrian slid a nervous glance to the bedroom door. "No, really. You've been there for me plenty of times."

Adrian noticed Skylar's gaze roam about the room and felt himself grow a little more anxious.

"I met Rheon and Petrof," Skylar said as if they were catching up over a cup of K'feinno. "They seem nice."

Adrian nodded. "Yeah, they are."

"They said this was Phoenix's apartment."

"Did they?"

"They did." Skylar's voice hardened slightly. "Where is she?"

"Getting dressed." The minute the words left his mouth, he knew it had been a mistake.

Skylar's brows shot up and his gaze took in Adrian's appearance, seeming to finally notice Adrian's state of undress for the first time. "Oh, hell no. You and my *daughter?*"

Before Adrian could duck, Skylar hit him squarely in the jaw.

The impact knocked him back a couple of steps before he could right himself. Immediately his temper flared. "Old man, it'd be a damn shame to kill you after I've gone to so much trouble to save your sorry ass."

"You slept with my daughter." Skylar pounded his chest.

Adrian wanted to tell him that they'd gotten very little actual sleep the night before, but didn't think that would help matters. "I love Phoenix, and I'm going to marry her. I'd like your blessing but I don't need it. I only need Phoenix to say 'yes.'"

"You mean you haven't asked her yet?" Skylar chastised him. "Why the hell not?"

Adrian's head was spinning with how quickly the old man's attitude was changing. "*Krauk*, Skylar. We've been a little busy lately. I'll get to it."

Skylar pointed a finger at him. "See that you do. I don't want you to make the same mistake I did. Now, tell me what happened after I left."

Phoenix stood by the door, waiting for the emotions on the other side to simmer down before she walked out. She'd brushed her hair and dressed, but there was nothing she could do about her flushed face or the sparkle in her eyes that came with being in love.

Smoothing the fabric of her tunic, she hoped her father would like the way she looked; would like her. She knew it was childish to feel that way, but she did. Finally, realizing she couldn't put it off any longer, she opened the door and stepped out.

Two sets of male eyes stared at her. She glanced nervously at Adrian, feeling his encouragement and support. She gave him a nervous smile before turning to her father.

He was taller than she expected, about Adrian's height, and his hair, now washed and cleaned, shone with the same auburn color as her own, only his was streaked through with grey. He was thin, but in surprisingly good health considering what he'd been through. As his brown eyes studied her, she hesitated, unsure what to do.

As if suddenly aware that he was staring, her father cleared his throat and shook his head. It took him a couple of tries to find his voice. "Forgive me for staring. You are the very image of your mother. So beautiful."

"Hello, Father."

She saw a tear slip from the corner of his eye and trail down his cheek. "I'm sorry we never met in person. I wanted to be a part of your life but I couldn't risk endangering you. The game room was the only way I could think to be with you."

Her own tears started before he'd finished speaking and before she knew it, she'd crossed the room and flung herself into his arms. "I thought I'd lost you and we'd never have a chance to be together."

His arms wrapped about her, holding her tightly and it was as she'd always imagined it would be. "We may have lost the first twenty-four years, but I'm retiring and will be around as often as you'll have me."

She leaned back to smile up at him. "Really? That's wonderful."

They walked over to the couch in the living room and sat down, her father holding her hand as if afraid to let go. "I want to thank you."

"For what?"

"For caring enough about your absentee father to go look for him." He smiled. "And especially for the positive emotions you sent to me. That was you, wasn't it? It's my good luck that you inherited my telepathy."

"Actually, I also have some of mother's empathic abilities."

Skylar looked down at his hands. "How is your mother? Is she doing well?"

Phoenix decided to take a chance. "She's lonely. I think she misses you. And I think you miss her, too."

"I do."

"You know, she never married."

Skylar gave her an interested look. "Is that right?"

"It is," she said with more conviction. "And since you're officially retired, I think you should call her."

Adrian made his way through the fortress to the landing pad, certain that neither Phoenix nor Skylar had seen him slip out. He looked around, amazed at the changes he saw. It had only been twenty-four hours, but the halls teemed with activity and smiling, laughing people.

Spotting the Black Jack on the landing pad, he walked over to it.

"Hey, stranger," he greeted Jack, who was standing close to a stack of boxes near the ship. The two friends exchanged a quick embrace. Emotional displays were new territory for both of them. "Thanks for saving Skylar."

"I wish I could take the credit," Jack said, "but the truth is, I almost lost him, first in Outer Fringe and then later, on the way to Veridian Prime. If it wasn't for Lena, we wouldn't be having this happy reunion."

"Lena?" Adrian asked.

"Yeah, Lena Alvarez."

"The Lyran engineer?" Adrian couldn't help but be surprised.

"The one and only," Jack said with a laugh. He quickly told Adrian about how Lena had first saved Skylar with a nanobot and then fixed the ship's engine when they overheated on him. "I'm telling you, we were lucky she was around." He paused a moment, studying Adrian's face. "How did things go after I left?"

Adrian filled him in and after he was done, Jack shook his head. "That was one hell of an adventure." He looked around. "What's next for you?"

Adrian didn't have to think about it. "I want to be here for Petrof. I'm the only one who's been through what he has. Plus, I feel like I owe it to Zarek's people to make sure they get back on their feet."

"And Phoenix?"

Now Adrian smiled. "I'm hoping to convince her to spend the rest of her life with me," he admitted.

Jack smiled. "Something tells me that won't be hard to do. I've seen the way she looks at you."

At that moment, a petite woman with short purple hair and large black eyes stepped into the open hatchway of the Black Jack. "Marsden. Are we doing this or what?"

Jack grabbed a box of supplies and carried it over to her. "Yeah, we're doing this," he said, handing her the box. "Lena, this is Adrian. Adrian—Lena," he said, making the introductions.

"It's nice to meet you," Lena said. "Don't worry about your boy, here. I'll keep an eye on him." Then she disappeared, carrying the box into the ship.

"So, I guess this is good-bye?" Adrian asked.

"For now," he agreed. "But I'll come back and check on you. By the way, give Phoenix a message for me. Tell her either I'm sorry, or she's welcome." At Adrian's surprised look, he chuckled and gave Adrian a friendly slap on the back. "When the time comes, you'll know which answer to give."

Then Jack grabbed the last box of supplies and carried them over to the ship. He shoved the box through the hatchway, then stepped into the opening.

Adrian couldn't help but feel like he was losing a significant part of himself. He and Jack had been together a long time. "I'll see you around?"

"You're damn right you will."

Then Jack closed the hatch door. Stepping back, Adrian watched as the ship took off and vanished from sight.

"Did Jack leave?"

Adrian turned to find Rheon and Petrof standing behind him.

"Yeah," he answered Rheon before smiling down at the boy. "What are you doing today?"

Petrof grinned, holding up a fishing pole. "Uncle Rheon is taking me fishing this morning."

Adrian smiled at the child-like excitement in his half-brother's voice. Maybe in time, Petrof would be able to leave Zarek and all the bad memories behind. Adrian hoped so.

"Petrof, would you go ask Gregor to pack us a lunch?" Rheon asked.

"Sure. Gregor makes the best sandwiches." Petrof handed his pole to Rheon and started to run into the fortress, but stopped short." We're still playing cards tonight, aren't we, Adrian?"

"Wouldn't miss it for the world."

Adrian watched the boy run inside, wishing he'd found him sooner.

"Neither of us knew," Rheon said softly beside him.

"Yeah, but it doesn't make it easier to accept, does it?"

"No, it doesn't." Rheon cleared his throat. "Look, I wanted you to know that yesterday, after it was all over, I went through the containment center and found several of Zarek's virtual-files. There was one of him raping my sister and then leaving her to bleed to death. You were never even with her. I know that now, but it occurred to me that you might still have had doubts about it." Rheon paused to collect himself before continuing. "I'm sorry I blamed you." He held out his hand and Adrian didn't hesitate to accept it.

"Thanks."

"I've got sandwiches," Petrof shouted, returning.

"All right," Rheon said with a smile. "Let's go."

Adrian watched them walk off together. It was nice to know about the files, but he'd already realized it hadn't been him. All it had taken was the love of a very special woman.

He walked into the fortress just as Phoenix appeared coming down the stairs, walking arm-in-arm with Skylar, who looked about as happy as he'd ever seen the man. When they reached him, Phoenix stepped into his arms and lifted her face to receive his kiss. It felt like the most natural thing in the world to him, and when he turned, he found Skylar smiling ear-to-ear.

"What are you grinning at, old man?"

Skylar held out his hand. "Son, I couldn't be happier about how things are turning out. I'm sorry I overreacted earlier."

Adrian shook Skylar's hand and another piece of his life fell into place.

Phoenix felt Adrian's love envelope her. She had the two most important men in her life with her and thought her day couldn't be more perfect.

She was wrong.

At that moment, they heard the sound of an approaching shuttle. They watched as it landed and the hatch opened, Phoenix couldn't stop the cry of delight. She pulled free of Adrian's embrace and raced outside to landing pad to hug her mother.

"I can't believe you're here," she cried.

"I received a communication from someone named Jack telling me I should come right away. He gave me directions and arranged for my flight."

"When was this?" Phoenix asked, curious.

"About twenty-three hours ago."

Phoenix looked around for Jack but saw no sign of him. Maybe he'd left already. If so, she needed to remember to thank him. She turned back to her mother. "There's so much to tell you. I don't even know where to start?"

"Some of it I know—like you've discovered your empathic abilities."

"Yes, isn't it amazing?" She laughed. "I'll have to be sure to tell the Grand Master next time I'm home."

Her mother smiled as she stroked a hand across Phoenix's hair in a familiar gesture. "He already knows. Who do you think organized our powers and made them available to you when you needed them?"

Phoenix felt her eyes go wide. "The Grand Master helped me bombard Zarek with all that pain and negative energy?"

"No, we're empaths, not telepaths. We helped you manage those negative emotions. Telegraphing them was all you." Her mother frowned. "I didn't realize you were telepathic."

"I inherited that from my father."

"Your father?" Her mother's voice cracked.

"Yes, you know—Skylar O'Mallen?" Phoenix waited to see if her mother would deny it. She didn't.

"What do you know about your father?"

Phoenix patted her mother's hand. "More than I've shared with you, I'm afraid. I've spent the last week looking for him and it's been quite an adventure, but I'll let him tell you all about it."

"He's here?"

They'd reached the front of the fortress and when they stepped through the door, they came face-to-face with Adrian and Skylar.

"Serina!" Her father's voice sounded husky as he stepped forward, his gaze locked on her mother's. "I never thought I'd see you again."

Serina took a tentative step forward, her hand raised as if she wanted to touch him to make sure he was real. "Skylar. . . is it really you?"

Phoenix suddenly felt like she was standing outside a window, looking in. Her mother and father were oblivious to everyone and everything around them.

When Adrian grabbed her hand and led her away, she tried to resist, but he proved too strong for her.

"Where are we going? I've hardly had a chance to talk with either of them."

"You'll have plenty of time to spend with them later. Let's leave them alone for a while, shall we? I think they need a chance to talk."

Phoenix glanced over her shoulder and saw her mother smile as her father reached out and took her hand in his. She supposed she could wait.

She and Adrian started back upstairs to where their apartment was located.

"There's something I want to ask you." Adrian trapped her against the stairwell wall so he could trail hot kisses down her neck between sentences. "I've been waiting for the right time and I finally realized I can't wait any longer."

"What?" She raised her hand to stroke his cheek and he turned to place a kiss into her palm.

"I love you." It was getting easier and easier to say the words.

A smile lit her face. "I know. You told me."

He smiled and ran his fingertip along the bridge of her nose, fascinated that he'd never noticed before how delicate a structure it was. "Get used to it. I plan to tell you often. You're the best thing to ever happen to me, Phoenix."

He felt her response wash over him in cascades of tender love and devotion that buoyed him—just as they had the day before in Zarek's chamber, in his hour of need.

"I love you, too, Adrian—I mean, Anthony."

He shook his head. "Call me Adrian. I haven't been Anthony for a very long time and I don't need the reminder of that old life."

"I understand—and for the record, I like the sound of Adrian Sun better."

He smiled. "I'm very glad to hear you say that." Holding her hands in his, he got down on one knee. "Phoenix, I don't want to live a life that doesn't include you in it. Will you marry me?"

After a moment of surprised hesitation, Phoenix's eyes filled with tears of happiness. "Yes, I'll marry you."

Smiling, he quickly rose to his feet, pulled her into his arms and kissed her. "I don't want to rush you but I think your father would prefer we marry sooner, rather than later," he told her when they finally came up for air. "And truthfully, so would I."

She laughed. "You'll get no argument from me."

He released her but tucked her arm under his as they walked together up the stairs.

"Speaking of the future," she said. "What'll we do? I mean, I know you want to stay here for a while and of course, I'd like to spend time with my parents, but what about after that? We can't stay here forever."

He stopped and pulled her up against his body, already hard at the prospect of getting her into bed. "We could."

She kissed him, then grabbed his hand and pulled him down the corridor, laughing. "No, seriously. We have to earn a living doing something." A mischievous gleam came to her eye. "I thought maybe I could earn money playing Endgame."

The image of her blowing away the room on the Black Hole filled his mind and he stifled his groan. "We'll talk about it," he promised, pulling her into the bedroom and closing the door. "Later. Much, much, later."

Also by Robin T. Popp

TEXAS AFTER DARK SERIES
Death at the Double R
The Ghost Whisperer's Gambit

NIGHT SLAYER SERIES
Out of the Night
Seduced by the Night
Tempted in the Night
Lord of the Night

THE IMMORTALS SERIES
Immortals: The Darkening
Immortals: The Haunting
Immortals: The Reckoning
Beyond the Mist

SUN SERIES
Too Close to the Sun